I0825081

FATHOM FALL

MATTEO L. CERILLI

BLOOMSBURY
CHILDREN'S BOOKS
NEW YORK LONDON OXFORD NEW DELHI SYDNEY

BLOOMSBURY CHILDREN'S BOOKS
Bloomsbury Publishing Inc., part of Bloomsbury Publishing Plc
1359 Broadway, New York, NY 10018
50 Bedford Square, London, WC1B 3DP, UK
Bloomsbury Publishing Ireland Limited, 29 Earlsfort Terrace, Dublin 2, D02 AY28, Ireland

BLOOMSBURY, BLOOMSBURY CHILDREN'S BOOKS, and the Diana logo
are trademarks of Bloomsbury Publishing Plc

First published in the United States of America in March 2026
by Bloomsbury Children's Books

Text copyright © 2026 by Matteo L. Cerilli

All rights reserved. No part of this publication may be: i) reproduced or transmitted in any form, electronic or mechanical, including photocopying, recording, or by means of any information storage or retrieval system without prior permission in writing from the publishers; or ii) used or reproduced in any way for the training, development, or operation of artificial intelligence (AI) technologies, including generative AI technologies. The rights holders expressly reserve this publication from the text and data mining exception as per Article 4(3) of the Digital Single Market Directive (EU) 2019/790.

Bloomsbury books may be purchased for business or promotional use. For information on bulk purchases please contact Macmillan Corporate and Premium Sales Department at specialmarkets@macmillan.com

Library of Congress Cataloging-in-Publication Data
available upon request
ISBN 978-1-5476-1652-7 (hardcover) • ISBN 978-1-5476-1653-4 (e-book)

Book design by John Candell
Typesetting by Six Red Marbles India
Printed in the United States by Lakeside Book Company
2 4 6 8 10 9 7 5 3

To find out more about our authors and books visit www.bloomsbury.com
and sign up for our newsletters.
For product safety–related questions contact productsafety@bloomsbury.com.

To everyone dreaming of a better world.
We'll get there.

FATHOM FALL

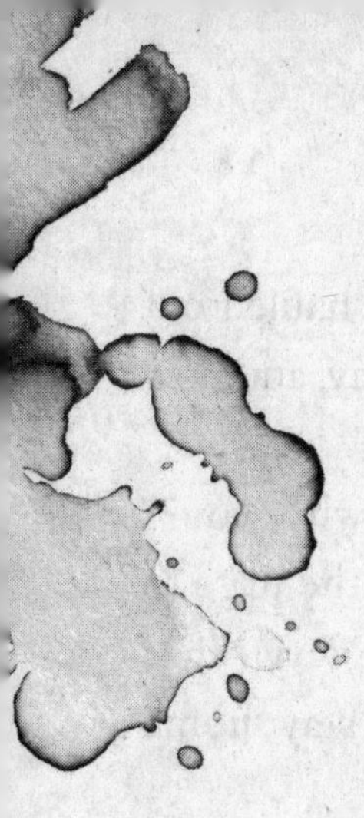

TUTORIAL

WYATT MANEUVERED A COLORFUL alien through a neon city, collecting lines of metal screws while the counter went up-up-up in the corner. He swiveled the controller, clicked to hide behind a wooden pallet while a human civilian trotted past, and then sent his alien slipping down a back alley. A cheery chorus of electronic zips and zaps sounded from the stiff band over Wyatt's ears.

LEVEL COMPLETE!

"Wyatt," his dad said through the poppy electronic soundtrack. "Are you going to join us in the real world?"

Busted. Wyatt flicked the game to pause, then pushed his Zip-Go Gaming Goggles up. The audio band shifted off his ears until he could hear only whirring AC. The flat virtual reality screen lifted away to show the bland interior of his family's Jeep.

Wyatt blinked a few times behind his chunky glasses, adjusting back to the boring world that was nothing like

Go-Go's Spaceship. He was already upset at being hauled out of his room to go somewhere boring on a Saturday, and now they wouldn't even let him play his game in peace.

"Why are you still dragging me to work with you?" Wyatt muttered, shuffling his feet and resisting the urge to kick the seat ahead like a tantrummy toddler. "Every other twelve-year-old on the entire planet gets to stay home alone."

His dad hummed and shrugged dramatically from the passenger seat. "Gosh . . . I guess we just love you too much to be away from you."

Now Wyatt *really* wanted to kick that seat.

He looked into the rearview mirror in time to catch his mom peering back at him. "You know, I think every other twelve-year-old on the planet would be proud that their parents work at Hydrexo," she said.

"We're very cool," his dad added.

Sometimes (often) Wyatt wondered if his parents actually knew anything at all. "Yeah, sure," he muttered. He should just drop it, and yet . . . "It's cool for *you*. It makes *me* look like a useless little Water Baby."

His mom sighed and drummed her fingers on the steering wheel. There was nothing she could say to change his mind: Wyatt Docherty had been called a "Water Baby" his entire school life, and he was tired of it. He should have had a better nickname by now, even a *bad* one. He had thrown up in gym class (more than once), done some pretty lousy class presentations, and had snorted juice out of his nose in front of the entire cafeteria, which should have opened him up to a thousand new and horrific nicknames.

But somehow, "Water Baby" still stuck, probably because his parents insisted on bringing him to work with them on Saturdays when everyone was at the mall or movies or wherever else people with cool parents got to go. Instead, both Wyatt's parents were wearing their Hydrexo HEAD ENGINEER hardhats, and Wyatt was hauled along for whatever emergency call they were on their way to fixing.

"We're almost there," his mom said like a sigh. She shot him a pointed look in the rearview mirror, more tired than angry. "Then you can go-go spacecraft all you want, okay?"

"Space*ship*," he corrected.

His mom put her eyes back to the gray road ahead of them. Wyatt understood there'd be no sense playing another level, not until he was set up in some Hydrexo office room where no one would bother him. Until then, he was stuck in the back seat. He flicked his thumbs across the controller still in his hands, just to get the annoyance funneled out before he said something meaner than he meant.

There was only one small consolation: from the other back seat, Leo shot him a wink as she pulled off her chunky headphones. A big, vintage market sticker was slapped on one side: a screeching black cat saying something about "solidarity," which was one of those words he'd only ever heard Leo use. She'd known him all his life, considering her family lived across the hall from the Dochertys and her little brother, Zav, was Wyatt's best friend. It made Lenore "Leo" Silva basically his older sister.

"A kid in my class peed himself in kindergarten, and they still brought it up at *high school* grad," she offered, tossing her headphones into her pin-covered backpack. She started to remove her jewelry too. Out came the silver lip ring and nose stud, and the dangly charms in her ears. Slowly, she started matching her boring blue HYDREXO INTERN polo. Well, besides her neon pink hair. Leo Silva never really blended in, which Wyatt admired. "Trust me, I liked being called a Water Baby *way* more than being called 'Pampers' for twelve years."

Yikes. Leo's parents worked at Hydrexo too, and so she'd also been called a Water Baby, but this was *Leo*. "It's not the same," Wyatt protested. He flicked his thumbs more, trying to find the proper words. Yes, her parents were also working today, something tax- or stock- or budget-related, but it was far more boring than Head Engineering. Far less *heroic*. "Your parents are just accountants—"

"*Just* accountants?" she asked, raising an eyebrow at him.

His cheeks flushed hot. "That's not what I meant. Just like . . . if *you* got teased 'cause your parents work at Hydrexo, imagine what *I'm* going through."

Her eyebrow stayed raised. Even he could hear how snotty he sounded. Wyatt gave up: he was terrible at talking. It always came out wrong and made him sound mean, or stupid. He didn't think he was either of those things, but his mind was always running way too fast to convince anyone otherwise.

"Whatever," he muttered. He clicked the controller a few more times in frustration. They were approaching the shadow of the Gardiner Expressway. Almost there. "Talk about your boring Hydrexo water stuff. Pretend I'm not even here." *I'll be a good little Water Baby and just shut up.* He knew better than to say that one out loud.

"So dramatic," his dad said, but took him up on the offer: he and Wyatt's mom and Leo got to talking about whatever they'd been called in to fix.

Wyatt knew Hydrexo was important, his parents were important, even Leo as their undergraduate intern was important, and he was just along for the ride.

The Jeep began to pulse with the vibrations of the plant. Wyatt grabbed his water bottle to stick the chewy rubber straw between his lopsided teeth, sipping to settle his stomach while he stared out the window. They rolled into the cold darkness beneath the Gardiner Expressway, where the huge support columns were smeared in graffiti, and then out onto the bridge over the Keating Channel. Beyond the guardrails, Lake Ontario shimmered faintly, not like shiny filtered water, but with the rainbow-y slickness of an oil spill. Rusty signs said swimming in the water was forbidden, and reminded residents to drink *only* from regulated taps. The crisp water flooding up from Wyatt's straw to cool his mouth had been rigorously sifted, filtered, and treated.

The sign had logos from the City of Toronto and from Hydrexo: Your Number One Source. They were approaching

Hydrexo's Lake Ontario refinery, producer of 50 percent of the continent's drinkable water, where his parents basically ran the show. Which meant they saved the world every day while Wyatt complained.

"They said it was something about the boilers, and the pumps," his mom was saying as the Jeep bumped back to solid ground, into the brown blur of the dirty-bricked, gray-skied industrial zone leading to Hydrexo. "The Lake Superior team said their pumps have been slowing down from incinerator buildup—maybe it's the same problem for us."

"Too much backup," Wyatt's dad said. They had to burn all the filth out of the water.

Wyatt pressed his face closer to the glass, staring up at the dark sky matted with clouds of incinerated pollutants. When they turned onto four-laned Munition Street, the pavement was coated in a layer of crackled dust from the hurricane-related storm a few weeks back, tracked through by the tire treads of huge construction vehicles.

"Did they get the pumps fixed? At Lake Superior?" Leo asked.

Wyatt's mom tapped her fingers against the steering wheel again. "They shut them down for a 'safety inspection.'"

"They can't just take the machines off-line whenever they get a bad feeling," his dad said. "People need their water," he added, in that quiet, almost secretive way he tended to around Wyatt. As if Wyatt wasn't old enough to know that people could (and did) die from dehydration.

Wyatt took a long, slow drink.

"But isn't it dangerous to run past capacity?" Leo asked. "I heard the safety committee talking about it."

"We have fail-safes. Emergency shutoffs," Wyatt's mom assured her. "That's why we need to fix the boilers before they go off-line."

Outside the Jeep, a construction crew was shouting and beeping as they laid new pipes beneath the road, ahead of a recently finished storefront row all marked as sold. Across, wooden scaffolds and bright construction netting corralled in two almost finished apartment buildings. A plastic sign proclaimed that they were the Future Homes of Hydrexo Families! "It'll be easier once we move out here, faster," Wyatt's mom said to the back seat. It took Wyatt a moment to realize that he was actually being spoken to. "Just a quick pop out and then we'll be done. We could even walk!"

Wyatt puffed out a bit of breath against the glass. Zav Silva got to stay home alone way back in their Jarvis Street condo building, because clearly his parents trusted him more than Wyatt's. Still, Wyatt knew that moving Hydrexo employees out here would ensure the equipment was always running at full speed, *and* would help cut down on emissions.

And yet, sometimes it was hard to believe that could be enough. That there was a solution to how difficult it was to filter water, how expensive it got as the demand rose, how the refineries were struggling to keep up.

Ahead of the empty apartment buildings, the sidewalk was filled up by a clustered line of tents, and shopping carts full of bags or packs or empty water tanks. People stood among them, some of them in clothing so faded and worn through that it was hard to tell them apart from the tent canvas, especially under the murky sky that turned the spring day to shadows. When it came down to surviving, water was more important than rent, or new clothes. Some of the folks on the street were wearing Hydrexo polos too, from an odd day labor shift they'd had at some point. Wyatt noted how his parents kept their eyes facing forward down the street: day laborers were supposed to leave the shirts after their shifts, so it was better to pretend they hadn't noticed them.

But keeping eyes front didn't stop the street folk from seeing their Hydrexo-blue Jeep rolling past—their eyes tracked Wyatt's window. The straw of his water bottle began to taste awful. A sick mix of pity, anger, and guilt twisted around in his stomach, churning in time to the chug-chug-chugging in the ground that seemed to make the dark neighborhood pulse. Past the intersection, the Hydrexo Outpost's signs glowed in the gloom, showing that the water price was now two dollars per liter. That was higher than last time he was here, probably because Lake Superior was down, and the boilers were acting up. So of course his parents were better needed at Hydrexo than back home. Of course he was better off being quiet in their office.

The world was terrifying, and Hydrexo was the only defense against everything going from bad to worse. What else was he supposed to do while his parents saved the world?

He was just a Water Baby.

There was a clatter of metal pins as Leo pulled her

backpack up into her lap, opening it to her usual assortment of Ziploc bags. Wyatt and Zav helped her pack those every so often: preloaded Hydrexo cards, and metro cards, and little handmade 'zines with the addresses of city resources like safe injection sites and mental health counselling written in Zav's very tidy handwriting. Leo got the money from all over: bake sales, donation drives, even some underground concert that Wyatt wasn't allowed to go to, which sucked.

The chug-chug-chugging in the ground was growing louder. Ahead, Wyatt's mom looked into the rearview mirror again. When she spoke, she sounded even more tired than when Wyatt pestered her. "We have to get those boilers fixed first, Leo," she said as the Jeep crawled up to the security gate. More street folk were gathered on the sidewalk, craning their necks through the gate to see if any Hydrexo Cares street outreach members were coming out with day job offers, or free samples. "You can hand those out after. Promise. I'll see if we can give you some mini bottles too, some of the damaged stock."

"Do you have extra Outpost cards? So they can buy snacks in the store?" Leo asked. "In case folks already have water."

Wyatt's parents shared a quick glance. "The Cares team will be out at some point today," Wyatt's dad said. "Maybe you can go to the park with them."

Leo swallowed, fingers holding tight to her bag. "I guess," she said.

Wyatt tried to help. "You have to fix this first," he said, "to keep prices good."

Leo shot him a look, eyes narrowed, but mouth quirking into a smile. "We will," she said. Her, not him, but he figured now wasn't the time to feel left out.

Wyatt's mom rolled the window down for the security guard. A smoggy gust of chemical-smelling air slipped in through the car, chasing out the cool AC. While his mom showed her ID badge to the guard, Wyatt leaned forward to peer past the gate. Even from so far back, the Lake Ontario refinery was almost too big to see properly. Wyatt knew that this building was the only thing sparing everyone from dehydration—his throat hurt when he looked at it, a mix of fear and awe.

A huge domed shell covered the settling tanks where they treated the lake water, a colossal factory in the middle let off black smoke from the incinerated pollutants, and a water tower stretched from underground right up into the clouds. The chug-chug-chugging was the sound of an aquifer beneath Hydrexo pumping water in and out at all hours, sloshing vibrations through the entire zone. Water surged from here out to the pump centers in every neighborhood in every city, even across the border. There were plants in other places, a big one at the top of Lake Superior and some smaller spring plants in piddly little towns, but this right here was the mothership.

In front of it all, just beyond the gate and a small courtyard with a tidy flower garden in the middle, a tall office building rose up with a water-drop Hydrexo logo staring down on all of them. In the dull gray industrial zone, amid the swirling clouds, it seemed like it was glowing, shining water-colored waves through the windshield to glint across the lenses of Wyatt's glasses. He didn't love being a Water Baby, but he did love Hydrexo and everything it stood for. A billion-dollar water empire in a world where water was scarce, and getting scarcer. As always, he felt breathless to see Hydrexo in person, and yet somehow crummy to know that he was about to march right in there just to play *Go-Go's Spaceship* while his parents and Leo saved the day.

Every time someone called him a Water Baby, it just reminded him how useless he was.

"I get it, Wyatt," Leo told him softly. She sat back in her seat, her INTERN hardhat on, but no smile. "They're just jealous, the other kids."

"It's bullying," Wyatt said.

Leo's mouth twitched. "Bullying is when they have more power than you. This is just teasing."

He was about to tell her to leave him alone, but this was Leo: no matter how much he pretended she didn't know what he was going through, she did. And now she wasn't a Water Baby anymore, was instead taking university classes to become an engineer.

"Hydrexo pays well, and everyone knows it," she explained. Outside, a boy barely older than Wyatt, his eyes sunken under greasy hair, looked through the high chain-link fence. "We have a better start than most other kids—we can use it to help. You're not *just* a Water Baby." She had her finger on the window roll-down button, her other hand in her backpack, like she might still try to hand out street packs while the security guard fiddled around with opening the gate. "Do something to prove it, huh?"

He blinked at her. Finally, she wasn't just telling him to stop complaining. But as he opened his mouth to ask what sort of thing he should do while he was so small and unsure, something strange happened. Wyatt wasn't sure what it was at first. Past the window, the people on the street paused too. Leo's fuzzy eyebrows dipped together.

It felt like the whole world had gone on mute.

Wyatt realized the chug-chug-chugging had stopped. His stomach dropped.

"Those awful boilers," his mom hissed. The security guard hit the button, and the arm started rising. She was already revving the engine, like she'd go careening in fast as a superhero car chase. "We need to go to the data team first, to get the computers' error reports—"

That was when it went from weird to worse.

BOOM—oom—oom—oom.

Before he even saw what was happening, Wyatt understood there had been an explosion. He just *knew*, deep in his stomach, like how he figured animals knew when to run, except he was trapped in a car and wasn't the adult with a foot on the gas.

He looked at the Hydrexo office building as the world moved in slow motion. The glass on the bottom half of the building shattered out, followed by torrents of dust. An orange glow ripped upward past every blown-out window to light the dust and smoke into clouds of fire that just kept getting bigger. And then the Hydrexo office building was getting shorter—no, it was collapsing down. All of the bottom half was being disintegrated by fire, and the top was replacing the bottom.

Wyatt was screaming, but couldn't hear himself.

Air rushed out in a shock wave. The metal gate and fences groaned and tilted forward. The Jeep lifted off the ground and flew backward through the air along with the people waiting on the sidewalk. In the slow-motion moment where Wyatt rose off his seat (he gripped his video game controller in one hand, his water bottle in the other, and could grab nothing to steady himself), he saw the gray-clothed, chapped-lipped, dehydrated people being thrown through the smoke with their clothes already singed from the heat. Wyatt heard the spare water bottles in the back of the Jeep sloshing around. His parents shouted, Wyatt screamed, but Leo was silent.

Somewhere in that building were her just-accountant parents. They weren't going to bring samples to the park. There weren't going to be any samples to bring.

The Jeep hit the pavement and rolled, crunching them all up inside while the biggest water refinery on the continent collapsed.

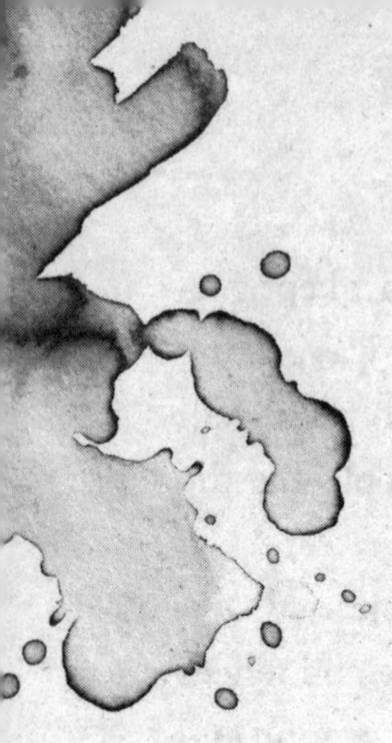

. . . LOADING . . .

THIS IS CBC NEWS.

What you are seeing right now is current footage of Toronto's Lake Ontario Hydrexo Water Refinery Plant, where only forty-five minutes ago at 11:54 a.m. Eastern Standard Time, all boilers exceeded their capacity, resulting in a devastating explosion that has destroyed the plant's office tower and damaged the remaining buildings. Nearly eight hundred employees are missing as rescue teams sift through the rubble. Personnel report that boiler levels had been fluctuating all morning, with lead engineers Andrew and Rebecca Docherty en route to assess, claiming it may have been the result of clogged pipes. The Dochertys are currently being evacuated to St. Michael's Hospital and are unavailable for further comment. Hydrexo's board of directors has released this statement.

"Boilers are a sensitive part of our process: they have the combined power to level buildings, and depressurizing from false alarms can result in hours of downtime and lost product. To ensure we're operating both safely and effectively, we use an electronic system of underground sensors and state-of-the-art risk-analysis code to

automatically depressurize any boilers that are exceeding capacity. While much of the system was destroyed in the blast, which makes it impossible for us to manually detect faults in the sensors or boilers, the system's feedback responses are being retrieved from our data center. We will investigate this data to provide answers and solutions."

As calls come in and rescue teams continue to search, hundreds from the boiler room labor crews and the administrative offices are already reported dead. Search and rescue for any survivors is ongoing. Hydrexo CEO Peter Davids assures consumers that while the boilers have been damaged, they will be replaced by the end of the month, returning production to standard levels. Water prices may rise in that time, so reduce use, fill your emergency tanks, and—

This just in: we're receiving reports that Hydrexo is unable to reach their Lake Superior refinery in Northern Ontario. It seems we are unable to provide video at this time. On the line now, we have Hydrexo CEO Peter Davids:

"I can't disclose all the details, but while attempting to contact the Lake Superior plant to inform them of the Toronto explosion and additional production needs, we discovered that their communications have gone off-line. We've dispatched helicopters. We're trying to reach the employees by their own devices—"

"Sir, are you suggesting that there may have been a similar incident?"

"I can't confirm at this time."

"If personnel aren't responding, does this mean there are no survivors?"

"It may just be the cell towers—the area is remote—"

"Is this targeted? Should the public worry?"

"We're doing all we can to investigate—it could just be a poorly timed digital failure . . . To the public, ladies and gentlemen, we're going to need your help until this is resolved. We only have minor spring plants running now—by god, just those—and it will take some time until Lake Ontario is back up. Even then, demand will be higher than ever. If there was ever a time to band together, it's now."

Thank you, Mr. Davids.

Ladies and gentlemen, this is a dark day. Hydrexo's Lake Ontario and Lake Superior refineries supply roughly 75 percent of North America's water, and with only minor spring plants remaining, water prices are expected to rise exponentially. Still, government officials urge the public not to panic. Rations will be announced by midnight tonight, with fill limits adjusted according to household census data and private business information. Until then, please turn off any nonessential water sources such as fountains, pools, or sprinklers, and restrict personal water usage. In Toronto, police will be issuing fines to anyone loitering near public fire hydrants. Cooling centers for the city's unhoused populations will also be closed until further notice. We recommend sheltering in place until the rations are announced. Details forthcoming.

THIS IS CBC NEWS.

LEVEL 1

WYATT RAKED ALL HIS textbooks into his backpack, where they crunched against the litter storm of abandoned notes at the bottom. His teachers practically begged him to type his notes, but even if the school counsellor called it an "ADHD accommodation," he knew it would just single him out. Starting high school was bad enough—he didn't need to give his classmates any more fodder.

Wyatt slammed his locker, another beat in the hallway ringing with loud laughter, and louder teachers telling students to quiet down. He turned toward the exit, hoping he could just slip away, but three girls with their arms linked caught his eye as they passed.

"That's the Water Baby—Docherty, like the head engineers," one of them whispered, as if he couldn't hear her barely two steps past him. "They were there when it blew up. That's why he has to talk to the counselor all the time. He's like *traumatized*." She looked back over her shoulder at him.

Wyatt stared, scraping his lips across his braces to funnel out the frustration. She didn't turn away. Instead, she gave him a slight smile and a wave, even though she'd never said a word to him in her life.

He'd thought getting nearly blown up and surviving would give him some sort of tough street cred, but there'd been no cool scar, or even a cast to sign. Just more whispering, some with pity, some with vindication, like he'd gotten something he deserved for being a well-off Hydrexo kid.

Wyatt broke eye contact first and returned to his backpack. There was no use feeling cheesed about any of it. The explosion was more than a year ago. He was past it, all right? School wasn't going to get any better, but it was just an obligation. He'd rather focus on the one thing he was good at.

Now that school was out, he took his Zip-Go Gaming Goggles from the side pocket of his backpack. They had some sort of data blocker that made it impossible to play on school grounds or near most businesses, so he just perched them in his hair like so many other boys walking past. Most of them were wearing Zip-Go merch, retro design T-shirts with Zip-Monsters or Go-Go the alien. Wyatt wore his standard oversized, slate-blue *Fathom Fall* hoodie. He liked to think it made him look bigger than he was . . . he was still the sort of fourteen-year-old who made the seniors laugh about kids getting smaller every year.

And yet, despite being small with chunky glasses and braces, Wyatt slung his backpack on and held both straps tight, keeping his forearms facing out as he eased into the crowd of exiting students. In the flood, an older boy wearing his Goggles on his head saw the personalized printing on Wyatt's sleeves: on one side, three fat stars to show his ultra-high score ranking, and on the other, his *Fathom Fall* username:

DoctorDoctor

"Whoa, DoctorDoctor," the older boy read, smiling like he knew that name.

Wyatt tilted his chin up, nearly gloating as he matched the boy's stride. "Yeah, that's m—"

"Tell your brother he plays a mean game," the boy said, then took long-legged steps to join his other tall friends.

Wyatt scraped his lips against his braces again, resisting the urge to flex out his tight fists—he'd learned early that it wasn't a very "socially acceptable" fidget. The guy would rather believe Wyatt was wearing someone else's hoodie than that someone so small and scrawny and weird-looking had earned it himself. If that hadn't happened to him so many times since *Fathom Fall* launched last spring, Wyatt would have screamed.

No use being upset, at least not now. Wyatt had a plan to fix everything, and he wasn't getting any further along by fuming in the halls of his boring school.

He straightened his posture and ducked around elbows and backpacks and conversations about math quizzes to exit into the still-persisting, early-November heat. Outside, thick clouds blocked in a haze that smelled like melting rubber from the football turf beyond. Students milled around, sticking to the cooler shadows while they waited, or else streaming from the steps and splitting off in groups in every direction. Wyatt turned alone toward Harbord Street, a "lone wolf" as his dad always said, which was a nice way of saying he hadn't made any solid friends since starting at Central Technical School. He wasn't too upset about it, mostly because there wasn't a good way to change it, so why bother moping? Wyatt just pressed forward down the long path of bleached white pavement with sweat beading under his hoodie and jeans. He hoped they got a good winter this year, some sort of break from the heat, but figured it'd just be the usual ping-pong between tundra deep freeze and smoggy thaw.

He had just clanked over a manhole cover (painted with the standard little yellow fish, a cheap reminder not to dump any more toxic crud, as if that would make a difference), and was about to turn out onto the sidewalk when he noticed a boy under the school's shade guard, sitting on the most chair-sized boulder of the painted rock garden. Over the boy's shoulder, Wyatt saw a notebook full of sketched cartoon creatures breathing fire and flood and whatever else. Zip-Monsters. The boy's dark hair was greasy, his clothing faded, and he swayed a bit as he sat.

Wyatt might have kept walking straight past, except as he went, the boy looked up from under a limp slice of bangs.

A car passed them, and students talked in the far-back distance, but that was the only sound. Otherwise, nothing but silence as Wyatt "Water Baby" Docherty stared at Xavier

"Zav" Silva, who had once been a Water Baby too, until one catastrophic event brought his world down with it.

"Oh . . . hey," Wyatt said. He swallowed, unsure where to go from there. He stayed just past the corner of shade, blinking at the Zip-Monsters in the school-issued notebook, trying to find anything to say. Zav had always been a good artist, quiet but clever. "Those, um . . . those are good."

Zav stared at him, not bored or upset or anything, just blank with his nubby yellow pencil paused.

"Do you still play?" As soon as Wyatt said it, he knew it was a mistake.

"Sold the game," Zav said. He'd always had a lisp, from a cleft palate that left him with a snarling scar so faded Wyatt felt certain no one else noticed it now, especially when dehydration slowed his speech. Zav swallowed dryly before he managed the next word. "You?"

Wyatt shrugged. He was grateful to move—it made some of the prickling in his ribs fade back, even if it couldn't chase the frustration that he'd said something so clueless. "Not really." He tried to turn his forearms to show the branding on his hoodie, but realized it just looked like an awkward little chicken dance. His stomach churned. "I play *Fathom Fall*. Not for kids, not like before—not that I didn't like *Zip-Monsters* and all but . . ."

Rambling. He stopped himself. Yeah, *Zip-Monsters* was for kids, or maybe for overgrown nerd adults who didn't know when to let things go, but it was hard not to feel a bit nostalgic seeing Zav with his drawings. They'd bought their

Zip-Go Gaming Goggles on the same day, nine years old and practically vibrating in the game store. At school, on top of both being Water Babies, Zav had been too quiet and Wyatt too awkward, but between Wyatt's sprawling trivia memory and Zav's clever strategy, they'd been a perfect team. They spent a month of after-school sessions building and training six Zip-Monsters, until the moment they were ready to enter the ring. He and Zav had sat shoulder to shoulder on Wyatt's fire escape as they watched their scrappy little team climb the bracket. It was the first time Wyatt ever hit the top ten—it had only been for three minutes, but it was still something, and he and Zav had done it together.

Then Zav's parents died in the explosion, and the Hydrexo Cares social workers helped him and Leo move out to somewhere more affordable in Little Portugal (within blocks of where their parents had grown up, which seemed nice). Leo quit her internship "'cause there were too many bad memories," and Zav moved schools. Wyatt had tried to invite them over a bunch of times, but they kept rescheduling. It sucked, but he guessed it was because their neighborhood was more exciting and exactly what a nineteen-year-old and twelve-year-old needed when trying to move past their parents' deaths, whereas Wyatt would only remind them of what they'd lost. He'd chosen to believe that the Silva siblings were doing all right.

But then he and Zav wound up at Central Tech together, where it was impossible not to notice how Zav smelled like Axe and powdery dry shampoo to cover the scent of rarely washed clothes and dehydrated breath that chewable toothpaste tablets couldn't touch. Apparently, even double-income Hydrexo savings ran out. It was too late to stop it, or to even know what to say after years of saying nothing. If there was a switch to flip that would put it all back, he would.

"You . . . you going home?" Zav asked, probably because Wyatt was just standing there staring. He nodded to Wyatt's hoodie. Only then did Wyatt realize that Zav was wearing Leo's old Hydrexo INTERN polo, faded from blue to gray. "To play?"

Wyatt supposed it was obvious. "Yeah. You waiting on Leo?"

Zav slipped his notebook into a Libraries Are Punk Rock! tote bag, definitely Leo's. "Yeah," Zav said. Another slow, dry pause as he swallowed. It sounded like every word was hard, which made Wyatt feel even worse for bothering him. "Should be here soon."

For some reason, the thought of seeing Leo sent a spark of terror through Wyatt's bones. It was already so much to see Zav like this. What was he supposed to do? *Could* he do anything more than give Zav his water bottle or some money? Would that be a nice gesture, or would it just look patronizing? Was he making Zav feel bad just by existing, reminding him of everything he lost? Was it kinder to leave him alone forever?

How the heck were they supposed to start again when their spots could have been so easily reversed if it had been Wyatt's parents inside? In the heavy, awkward silence, Wyatt remembered the sounds of everything collapsing.

No one had prepared him for how fast things could change, and how bad they could snowball.

There was a rush of wind as a larger-than-average vehicle passed behind him. Wyatt turned to see a red-and-white TTC bus. Along the side, a bright advertisement was adorned with the CBC logo and Hydrexo sponsorship tag.

From the studio that brought you Zip-Monsters,
Panda Parade, and Go-Go's Spaceship . . .
The fall of humanity is at hand . . .
FATHOM FALL
(Rated M for Mature)

Sign up now for our: Toronto-Area Championship
"FATHOM FALL: OPERATION HOSTILE"
Friday November 12th 9 AM EST

A shock wave sped from Wyatt's brain down into his feet. He needed to get home, to check the mail. And, also, that was his bus.

"Gotta run," Wyatt said. "Uh . . . see you," he choked out.

"Okay," Zav said, but Wyatt was already turning and rushing past all the tidy little shops of Harbord Street, dodging A-frames advertising iced drinks and discounts for bringing reusable cups. His stomach churned with guilt, but at least that was over.

He cut across the crosswalk, ignoring other students who shouted things like "Run, Water Baby!" He grimaced and ran faster even as his shoulders ached under the weight of his backpack and his legs began to burn. He had to get home ASAP.

A block ahead, the bus stopped at the post to let on a few other students. Idling exhaust billowed up past the *Fathom Fall* advertisement on the back: two Bluddite monsters looked like they were tearing through the bus's metal with their long claws, showing their creepy human bodies covered in hundreds of kelpy-looking fins, staring toward him with their bulbous eyes and eel-like mouths waiting to puncture his skin. The tagline was written in a drippy font.

**THEY CAME FOR OUR WATER,
BUT THEY'LL SETTLE FOR
YOUR BLOOD.**

The bus chugged up again like it would drive off, but Wyatt forced his legs to move even faster and dove up to the front, panting and red-faced and waving his hands sort of pathetically. Faces stared out at him through the windows—he ignored someone's obvious phone camera snapping a picture. Thankfully, the driver clunked the doors back open to let him stumble in. He gave a silent thank you–ish nod and fumbled his wallet out to slap it against the fare collection scanner. There was no reassuring *ding!*

Come on, he thought, trying to fish his metro card out while the bus idled. He could feel so many eyes staring at him, and the insistent urge to yell at them to back off.

"You playing in that competition?" the driver asked him. He looked up to see her motioning to his hoodie, and then back down the bus where every available advert space was filled by *Fathom Fall* or Hydrexo.

Not now. "I-I signed up," Wyatt muttered, trying not to sound rude or frustrated. His card was stuck against the sweat-damp leather of his wallet. "I'm waiting to see if I'll get a recruitment pack—they only let ten people in and—"

Finally the card came free.

"Ooh, recruitment, fancy," she said. He could tell she wasn't taking it seriously.

He hunched his shoulders further than his usual poor posture. "Uh, sure," Wyatt muttered. He smacked the card into the reader, which mocked him with an immediate *ding!* and cheery green checkmark. "Thanks," he muttered, then bustled back into the belly of the bus, trying to avoid the other kids' stares.

There were no available seats, so he stretched onto his toes to grab the hanging strap and stumbled when the bus started up. On the advertisement banners above, Hydrexo announced that stock investors could slash their water costs. The bus windows framed a rooftop billboard showing a rock garden full of brightly painted stones, reminding citizens to Be a Water-Wise Neighbor: Conserve for the Future. The entire building—apartments above, and storefront below—was empty, and had been for months. Wyatt passed a few too many buildings in the exact same situation. The sidewalks were unusually empty.

Things were worse since the explosions; the Lake Superior plant had been destroyed by a similar blast, seen in photos that circulated on the news for weeks. No survivors. They traced it back to faulty sensors, one of those freak things that blew up into a multimillion-dollar lawsuit that was still slogging through court even after the media moved on. There were bigger problems to focus on, like how the Lake Superior refinery was too remote to fix as quickly as the one at Lake Ontario, which had reopened and tried to play catch-up.

Meanwhile, the country *had* spent the past year and a half banding together: they switched from flower gardens to rock gardens, and took showers instead of baths, used paper instead of plastic, converted fields to turf and took transit more than cars in an attempt to stop the water-scarcity problem at the climate change-y root. All these small changes would help, they'd been promised. Give it some time and it'd be back to normal.

None of it could stop the simple fact that there just wasn't enough supply for the demand. His parents had rushed back to the refinery the second the hospital cleared them, to spend half their time engineering solutions and the other half featuring in heartfelt investor videos about dousing for wells and dropping water on crops. And all the while, prices on everything else went up too. Businesses closed and no one moved in. Rent kept going up even while neighborhoods slowed down. Wyatt didn't know how anyone could still afford to live in Toronto; besides that they were all clinging to the hope that they'd be able to rebuild the Lake Superior refinery and fix everything. That the carbon tax, or recycling, or whatever else would fix the climate. That "the housing bubble would pop," as his dad always said, and liven the streets up with shops and tenants.

That there would be a moment, someday soon, when everything would feel normal again. After so long of the same, it was hard to believe it ever could. The bus meandered past Queen's Park, avoiding a blockade of police cars and parked horse trailers that signaled some distant protest outside the Premier's Office. The world was so messed up.

But Wyatt didn't have any means to fix it, and so couldn't care. Not *didn't*, but *couldn't*, the same way he couldn't stop his parents from working so much, and couldn't stop Leo and Zav from moving, and couldn't stop himself from failing even more math tests than usual because all his dreams were filled with smoke, and he was exhausted. That was just the way things had gone, couldn't change it.

He refocused his eyes to catch his reflection in the window, of his big glasses and braces and choppy hair and curdled-milk-colored skin, and understood why no one believed he was good at anything besides being the Water Baby Docherty kid.

He couldn't change the world, but he could change *that*.

He just needed to be given a chance.

LEVEL 2

WYATT TOOK THE BUS to the subway station, where the train was stalled for over half an hour due to a "person at track level"—the announcement wasn't unusual, but always annoying. Wyatt grumbled and sunk down into a seat. A pair of transit cops wandered in, spot-checked some metro cards, and then exited again in a bit of a hurry. Wyatt figured someone had hopped the gate. Then the doors finally closed and they sped off.

Despite the delay, Wyatt eventually slipped through the revolving doors of his condo complex. The lobby was empty, besides a light fountain rippling like water, and the head security guard, Mr. Greene, an older man who still called himself a "doorman" despite his Kevlar vest. Before Wyatt could even open his mouth, Mr. Greene shook his head.

"Sorry, sport," he said. He'd known Wyatt since he was a toddler, so there was no sense in arguing that he was too old to be a "sport." "No recruitment letter."

Wyatt's hands grew clammy. The competition was in a week—half the contestants had already been picked. He only recognized one: B_Townz, a player from Brampton who streamed on Twitch and was kind of a legend, the first person to really blow up playing *Fathom Fall*. He went live a few days ago to show off his recruit gear—a cool competitor's jacket and one-of-a-kind knife just like from the game. Wyatt was torn between fanboy-ish fascination and raging jealousy.

"I'm sure you'll get picked soon," Mr. Greene said. "Didn't you say you have a pretty high score?"

Wyatt resisted the urge to roll his eyes. Didn't any adults know *anything* about *Fathom Fall*? "They aren't recruiting based on scores—the website says they're picking randomly," he said. Then again, from thousands of players, they just happen to pick the guy who's already a gaming superstar? There had to be some sort of *algorithm*, or whatever, bringing in a team they knew would get the most views?

Mr. Greene blinked at him. He chose the absolute worst thing anyone could say: "Well, it's not the end of the world if you don't get picked. It's just video games—no one's dying, right?"

Wyatt's jaw tightened. Winning this competition was the *only* chance to show how good he was at *Fathom Fall*. His parents had bought him a ticket, but it wasn't enough to just sit in the audience, even if it'd be maybe the only place in history where the people around him understood how cool *Fathom Fall* actually was. That wouldn't be enough, not if he was still *just* Wyatt Docherty, spoiled Water Baby. Even cool gaming friends would learn that eventually.

Sure, no one was living or dying by this competition, but Wyatt had a chance to make a name that was only about him. He could be important too, in his own way, as DoctorDoctor.

"All right," Wyatt said, standing stiffer. "Keep me posted."

"Yes, sir." Mr. Greene gave a jokey salute.

Wyatt gave a half-hearted, two-finger salute that he hoped looked a lot less ridiculous, then walked on through the wide lobby to the stairwell. He trudged up to the first floor, which had been converted to offices after the administrative tower blew up. The plans to move Hydrexo employees out near the refinery had been stalled until Lake Superior was back up and running, and most everyone who lived in Wyatt's downtown neighborhood had been Hydrexo workers anyway, so the company cut out the middleman and bought the rest of the building instead. It didn't change much for Wyatt's parents and the other technical workers, but at least the admin staff were cutting their emissions and boosting productivity, or whatever.

It also meant more Hydrexo kids wandering around, which might have been nice if Wyatt knew or cared how to socialize. When he turned around the bend of the stairs, he saw a girl sitting on the top-most step, legs stretched out to the banister. Ava Maraj was his age, South Asian, and the last time he'd seen her, at some back-to-school Hydrexo Cares charity party his parents forced him to, was exactly the same height as Wyatt when he *didn't* slouch. Mortifying. He suspected she lived in the building too given how often he saw her, but wasn't exactly keeping tabs on specifics. Better to just duck his chin and move on before he could embarrass himself.

Wyatt was just going to ask her to move and keep on trudging, until he realized that Ava's flat black curtain of hair was falling around the wide shape of Zip-Go Gaming Goggles. Wyatt figured she'd be playing *Go-Go's Spaceship* like he used to, or *Panda Parade*, or, you know, something else for girls, especially ones wearing pink sneakers and pink shorts and a pink Hydrexo T-shirt.

But games each came with their own special controllers: *Go-Go's Spaceship* was just a little rectangle with a clicky swivel ball, *Zip-Monsters* a tracking canvas and stylus, and he'd seen people playing *Panda Parade* with a small square with two buttons on the front and four on the back. Her controllers were way more familiar.

In her right hand, Ava was holding a small blue water pistol with three code buttons on the grip, a working trigger and safety button, and a spring-action magazine. He watched her snap the magazine in and out, reloading another blaster cartridge. She raised her arm up as if shooting near the ceiling, steadied her aim with one half breath like any player learned in the basic training level, and pulled the trigger to fire off a blast. Wyatt could just hear the liquidy-electric *SHWOOP!* sound of a laser shot. In her left hand, she clicked a swivel ball in and jammed it forward to send her character sprinting, then swung her arm through the air to land a motion-sensor sucker punch. She hit the code on the right hand to switch from the long-range aqua blaster to the close-quarters knife before swiping across the air.

"Gotcha," Ava said. She wasn't smiling; Wyatt had never seen her look anything less than gravely serious.

He knew he shouldn't interrupt her, but was surprised. "*You* play *Fathom Fall*?" he asked.

She jammed all the buttons at once to pause. The flat visor of the Goggles turned from black to transparent; behind them, her brown nose was already crinkled up, and her eyes narrowed. "Thanks," she said, dry. "You're lucky I wasn't sneaking up on anything."

The volume sensor . . . right. "Sorry," he said, "I just . . ." He waved at the gear. "You play *Fathom Fall*," he said, not a question now.

"Why do you care, Docherty?" she asked.

He was actually surprised she knew his name. Now that he was talking to her, he didn't know what to say. Wyatt didn't do a lot of talking to people his own age, especially not girls, especially not girls he thought were cool. "I dunno," he said. "I didn't think girls liked that kind of stuff."

She just stared at him. His skin started to tighten. He shouldn't have said that. He wasn't good at knowing what to say, ever. He'd played group campaigns with girls before, but they didn't exactly become regulars in the servers . . . probably because people like Wyatt said things like that.

He tried to remember how to smile like a normal person, but his mouth kept twitching weirdly. "If you want, I can teach you how to beat the Lake Ontario refinery map," he offered. It was one of the hardest levels on Campaign Mode, where you had to fight back the Bluddites who had disarmed the boiler sensors to blow up the office tower. Wyatt's mom said it was "insensitive" that the game was based around real tragedy, especially the level where you had to clear the infestation of the Lake Superior ruins, but Wyatt had speed-run it loads of times.

Without another word, Ava unpaused and leaned back against the metal banister, clicking all the right keys to run forward and climb a lookout.

"A-are you signed up for the competition?" Wyatt asked.

She didn't answer.

"We can play together sometime if you want?" Wyatt asked.

Nothing.

"Helloooo," Wyatt said, but she just spun the volume dial on her left-hand controller to tune him out. He tightened his fists.

If she heard him, she didn't seem to care. "I have someone to play with already," she said, but didn't elaborate on who it was. Did she have a sibling? Wyatt honestly had no idea. Maybe he should actually start paying attention to the other kids in the building. "And I beat Campaign Mode before you even had the game, Water Baby." Then her gun was up again.

Wyatt thought that was a pretty bold claim from someone who had no idea that he'd gotten the game on pre-release, a special deal for Hydrexo families. Though, frankly, she might have done the same, so what right did she have to call *him* a Water Baby when he was sure her parents worked in that office back there? This was why he didn't do the whole "socialization" thing; it always went sour, because other kids were jerks. But he also remembered telling Leo that she didn't get what it was like to be him, because her parents were "just" accountants . . . he'd been a jerk then, and now he'd done it all over again trying to help someone who was playing pretty well without him.

If she thought he wasn't worth her time, he'd show her. Wyatt wasn't counting himself out. At the end of this, he could march right up to Ava Maraj looking just as cool as her.

After being forced to awkwardly hop Ava's legs, Wyatt ran down his hall, plucked the usual Hydrexo stock options pamphlet out of the crack in the door before unlocking it, and bustled inside. He didn't have time to sulk; he had to prepare for *when* he was picked.

Wyatt threw his backpack against the wall, kicked off his shoes, and swiped his controllers off the kitchen island where he'd left them. Because he *needed* to be picked. Wyatt got most things he wanted—new clothes, new games, trips to Canada's Wonderland and Disney World—and would have given them all up for just this chance to change anything. And not only would he be picked; he'd also win, get his face on cereal boxes, and put his name down in history, the first ever champion of the first ever *Fathom Fall* competition.

Good luck calling him a Water Baby then.

Both Wyatt's parents were still at work, and would be for a

while. He had enough time to play a round or two. The living room window was open, letting in a faint rumbling of traffic. He trudged over and thunked it shut.

Outside, cars ambled down Jarvis Street, passing the Outpost listing $3.62 per liter. It was a bit cheaper down here, where most folks didn't use the Outpost. Instead, they paid higher condo fees to be on the main waterline, in exchange for a lower price per liter. It cost more, but when there were rations (like there tended to be, since the explosions), the Outposts could only pump so much before they ran out, while the waterline kept running.

"People are always going to pay good money in bad times," Wyatt's mother told him once while he was trying to finish his dinner as fast as possible to get back to his game. She was always trying to get him in on water nonsense, and opening his own savings account, and making a budget for his allowance and birthday money. It was annoying. "They're paying for a sense of control—Hydrexo's stock tripled after the explosion."

"We need that to get Superior up and running," his dad had said, scratching at his thinning hair. "People are only going to accept price-climbs for so long before they get desperate and . . ." He'd looked to Wyatt, then stopped, which made Wyatt feel so condescended to that he wanted to scream. He knew what people did when they were desperate: broke windows, broke fire hydrants, drank from the lake or some puddle and died of *E. coli*, attacked the first person with a water bottle to pass. They wanted him to know about all this water nonsense, but they wouldn't even tell him the whole truth.

Wyatt *couldn't* care about water nonsense. He threw himself into the huge reclining chair and popped it all the way back. He pulled his Goggles from his hair and settled them over his glasses.

Water was his parents' business; this was his.

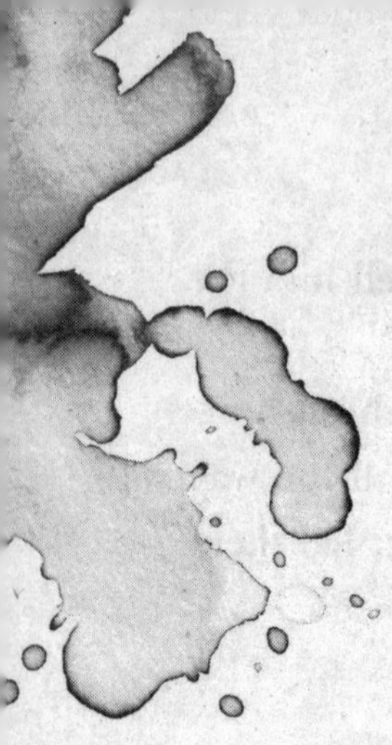

LEVEL 3

EVERYTHING WAS BLACK. THE game was taking a long time to load, as it sometimes did when the server was busy after school. The endless dark reminded Wyatt of falling unconscious after the Hydrexo explosion, the memory of chalky debris in the air, of the smell of gasoline and metal inside the clam of their crushed car tossed upside down. He tried to breathe in deep, and yet he was convinced that when his vision cleared, he'd see Leo's tear-streaked face, her pink hair wet with blood, feel her trembling fingers trying to cut his seat belt away from him with a pocketknife to drop him into her arms while his parents hung unconscious in the front seats.

"It's okay. It's gonna be okay," Leo had muttered. But it wasn't. It wouldn't be. Ever.

The screen flashed white. Wyatt swallowed sour bile to watch the red Zip-Go logo fade in, and Go-Go the alien pop his head up from behind. "Zip Go-Go!" he cheered, then winked in a shimmer of stars.

That was real, and happening right now.

The logo faded to a screen that looked like bleached cement. Through the bands over his ears, Wyatt could hear the echoing trickle of water, as if he was in some underground sewer. He was grinning, adjusting his hands on the controllers, narrowing his eyes in concentration. *Here we go.*

Sponsored by Hydrexo: Your Number One Source

The music roared to life, all dramatic drums and slow, ominous horns. A water droplet logo swooped into view on orange-gold wings like an eagle, soaring up to shine above the just-appeared words:

Fathom Fall
Press [Trigger] to Start

Wyatt did. The logo and words shot off the screen. Three other lines slowly appeared.

Campaign Mode
Brotherhood Mode
Leaderboard

Wyatt raised his shooting arm—aqua blaster crosshairs floated into view. His aim rose up and down with his breath, settling on the leaderboard. He pulled the trigger to a loud *SHWOOP!*, a sound somewhere between an electric fizz and a rush of water. The loading screen blinked up with the weekly letterboard announcement.

This Friday @ 9AM
Prevent the Fall of Humanity
Like Never Before at the . . .

TORONTO-AREA FATHOM FALL CHAMPIONSHIP

Under 16? Think you can hunt? Throw your number into the draft and you could be one of ten picked to test run Fathom Fall's top secret "Operation Hostile" mission, and win one of three $10,000 prizes, plus a lifetime supply of Hydrexo products! (Details available @ *Fathom Fall* website. Waiver must be signed by a parent or legal guardian.)

Wyatt forced himself to take a breath. He didn't know what "Operation Hostile" meant, only that he had to be there. The forums were speculating everything from a new level to a new map to maybe even some sort of spin-off game. If *Fathom Fall* had been out for a while, this could all be just some publicity stunt, but the game was barely six months old. Whatever this competition was, it was certainly the sort of thing that launches video game superstardom. If Wyatt could win, it'd be proof that he wasn't a waste of water.

He could earn something through his own hard work.

The music changed to patriotic, slow bugle music. Wyatt stood on a wide stage, with an audience of people in blue military-like uniforms. They were all clapping for him, a few whistling. A woman in the front row wiped her eyes. It was so *real*.

Wyatt "DoctorDoctor" Docherty turned around (a swivel of his left hand) and looked up.

The scoreboard glinted behind him. He always started his games like this, to know how much the standings had shifted around while he was at school. He scanned the "triple stars," the top three scores.

LEADERBOARD

Alpha_Test .... 99.9% Lethal

B_Townz .... 92.3% Lethal

Doctor Doctor .... 91.1% Lethal

Wyatt grimaced. He'd been in second just that morning. Alpha_Test was some dead silent unknown, maybe even a bot considering the name and the fact that no one had ever heard him speak when he showed up in a roster. But B? Obviously real, and already a star. He didn't have his face on cereal boxes, but he'd done interviews on CBC for "the new gaming craze your kids are definitely talking about," wearing shiny headphones and sneakers and a silk bomber jacket, looking like he belonged in an energy drink commercial already.

If Wyatt won the competition, could he change what it meant to look like a hero? Maybe heroes were going to start looking like awkward kids with glasses and braces and bad posture.

B had been picked, so the recruitment wasn't completely random: if Wyatt kept his score up, proved that he could play a good game, then he could be picked too.

He walked his avatar over to the broad-shouldered, heavily mustached man standing at the podium.

"We appreciate your valiant contributions to the Hydrexo Private Security Force," the General said, his usual dialogue prompt. The graphics were so realistic that even Wyatt's mom had been amazed when he forced her to look: all of the General's medals were lined up over his breast pocket, his gloves a stark white, the brim of his military-style cap glossy and perfect, and each letter of his Security Force badge gleaming gold. He swung his arm up into a salute. Wyatt saw himself staring back in the General's dark aviator sunglasses. Or at least he saw his avatar, just as broad-shouldered and tall, decked out in the coolest stealth-black fatigues and body armor from the in-game shop. "What do you say? Another round?"

Yes, sir. Wyatt swung his hand up into a motion-sensor salute, sending him back to the main page. He was raring to go, but he kept his heart rate steady.

This time when he raised his aqua blaster, he shot at Brotherhood Mode. The usual pop-up asked him to "select any Friend profiles" of people he wanted to play with. Zav's old account icon was still there in the eternity of Zip-Go's servers. If Zav had the game, if he was standing by alongside

Wyatt like old times, then one click from either of them would send them careening into the same server . . .

To play a game he couldn't afford, that fictionalized his parents' death?

Wyatt swallowed and swiped past that to get the show started.

Finally, the music and words faded to black. Wyatt heard the rough sounds of someone descending a rusty ladder, the gentle splash of feet hitting water. The game amplified his own breathing back at him, played his pulse so loud it sounded like a drum, or like super-pressure heartbeats from hanging upside down in his car. The game wouldn't let him move, just kept him frozen to the spot, waiting, waiting.

"Game on," Wyatt whispered.

And then came a grating, humanlike scream.

Out of the darkness, the hunched shape of a Bluddite raced out. It was as tall as Wyatt's avatar, with wide white eyes like a dead fish, too-long limbs, and bright blue-and-orange scales where it wasn't covered in kelpy green fins like tattered clothing. It might have looked cartoonish if it wasn't running at him with hostile intent.

Still, Wyatt didn't even flinch. He just raised the bulky blue-and-orange blaster in his hands. His dad said it was modelled off Super Soaker water guns, relics from the days when you could shoot water at each other for fun. Now, Wyatt clicked off the safety and pulled the trigger.

SHWOOP!

A blast of white-blue energy shot into the Bluddite's head,

spattering a very fake-looking burst of blue blood. It gave a whiny *bleghhhhh* sound before it dropped. Wyatt had only a moment to look at it sprawled dead on the black floor before it disappeared, leaving the pregame loading message:

Remember: Bluddite saliva is potent, acidic, and blinding. Keep your Goggles on at all times, and get ready to save humanity.

LEVEL 4

WYATT'S WATER BAR APPEARED bright blue and full at the border of his vision, along with the current time (3:40 p.m.), a map that showed only a spinning loading symbol, and his volume sensor glowing a harmless emerald green. Past those, Wyatt had been dropped into a covered vehicle, the bumps and jostles of the screen matching the rumbling in his hands and head. There were nine other people lined up on the seats beside and across from him. Their water bars and usernames floated above their heads, along with their lethal averages. He recognized some of them. Wyatt looked at each player, assessing their info.

All of them were looking at him. As the highest score, he sat in the lead seat. He got to talk first, thank you very much.

When he finally spoke, his volume sensor raised to an even-toned orange. "You're new," he said to a player named Z_Lion_Z sitting three seats down. He was wearing the default, slate-blue Hydrexo Private Security Force fatigues, and his average was blank; he hadn't played Brotherhood Mode before.

The rookie nodded. "I played the Campaign Mode," he said. He sounded like he might be Wyatt's age. He also sounded like there was traffic behind him, just a faint rumble like he was playing from his porch or fire-escape or something. Not good.

"That's for the story. Brotherhood Mode's not like that. The Bluddites here are mad vicious," Loop_D_Round said from Wyatt's left. He had an average of 75 percent, which put him in the top hundred, enough to earn three chevrons. His avatar was decked out in a neon bulletproof vest, even more vibrant against his bare black-brown arms where he'd added a Bluddite tattoo. "You figured out the controls yet? Us two can cover you if you need." He looked to Wyatt, holding up a peace sign like, "You and me? That all right?"

Wyatt smiled a bit. It felt good to be trusted. "On it," he said. He shuffled his grip on his aqua blaster, ready to give more formal orders, but someone else cut him off.

"Did you guys hear they picked another player? That makes six," a guy down the line said. Wyatt shifted his jaw. Four more spots. Now wasn't the time to panic. "Some random kid from Burlington with a *fifty*!"

Loop's avatar flipped his blaster in a circle. "I saw he was an Army Cadet," he said, all casual as he ran through trick codes, incapable of sitting still.

"Ugh, of course," another player said. "I bet the army or the Cadet program or whatever wanted him there—it's free promotion for them, and now they'll get more views from military nerds. Like that kid they got from 'Sauga who won that science fair thing—I bet they picked him 'cause now all the nerds are gonna watch their friend."

"There's gotta be an algorithm," Wyatt said, to nods. Maybe he was awkward in the real world, but in *Fathom Fall*, he had respect. Probably because no one knew he was a Water Baby, and because there were fewer opportunities to put his foot in his mouth when they had Bluddites to shoot.

Lion looked around the truck. "Did anyone here get in?" he asked.

Wyatt opened his mouth to say no, he would have heard if they did, but he was beat to it.

"Guess who got his letter this morning?" Loop said, with that 75 floating above his helmet. Wyatt almost flinched, surprised first, then frustrated. That meant there were only three spots left! Loop's avatar flickered through more codes, pulling a bunch of haughty little dance moves even while stuck sitting. "Gonna wreck all these wastemans," he said, letting his Caribbean accent flood thicker. Wyatt had already known he was Torontonian, but hearing local Patois slang just reminded him how *close* he was to someone else living his dream. "Catch me 'pon them big screens with my trophy."

"See! It's *not* random!" that same guy said. "Bet they'll pick a girl next just to get an audience."

Wyatt cringed, mostly because he'd been a jerk about girls playing *Fathom Fall* about five minutes ago. And now he was watching Loop get underestimated, because apparently gaming heroes were supposed to look a very specific way, and that wasn't Black or fidgety with an accent. Wyatt wondered if he should be backing Loop up, but didn't know what words to use.

"You got something to say?" Loop asked. Not angry, not awkward, but smooth in a way Wyatt never was.

The other guy shuffled, but got the guts. "I just meant they're hitting their diversity targets, aren't they?"

"Man, shut up with your forty-eight percent," another player called from the end of the line.

Wyatt opened his mouth, but didn't know what else to add. What if he just made the moment worse?

"And if they want to target little trolls who punch walls when their moms don't bring them enough pizza rolls," Loop started, then formed a sarcastic heart with his hands, "then I'm sure you'll get a call next, 'kay, fam?"

Lion snorted, and then the whole truck roared up in laughter, even Wyatt, despite the disappointment still churning in his stomach. The other guy promptly rage quit. Loop went back to flipping his blaster around, unbothered.

Loop was in the competition, and confident even when other kids were being shitty. He was everything Wyatt wasn't. Even if Wyatt was happy for his gaming acquaintance ("friend" was pushing it—he'd never had the guts to reach or anything, even though there was always the possibility that they actually lived very close to each other), it still hurt.

Wyatt pressed his lips together. "Anyone else wanna be an insecure jerk?" he asked, trying to keep his voice bassy and round and avoid tangling his tongue. It was easier in *Fathom Fall*, where he knew exactly what he was doing. "Or can we just play the damn game?"

"Say less," Loop breathed. He shot the guy at the end of the line a little peace sign "thank you."

Wyatt reminded himself that Loop wasn't responsible for Wyatt still not being picked, and probably had just as much to prove as Wyatt did. Wyatt decided to just be happy for him, or at least pretend.

"Hydrexo Private Security Force, you are about to be released onto the Keating Channel," a calm woman's voice said.

Wyatt pushed his avatar up to its feet and strode for the back of the truck. Lion's avatar followed in flinching jerks. Ahead, the canvas flaps fluttered, light and dust sparkling through them.

"Bluddites have overtaken all Hydrexo locations, threatening life as we know it. The objective is simple," the woman's voice said. "Hunt as many as you can before they hunt you. Your score will be the group's kill count at your time of death."

Wyatt looked around. The others were readying their blasters, bringing them up to their eyes and practicing their breathing. In and out, in and out, slowly in through the nose, and out through the mouth. Wyatt was sure half of the players would fall away within the first ten minutes, but he'd soloed Keating Channel missions before. As long as the score was high when *he* died, it didn't matter what the others did.

“The fall of humanity is at hand,” the woman said. “All forces deploy in three . . .”

Wyatt looked back at the others, but everyone was just avatars, so he couldn’t tell what they were feeling. “We have to get over the bridge,” Wyatt tried to say before they’d run out of planning time. “As fast as you can.” Most of them nodded. Loop was still dancing . . . Wyatt wished he’d take this seriously. He knew it was a video game, but it was *his* video game. And he didn’t like anything as much as he liked playing it.

“Two . . .”

“Keep blasters ready,” Wyatt said.

“One . . . ,” the woman said.

“Don’t worry about being quiet,” Wyatt said, trying to get out the last of his expertise, especially as someone’s mic let off a shriek of truck tires. Probably Lion . . . Wyatt would have to work double time to keep the patrol hidden, though even then, he doubted Lion would last long. At least then he’d learn. “They already know we’re here, so let’s murk ’em.”

“We’re counting on you, soldiers,” the woman said. The truck stopped. Loop whooped and flipped his blaster. “Mission a-go.”

Time to move.

LEVEL 5

WYATT SLAMMED THE LEFT-HAND swivel forward to race from the back of the covered vehicle. Canvas slapped against his helmet; then light burned across his vision so bright his eyes hurt. That was when the screeching started.

Wyatt blinked sideways to see two Bluddites scrambling over the metal guardrails of the channel bridge, their ruff-like gills fanning out with every scream. He kept running and fired two blaster shots that hit right between the eyes on both. There was a splatter of blue blood—they both fell back off the bridge with twin splashes and *waaah* sounds. The kill counter gave a *plink!plink!* as it rolled to 02.

Wyatt heard more screeching, and the sounds of claws on metal. He looked back just long enough to see the other players racing after him—Loop first, and Lion. One player paused as he got out of the truck, as if trying to remember the way to sprint. Beside him, a Bluddite leapt up the side of the bridge and crouched on the railing, just next to the hyper-realistic No Swimming—No Drinking sign. The Bluddite tilted its head like a curious, bug-eyed, eel-toothed dog.

"Heads!" Wyatt shouted.

The player looked up long enough to see the Bluddite and know he was toast before it leapt for him. Its claws caught into the front of his body armor and dragged him sideways toward the other side of the bridge. "*Crap, crap, crap*," the player said, voice already fading quieter as he was pulled away. His avatar flailed, but he was hauled off the bridge and into the water.

"Loser!" someone shouted.

Wyatt's player counter, center bottom of his screen, dropped to **9**.

Wyatt turned back and kept running. All around them, Bluddites scrambled out from under the guardrails, or else bashed up through the weak spots in the bridge. Wyatt shot for the head.

"On your six, Doc," Loop called as he and Lion positioned themselves behind Wyatt while the other six—no, five now as one more avatar collapsed under a swarm of Bluddites—players followed suit, shots still flying. "Lion, don't get eaten."

That wasn't very helpful. Wyatt tried to offer something better: "Make sure you're looking out for—" His controllers started to rumble. "That," he said, just as a colossal Bluddite the size of a car crawled up from the end of the bridge.

"O-okay," Lion stuttered.

"Now you shoot it," Loop added calmly, nailing down a few more crawling up the sides. "Just in case you forgot."

Wyatt didn't have time to roll his eyes. The monster Bluddite raced forward on all fours and then reared onto two feet. Lion fired two shots for its torso. Neither pierced the hard shell, only sprayed two puffs of blood. "Shoot the *head*," Wyatt added.

Loop laughed.

The Bluddite kept coming to swipe a hand toward the three of them.

"Down!" Wyatt shouted. He sent his avatar front-rolling toward the edge of the bridge, where he caught sight of another Bluddite slithering up the support column. Wyatt deftly switched to his knife and swiveled to land with his back to the black water so he could keep eyes on the boss-monster. He jammed his knife backward to a piglike squeal and victorious *plink!* before the Bluddite splashed down into the water. Ahead, the boss-monster swiped again. Loop and the others scattered. Lion was too slow, still standing stunned.

"Front-roll!" Loop shouted.

"Hold two and three and swivel—" Wyatt started to say, but the boss-monster's claws had already collided with Lion. Someone on the call snorted. Lion's avatar flew like a rag doll into the guardrail, where another Bluddite was waiting. Before he could even recover, its teeth had already snapped into the side of his throat.

"Tough break," Loop said. He fired off a few scattered shots—only one of them hit the Bluddite he was aiming for. Maybe if he just *focused*.

"Oh m-man," Lion groaned, the game already distorting his audio, crackling it up.

Lion's avatar shriveled, tanned skin graying below his

Goggle-visor as dehydrated, powdery blood sprayed from the two holes on either side of the Bluddite's mouth to spatter out over its ruff of gills. The Bluddites came from the sewers to drink the clean water at the Hydrexo plants, but they'd take the water from your blood if they had to.

Lion's avatar died, and disappeared from the game.

"Deadweight," someone said, trying to hide it in a joking cough. Wyatt unfortunately agreed—at least now they wouldn't have to worry about that traffic rumble through Lion's mic.

"Guess we biffed on babysitting," Loop said. His avatar yanked Wyatt's back up to his feet before flipping his blaster around.

"I hope you take all this more seriously when you're competing," Wyatt said as he knocked down the Bluddite that killed Lion. The boss-monster turned to him with a scream so loud Wyatt's head and hands vibrated.

Loop flipped his blaster again, backing up a few steps. "Life's too short."

Untrue. Life was very long, and very boring, but not here. And if Loop was going to waste his recruitment, Wyatt wouldn't.

He aimed between the Bluddite's eyes, steadied his breathing in one perfect moment, and fired a kill shot.

He was already running before the huge Bluddite hit the ground and disappeared, raising their group score by a boss-worthy five points. Wyatt and only five remaining players scrambled off the bridge, Loop turning back to lay down cover fire to scare off the final few Bluddites trying to follow them onto Cherry Street.

"Go right," Wyatt instructed. He turned off the road toward the cement silo lot. In real life, the Hydrexo zone had paused construction after the explosions, leaving trucks and cranes and pylons scattered around. The game was realistic down to every hiding spot, which made it a perfect place to regroup.

Wyatt hit the code to jump up onto the chain-link fence, swinging over the top and down to the cracked pavement. The other players followed him to take cover behind a construction portable. They all crouched low into the shadows, barely daring to breathe. The dust in the air floated silent and steady. Loop was still flipping his blaster around. Wyatt ignored him.

Wyatt's volume sensor had been at a red the entire run, but now it was sitting at a harmless green. It would stay that way without Lion's background noise. Wyatt herded the other players behind him before poking his head back around the faded corner of the portable: a few Bluddites were meandering on four legs down Cherry Street, heads swinging around to catch sight of them, gills fluttering to funnel sound into those bony holes on the sides of their heads. One slipped under a manhole cover, and the other walked out of sight. There was a *crunch* and *clank*, a loud *pop*, and then a showering of water from a chewed-through fire hydrant. It would cover more noise, which might do Wyatt and his patrol a favor.

He turned back to crouch in the pipe-filled shadows

between the silos, where the already overcast light couldn't reach them. Only one of the players had taken a major hit that tanked his water level by half; the rest of them, Wyatt included, had only lost a few hydration points from running. They should find some Power-Ups, just to be safe. There was a restaurant nearby with some bottles in the fridge.

Wyatt was about to head off for it when he heard what sounded like voices coming from behind the silo on his left. There were a few garbled human words, but mostly toddler-like babbling, nothing coherent.

Wyatt clicked codes into the left-hand controller: his avatar held a finger to its lips, then raised a fist to signal the patrol to stay, that he'd go around. Loop stepped from the group, hand signals flickering to say he could come too.

Wyatt narrowed his eyes. Was he being petty? *No*, he signaled. Loop was already picked, but Wyatt still had a reputation to uphold until he could join too.

Loop gave him a big old thumbs-down, but stayed where he was.

Wyatt walked toward the sounds with his shoulder so close to the silo it nearly brushed a line out of the dusty film. Shadows moved on the third silo ahead. They looked almost human—something in the way they were standing, like tall people with big scarves and helmets. But Wyatt knew what they were, and he also knew that if he wanted to keep from getting ambushed, he'd have to step carefully and stay silent. He counted about six shadows on the wall, though he couldn't see around the bend yet. There could be more waiting.

His best bet would be to roll a hurricade, *Fathom Fall*'s neon-orange version of a grenade, and hope it injured or distracted them enough that he could finish them with his blaster. As he pulled a hurricade from the pocket on his belt, he heard a faint clicking sound, different from the usual chug-chug-chugging and lake-water-lapping soundtrack. It sounded like a window opening. There was something strange about the sound, muffled like background noise amplified through his headset. Wyatt's volume senser flickered faintly—he froze where he was, listening until his ears strained—but his senser quickly cooled back to green.

Surely it was just a game sound effect that he wasn't used to yet. Perhaps there had been an update patch, and the other players had found out that the locked construction cubicle was open now? As long as the Bluddites didn't hear them, Wyatt figured there was no harm. He had a game to win.

He was close to the edge of the silo, moving slow and careful so that even his boots didn't crunch on the gravel. He'd stopped breathing, mouth pressed into a frown, brow furrowed in fierce concentration. He was just close enough to roll the hurricade around the corner when the mysterious sounds returned. There was a loud *click*, followed by a steady *kshhhhh*, like rushing water. Wyatt's volume sensor sparked from green to orange. His eyes widened.

The sounds were *definitely* coming from somewhere in the room around him while he played. That wasn't as frightening as the fact that his blaster was strapped to his back. Just as he tried to hit the code to throw the hurricade and grab at least his sidearm mini-blaster, there was a shrill scream.

Wyatt didn't have a chance.

The Bluddites came from all over. While Wyatt's volume glowed orange to say *something* was making noise on his end, and that rushing sound echoed in his ears, they raced around the corner and leapt down from the silo tops above him, landing with hard splats and cracks and puffs of dark dust. Wyatt tried to stagger away. A Bluddite launched straight for his chest. The world tipped backward. His controllers and Goggles pulsed hard as he smacked into the dirt. His heartbeat echoed back at him. A haze of maroon closed in around his vision, framing the Bluddite sprawled atop him.

"Jokes!" he heard someone shout as teeth lunged for the right side of his throat. He jerked his head to the left to give it a face full of gravel. He tried to pull his knife, to stab hard enough to break the shell beneath its kelpy fins, but his right-hand controller vibrated uselessly. He turned his head to see that another Bluddite had chomped down on his forearm, spraying powdery blood solids across its gills. Wyatt's water level was tanking fast.

Frantic, he looked back to his front where the Bluddite on his chest opened its round mouth to screech so loud Wyatt's ears rang. Toxic blue spittle landed on Wyatt's visor where it sizzled as it evaporated. Wyatt dropped the useless hurricade and swung out with his empty left hand—he squeezed all his fingers to grab a fistful of wavy green fins on the Bluddite's side. He tried to yank it off, but he was too late to do any real damage. That hidden corner was suicide if you weren't dead quiet, and Wyatt was about to be dead *dead*.

"No, no no no," Wyatt heard himself muttering as the Bluddite's horrible head tore toward his throat again. His pulse raced behind his eyes in pure panic. How was he going to lose like *this*? He could hear voices in the distance, lively laughter. Even through his thudding heartbeat and that strange rushing, he was sure Loop had said something sort of sarcastic and totally unhelpful. So casual.

Loop was getting everything Wyatt wanted, and he didn't even seem to care.

A spurt of blood shot across the Bluddite's scaly face, followed by a dry wheezing-sucking sound from Wyatt's avatar. With that, his vision split into parched fractals until the whole screen had dried to dull gray-white. The controllers went still. His hands tingled, cold.

"This is bullshit," Wyatt said quietly.

That woman's voice came back. "Game over."

17% Lethal

*(78% Total Lethal Average, * 68th)*

Press [Trigger] to return to Main Menu

Wyatt lay staring at the blood-red words, stunned. He blinked twice and then pressed all the buttons, snapping the game to Standby Mode and staring at the real-world ceiling over his head.

The utility symbols were all still there: a default water level (which would go down at the usual rate of dehydration, and a bit faster if the Goggles sensed that his heart rate had gone up), an angry volume sensor, the time, and even a vague satellite map in the bottom. And yet, the afterimage of his new low score floating in the middle seemed burned into his eyes. From third by the tiniest decimal points, all the way out of the top ten, even out of the top fifty, straight down to sixty-eighth.

Maybe he really was just a Water Baby, some spoiled kid with parents cooler than him. No one cared about the sixty-eighth kid—you didn't even get *one* star for that! Three stars for the top three, two for the top ten, one for the top fifty, and then right down to three stupid chevrons just like Loop. It wasn't like they'd send some *Fathom Fall* rep to take back his hoodie, but if he wasn't picked before this, how did he expect to be noticed now? And when other kids already insinuated that he hadn't *actually* earned three stars? He'd never had the confidence to correct them, but at least he'd known they were wrong about him.

Maybe they weren't.

Maybe Wyatt had been wrong about himself.

"Dammit," Wyatt tried to say, but his voice came out as a quiet hissing sound. He could try to play another round before dinner? Or two? He'd have to get a perfect score to move up even a *little*, then keep that up for a few days to get back to where he was. Could he manage it before they picked the last three competitors? If he stayed up all night, he could fit in a bunch of rounds. And maybe he could fake sick and stay home from school the next day?

Yes, yes. He'd do that. His score would climb, maybe even before anyone noticed it had dropped. He prepared to spend the next twenty-four hours in his Goggles, or the next week if he had to—whatever it took to make the competition.

He refused to accept defeat, or to think he was powerless.

As his heartbeat and breathing began to quiet, Wyatt remembered that he'd been sabotaged. There'd been a sound on his end, one that was still tingeing his volume sensor orange even as it faded to background white noise. Now he heard it clearly: running water. Not a drip, but the clear rushing of a tap on all the way, and the bubbling, frothy splash of something interrupting the flow. It wasn't a bad sound, not even a dangerous one, if he ignored how a running tap would spike their waterline bill and get him a talking-to, but Wyatt went numb.

The sound was from right behind him, just through the bathroom door, and he was the only one home.

LEVEL 6

WYATT SAT UP. A thin beam of sunlight glinted against the wide TV screen on the wall next to him, shot out from between the half-open blinds. He heard cars ambling down Jarvis.

That was wrong. He remembered shutting the window, and leaving the blinds up all the way. The bubbling bathroom tap was loud in the empty condo.

"M-Mom? Dad?" Wyatt tried to say, but it came out as a whisper.

Wyatt's heart thudded in his chest again, echoing through the Goggle straps still set over his ears. He turned around in the dim room to see a thin line of light around the bathroom door. It looked like a video game checkpoint: *press [trigger] to open*.

Wyatt didn't like this at all. He scraped his lips against his braces, trying to put his racing thoughts in order.

He swung his feet off the reclining chair. He realized that he'd swiveled his thumb on the left-hand controller as he stood—it was always odd to use his real legs after playing

Fathom Fall. The bubbling sounds didn't stop. He stepped forward, limbs locked, blinking behind the flat plane of his Goggle-visor and his glasses. His hands cramped around the controllers so hard he thought he'd have to snap his fingers to let go, so he didn't. He stepped up to the door, hooked his toe around, and pulled it all the way open to the bright white of the bathroom.

His first thought was to scream, but he felt *nothing*. Fear had zapped away every reasonable response.

In the bathroom light, a figure was crouched over the sink. It was no bigger than Wyatt, its long, slimy legs curled under it, face jammed under the faucet, one scaly blue-and-orange hand braced across the sink, the other gripping the tap as it slurped. Water splashed everywhere—across the counter, on the floor, dripping in long rivulets from the thing's scaly face to bead off the edges of its feathery gills. There were veins in that thin skin, and in the fins along its back and on the end of its tail. The kelpy bits hung ragged. The scales shone individually. That was what made Wyatt sure this wasn't some weird dream; even with his utilities still visible in Standby Mode, this was realer than even *Fathom Fall*'s top-tier graphics. His whole body turned cold.

Wyatt opened his mouth, but all that came out was a dry, crackling fizzle. It was enough. Among the utility symbols, the volume sensor blinked from urgent orange to violent red.

The Bluddite looked up. The *Bluddite* in *Wyatt's bathroom* looked up. Wyatt saw himself reflected in those Ping-Pong ball eyes, watched the water drip from its chin. From a few feet away, he could see straight into its mouth—there were four lines of teeth before it was nothing but red, then darkness.

The muscles in its throat contracted into a series of careful clicks before it compressed to a croak: "*Wyattttt?*" The voice sounded familiar, like the Bluddite might have been mimicking something it overhead, but far too whistly to be human. He realized it wasn't coming from the thing's mouth, but the two bony holes beneath where blood solids spurted from.

The only warning he was given was a small bristling of its gills. They expanded, as if to filter sound down into those ear gaps, and then suddenly there was a squeak like running shoes on the gym floor, and the thing lunged for him.

Wyatt yelped and dodged aside. His feet tangled under him, sending him collapsing into the side of the bathtub while the Bluddite fell into a pile on the floor ahead. Everything smelled like rank sweat and something rotten. The Bluddite got its armlike legs back under it, shook its head with a cartoonish *bugga-bugga-bugga* sound. Wyatt was still holding his controllers—he hit the code for the close-range knife before realizing. The closest thing to a weapon in the real world of his bathroom was his dad's straight razor on the counter ahead.

The Bluddite's gills fanned out as it screamed: "*SsssrreeeeEEEK!*" Wyatt's eardrums pulsed painfully. Under all the screaming, its throat contracted and clicked and spat in a garble of gibberish humanlike sounds. Suddenly the Bluddite was diving for him again.

Legs! he realized, and when it reached toward him with all its terrifying teeth and claws, Wyatt reared his leg back and kicked hard for its face.

He had never been very coordinated, and the Bluddite wasn't slow. It ducked in time for Wyatt's heel to strike the center of its smooth, bulbous forehead rather than crushing its nose or one of its terrible eyes. A mouthful of blue spit flew out to splatter across the front of Wyatt's Goggles, far too close to his very vulnerable eyes. It sizzled and evaporated.

The Bluddite collapsed backward. Its fin-ridged spine slammed into the doorjamb.

Wyatt fell forward to his knees. Every part of his brain was sending signals, every nerve in his body *awake*. But just as he was pulling himself up by the cabinet, reaching for his dad's razor so he could spill blue blood before his own got slurped up, the Bluddite scrambled forward out the bathroom door. It was going for the window, back out toward the rest of Toronto!

Wyatt's teeth gritted. He swept up the razor and turned to follow it.

His foot landed on something hard. Only once he was beginning to lean forward did he realize it was his controller. Wyatt's lungs tightened—he lurched so he wouldn't crush it, but the sink was still on, and so when Wyatt's second socked foot hit the tiles, it slipped out from under him. He let go of the razor, fell out through the doorway, couldn't get his hands braced in time. The floor came at him like a punch.

Wyatt's cheek slammed off the living room laminate so hard his head bounced and crashed down again. His Goggles and glasses went sliding away from him. Everything was ringing and hazy.

Wyatt tried to look up, jaw hanging slack and his brain shifting around in his skull. *Stop*, he wanted to say. Ahead, a vague gray figure swung up into the window, gave him one last look, and then was gone.

The Bluddite was gone. The Bluddite that had *attacked him*. That had been so real he could see the veins in its gills and fins, every scale. So real that his feet had touched it. The real-life monster. The thing that used to be pixels, but now was all teeth.

And had escaped.

The sink still bubbled as Wyatt lay alone on the cold floor, feeling the wet tiles under his legs, and knowing what he had just seen. Anyone else might not have known how to handle it, and anyone else wouldn't know what this meant.

Bluddites came for our water, the last drops we had, but they'll settle for our blood.

He was already fading unconscious, maroon creeping at the edges of his vision. If Wyatt was just a dorky kid, just a spoiled Water Baby, he would have let himself pass out. But he wasn't. Something terrible was in Toronto, and he might be the only one who knew.

Wyatt forced himself to sit up, forced his soupy skull to rest back against the doorframe, and fumbled his phone out from his pocket. He clicked the button.

"Nine-one-one," he hissed into the speaker.

LEVEL 7

WYATT WAS FIGHTING TO stay awake. In the black of his vision, he could picture an avatar-like version of himself thrashing through bright blue swarms of Bluddites with his close-quarters knife. He knew that if he stopped slashing, or if he stopped punching with his other hand, or if he stopped kicking (which was a new function for real life and not video games), he would die. This call was life or death. There was a Bluddite in Toronto, and that meant things were wrong, like the world had split down the middle and started letting monsters out from under the bed. Monsters who wanted their water, had already taken a drink from Wyatt's waterline, and could come back for more.

It was impossible, or should have been.

"Emergency," he heard a woman's voice say, like mission control in *Fathom Fall*. It echoed down around him while he slashed and spat and screamed in his head. The bathroom tap was still running, rushing through his thoughts. "Do you require police, fire, or—"

"Hydrexo Private Security Force," another voice said,

slurring through the sounds. Wyatt took a second to realize it was him. In his delirious fight to stay conscious, he imagined a Bluddite lunged for his throat. He punched it hard in the skull. It sent a painful jolt through his knuckles. In video games, it just rumbled; in real life, you hurt too. "Th-the-there was a Bluddite in my bathroom. Like from *F-F-Fathom Fall* but *real.*"

There was a pause. Kick. Punch. Stab stab stab. The Bluddites made those funny *waaah* sounds . . . Wyatt didn't find them very funny anymore.

"Can I have your name?" the operator asked.

DoctorDoctor. "Wyatt."

"How old are you, Wyatt?"

"Fourteen," he said, though it came out *fourrrrr-teeeenn.* He could hear his voice fading down. He just needed to tell someone. He realized too late that the Hydrexo Private Security Force wasn't real, or at least not like it was in *Fathom Fall*, but the military could be a close second, right? All he had to do was send up the flare. "I live at 200 J-J-Jarvis. Apartment 2012. It went toward Jarvis—"

"I'm sending police and paramedics to your location, Wyatt," she said. "Are your parents home?"

She thought he was just a concussed, panicked kid. And wasn't he? In his dreamscape, he shrunk a foot. He hadn't realized he had been his avatar before, a hulking security agent with the coolest stealth-black gear and wide shoulders, and now he was just too-small Wyatt in his too-big hoodie with bulky glasses and not even a knife.

"Can you tell me where your parents are?"

No no no. The dream-Bluddites were closing in on him from all sides. *Water Baby*, one whispered, spraying searing spittle against his face. *You're just a Water Baby. You're just a spoiled little kid in a big bad world. Did you think you were a hero, Wyatt? You didn't even kill it. You let it get away.*

"It was real," Wyatt said. "I almost had it."

But before he could say more, the Bluddites closed in over him.

Wyatt lost the fight, and fell unconscious.

LEVEL 8

"IT'S THAT GAME, ANDREW," Wyatt's mother hissed. She had been crying—her voice was still wet and fierce. "All he talks about now is 'kill' this and 'lethal average' that. I can't remember the last time we had a dinner where he didn't talk about shooting something—it's *sick*."

"That's just what boys are into," Wyatt's dad tried to explain. He sounded as exhausted as Wyatt felt. "All the other kids play it too. If there's anything that could get him to start making friends—"

"Well he hasn't," she said. "Maybe *because* he's always playing it."

"Becca," his dad started.

"He thought he saw a Bluddite," she snapped. "It's messing with his head."

Wyatt was lying in his bed, staring at the streetlight shadows roving across his ceiling. He was back in his *Fathom Fall* hoodie—his mom had put it through the wash while Wyatt's dad met him at the hospital, and the police surveyed the bathroom and window and fire escape. They were looking for evidence of a break-in, which was easy enough to find. The window was unlocked, the fire escape ladder had been pulled down, the building manager agreed that they needed to put security cameras in the alley and alarms on the windows, and the case was closed.

As if that would stop a Bluddite. Wyatt knew no one believed him. That ached as badly as his "minor" concussion. None of this felt minor.

Wyatt could only hear their voices if he strained, which hurt his still-soupy head. "I don't think that's the game," Wyatt's dad said. "Someone broke in and gave him a concussion. He's just rationalizing it with what he knows." Wyatt didn't like the sound of that, especially not when his dad's voice thinned. "He needs to talk to someone. What's our therapy coverage like?"

Wyatt's brow furrowed. His throat was dry, not from thirst, but from a feeling like he might burst into tears. That was some real baby crap. He hadn't cried when the police gave him condescending frowns at the mention of a Bluddite in his Jarvis Street condo, and he hadn't cried when the paramedics asked if he smelled anything funny before he passed out, or saw anything else he thought shouldn't be there, so he wouldn't cry now. He just needed to figure out what to do next.

"I'll ask HR if they have any recommendations for a therapist," his mom said. "Not just for this. I know he said he was fine about the explosion, and starting high school, but he's just so . . ."

"Quiet," his dad offered. Wyatt didn't understand that, considering his mom had just been saying he talked too much about the one thing he enjoyed, but he figured it was more about what he wasn't saying. Nothing about school, or friends, or wanting to meet more kids in the building, because all of that *sucked*. *Fathom Fall* was the only thing he was good at, the only thing he enjoyed, the only moments in his days where he didn't feel totally useless.

Wyatt felt utterly betrayed, and utterly alone.

"Something's wrong. Something's *been* wrong, and we didn't notice. I don't want him playing that game anymore," his mom said, firm and final. "He has a concussion; the lights can't be good for him. I don't care if he hates us for it, but I want just two weeks of no *Fathom Fall*. We can talk about it after."

"And the competition?" Wyatt's dad asked.

Silence. Wyatt didn't even know if he cared about the competition anymore, not when there were *much* bigger worries, but he wanted one of them to realize what they were taking from him.

"Maybe we can take a personal day instead," Wyatt's mom suggested, soft. "Take him go-karting. Just so he doesn't think we're taking away all the fun things."

Wyatt's stomach churned. It was nice of them, which was almost worse: the reminders that his parents weren't monsters either. They loved him enough to take time out of their superhero jobs to try to do the right thing.

It didn't mean they knew what was best for him.

He turned his head to the door. The General from *Fathom Fall* stared back at him from a poster there, wearing his dress uniform, all his medals and his clean white gloves, pointing right at Wyatt: *Will YOU prevent the fall of humanity?* Behind him, far in the background, the Lake Superior refinery ruins stood shadowed against the sun. That was the big finale in Campaign Mode: the Bluddites had blown up the refinery and then turned the whole place into a seething nest of brood mothers and eggs and swarming defenses, and you had to plant a bomb in there to bring the whole thing full circle. To burn them up and collapse them in, just like they'd done to Hydrexo.

The Lake Superior refinery never reopened. Maybe the refinery being overrun by Bluddites wasn't made up for the game. Wyatt's breath caught. Had even the Toronto explosion been Bluddites the entire time? How long had this been going on right under their noses? Why were they never told?

Wyatt heard his mom's light footsteps coming toward his room, so he shut his eyes to pretend he was asleep. The door creaked open, followed by clacking from his nightstand as she plucked his controllers and Goggles off the charging dock.

She paused there, standing over him. Wyatt opened his eyes to stare up at his mom. Her orange hair was still pulled into a refinery-regulation ponytail, but it was coming loose.

Wyatt's hands were in tight fists. "Taking my gear away doesn't stop what I saw," he said. His anger was turning cold, too prepared to be angry, larger than anger. She just didn't get it, which wasn't her fault. "It's real, and it's going to infest the city and take all our water."

Her eyes were dim. "I won't let that happen," she said. But when Hydrexo blew up at the beginning of all this, even his parents had been thrown through the air. And if the refinery was shut down for good under a Bluddite infestation, they'd again be just as powerless as their Water Baby son.

"It'll blow you up," Wyatt added. Chew out the sensors, just like last time, but bigger. "Like Zav's parents. We'll all die this time."

Her lips wrinkled tight. Was she going to cry too? She reached for his face. "I know you're scared," she started.

At first, he was insulted. But the truth was that he *was* scared. Scared of the Bluddites, and scared of the reminder that even his parents couldn't stop it. The same way they couldn't stop Hydrexo from exploding, or Zav and Leo from moving, or stop climate change and smog and heat from ruining the water no matter how many boilers they fixed or expansions they built.

The only thing they could control was Wyatt, or so they thought.

When her fingers brushed his clammy cheek, Wyatt rolled away from her, wrapping himself so tight in his blankets that he thought he might suffocate in them.

"We'll talk about this in a few weeks," she said, some final, last-ditch effort. "Maybe you'll understand then, or when you're older."

He wanted to scream that he wasn't going to get any older if they didn't stop this, but didn't. He heard her leave. The door clunked shut, and Wyatt simmered in the dark.

He turned his eyes up to see the Bluddite poster hovering above his bed. It hadn't been scary before, no more than having a poster with a vampire or a werewolf or any other made-up monster. But now as Wyatt looked up at the fishy eyes and lamprey mouth, and the ruff of fluttering gills while it screamed out toward the dark of his room, nervous sweat began to itch on his forehead.

Bluddites weren't just a threat to his score or a plea for popularity. Now they were also a thing that *could* get him, had almost gotten him, and might try again. Worse than that, they might target the last major filtration center on the continent. When that ran out, the Bluddites would look for blood instead. The city, the country, and the entire continent were falling toward total annihilation.

Someone had to do something. And if no one else would step up, this Water Baby would.

LEVEL 9

EVEN WITH A MINOR concussion, Wyatt was prescribed a week off from school. He woke up the next day feeling so exhausted and headachy that he couldn't do much more than lie in bed, drifting in and out of sleep despite the rattling of someone drilling new locks into the living room window. Every hour or so, he jolted awake in unexplainable panic, feeling that he'd forgotten something, like a test that he hadn't studied for, or that he'd left the water running. Then he realized—he was so used to checking his score and the mail five times a day that he wasn't able to break the habit.

"Bigger things, Wyatt," he whispered to himself each time, then looked at the Bluddite poster. He couldn't keep a train of thought long, but he kept going over his new plan.

Someone at Zip-Go had to know about the Bluddites, maybe even Hydrexo's board of directors since they'd sponsored the game, but Wyatt had no idea how to contact any of those people for answers. He was pretty sure if he wrote a letter that said, "Dear so and so, I saw a Bluddite. What should I do? Please write back," he wasn't going to be taken seriously. So instead of trying to get answers in a tidy, administrative way, he was going to hunt down the Bluddite that came into his home, and then he was going to put its head in his backpack and take it to the Hydrexo Private Security Force. Unfortunately, since he didn't know where the real-world stuff ended and the fictional video game stuff began, he couldn't be sure the Hydrexo Private Security Force existed. He *did* know that there was a naval reserves base on Lake Shore Boulevard, which seemed the next best bet.

The second day, Wyatt was well enough to read in short bursts, so he got to flipping through his *Fathom Fall Handbook*. He was pretty sure the book went against his parents' *Fathom Fall* ban, but they weren't home, so he was safe to study up on all things Bluddite. If Wyatt had been attacked by some other video game monster, there might be a problem, but he already had most of this memorized. Bluddites traveled in packs, no one knew where they came from, but they probably existed on every continent, yadda yadda yadda. He classified it all in his head as "real-world info" instead of "video game info." Usually he had trouble focusing on actual facts, and even now he had to blink through concussion-induced splotches of light and shake his foot the entire time to stay locked in, but this was too important not to try.

It was the day before the competition when Wyatt was finally feeling back in working order. He hadn't gotten a recruitment letter to the competition, not that kiddie stuff like that mattered anymore. He was going to hunt his real-life Bluddite, and march that evidence right down to the naval base. He just needed his parents to leave for work. They were going to do their part to keep the water running, and he'd do his.

Wyatt sat at the kitchen island, eating his cereal and staring at the *Fathom Fall* General printed on the box. Outside the locked windows, the Outpost water price had climbed another fifty cents. Before, he would have looked away and considered it too big and sickening for him to care about. Now, he realized he had some hand in fixing this.

The news was playing. Wyatt gave it half his attention.

"Strange news from Toronto this morning, where the city water regulators report high levels of wasted water from multiple hydrants opened in the early hours of the morning," the reporter said, with that specific reporter voice. Wyatt was simultaneously thinking of the *Fathom Fall* Toronto sewer maps, and how some "urbex" person on Reddit had said they were actually accurate. When his dad flicked the volume up a few more notches, Wyatt tuned in closer to the news.

"Officials say that while wasted water had dropped down to two percent since hydrant tampering was deemed a misdemeanor in the early summer, we're now seeing numbers as high as fifteen percent."

Wyatt turned just as the screen changed to show an open fire hydrant. There were police lined up around it, arms linked to form an outward facing barricade while the gushing water splashed in bright rainbows behind them. The buildings suggested it was near the Hydrexo zone, or at least outside squeaky-clean downtown: he could see broken windows and a large scrawl of spray paint reading, "WHATS YOURS IS MINE!" behind the hydrant.

"Public hydrants can be opened only by authorized personnel, with specialized keys. It is yet unclear how vandals were able to break through. There have been reports of opened hydrants all over the city, which explains the recent rise in water prices to an average three dollars and ninety-five cents a liter," the reporter continued. "Remember, ladies and gentlemen, tampering with public water *is* a crime. If you see something, say something."

He *had*, and yet? Wyatt resisted the urge to be bitter. Here was the proof that something awful was happening, and getting worse.

"In other news, unhoused individuals clashed with Toronto police in a dawn sweep of the Christie Pits park, with local activists speaking out regarding city shelter crowding . . ."

Wyatt's mom and dad had already launched into a conversation about tightening up on water waste by rerouting the public water away from "hostile areas," which Wyatt knew meant areas where people grew desperate enough to try to break into public waterlines, though they were rarely successful. This was more than that.

Wyatt sat eating his cereal while the police were chasing their tails looking for some*ones*, but Wyatt knew the real culprits were some*things*. Bluddites could gnaw right through those locks—you saw it all the time in the games. They ate through hydrants and destroyed the boiler shutoff systems to cause the explosions. They'd follow the water wherever it was, even into the populated streets, if they were desperate enough, or when there were enough of them to make every neighborhood a hostile zone. No amount of rerouting would stop them.

No one would believe me if I told them that, Wyatt thought. He crunched harder on his spoon. His ears were rushing like the loading screen. *But I'm going to fight back.* He'd kicked the thing, hurt it, and he would again. Wyatt Docherty knew all the codes and tricks and tips, so if there was ever anyone best suited to rip Bluddite guts out . . .

"*Wyatt*," he heard his dad say. A hand had closed around his to pull the spoon out of his mouth. Wyatt realized his jaw ached from how tight he had it clamped. His dad looked at him across the kitchen island with his eyebrows pressed tight together. His mom stood just behind, holding her work bag and staring at him with her mouth agape.

"You'll pop a brace. Do you know how much those cost?" his dad said. But the worry in his eyes seemed bigger than an orthodontist appointment. "Didn't you hear me telling you to stop?"

Didn't you hear me say there was a freaky alien monster in here trying to kill me? "No," Wyatt said. He dropped the spoon back onto the counter. He set his mouth back to a stern, straight line. "Have fun at work."

His dad stared at him longer before letting go of Wyatt's wrist. "Tomorrow," he started to say. Wyatt wondered if he'd changed his mind about the competition, which would be a nice gesture. "I know we said go-karting, but with the waste numbers going up . . ."

Of course. It wasn't the first time they'd cancelled an outing for work. Wyatt couldn't be upset about it. "You have to keep the water running," he said easily. "Don't worry about it."

His dad's eyes shifted back to his mom. She swallowed. "Rest up today," she said. "Call Mr. Greene if you need anything."

He didn't need to be babysat. "Okay," Wyatt said. Finally, they left, huddled close together. He'd bet anything they were talking about him. It didn't matter.

When the door closed behind his parents, Wyatt's face fell. The TV was still running—the *Fathom Fall* logo smeared across the screen, while the ticker banner ran:

MONSTERS IN TORONTO?

Wyatt's stomach dropped. Of *course* his parents would leave the second the news was useful. He turned for the screen, braced to run and grab them.

"Reports of strange monster sightings have been flooding in all throughout Toronto, from terrified young fans of the Zip-Go game *Fathom Fall*, who claim they saw so-called Bluddites lurking around the city," the reporter said. Game footage popped up on the screen, of the slowly rotating Bluddite model that players could look at in the General's office. It was frozen on two feet, with its gills expanded mid-screech. Wyatt couldn't see the veins in its fins, though. "These sightings come just in time for the Toronto-Area *Fathom Fall* Championship, which will be taking place at the Hydrexo Centre tomorrow morning and streaming on more than a dozen TV channels. Ten randomly selected competitors below the age of sixteen will compete for a top three title in 'Operation Hostile,' a new game mission that promises to be like nothing fans have seen before."

"Get back to the Bluddites," Wyatt hissed.

"I'm not surprised Toronto's young people have been spotting Bluddites," a voice said. It seemed familiar, in a way that itched in Wyatt's brain and told him he should recognize it. The feed switched to a man in a Hydrexo office, where the glass windows behind him looked down upon the boilers. The man and the reporter were wearing Hydrexo-blue hardhats.

It was Peter Davids, CEO of Hydrexo, and the lead sponsor for *Fathom Fall*. He was a very average-looking person, white and wiry with thin metal glasses, young enough that his hair was still sandy brown and not yet gray, but old enough to have faint wrinkles bracketing his mouth. Wyatt had heard he'd taken on the company from his parents when he was just twenty-five, and now he seemed a similar age to Wyatt's parents. He smiled from the screen. "Kids have more open minds than us boring old adults, especially our *Fathom Fall* players. We're looking up, and they're looking in the sewer grates."

The reporter laughed. It was *so* condescending. Wyatt felt

a flash of anger rip through him, hotter still when the footage changed to a shot of a sewer grate. Below it was a Bluddite, clearly made out of cardboard.

"It's just clever marketing," Davids's voice said over the picture. There was another still image of a pack of Bluddites creeping atop one of the big electric billboards visible from the expressway into Toronto. They were accurately sized, so Davids was right that only someone paying close attention would see them. The reel flipped to another shot, of a screeching, attack-ready Bluddite pasted under the glass floor of the CN Tower's observatory deck. It even had the date and time of the championship printed beside its head.

Those all looked so fake. Why would anyone report *that*?

Wyatt had made one of those reports. Now he knew there were other kids who must have done the same, and didn't believe they'd misunderstood some marketing campaign. The problem was real, and all these adults wanted to do was treat them like they were stupid.

"So, soldiers, use all the usual rules," Davids said cheerily. Hadn't Wyatt thought that Hydrexo knew something, considering they sponsored the games? Why weren't they confirming the truth? "Don't go near dangerous water, stay in groups, be home before dark. And tune in to your local broadcasting channel or the *Fathom Fall* website at nine tomorrow morning."

The footage flipped back to the news anchor talking about

Hydrexo stock going up, while a ticker reel reported a rash of park muggings. Wyatt turned off the TV.

Staticky silence fell over him, uncomfortable even in the morning light of his familiar kitchen.

Monsters in Toronto . . . Davids had said there was some marketing out there, but he *hadn't* said "You are not seeing monsters, so don't worry." Instead, he'd given those vague "stranger danger" warnings that would actually work against Bluddites. They weren't going to target a large group in a busy area, at least not yet; the only people who were at risk were people out walking alone, which Wyatt rarely was. The Bluddite in his bathroom could be a freak incident, like a rabid coyote wandering into the city? Could Bluddites get rabies?

"Stay inside, don't talk to strangers" wasn't going to work all the time. If the Bluddites were left alone long enough to populate the city, then soon it wasn't going to work at all! Wyatt had played levels on Jarvis Street, in buildings just like his own, and seen the shriveled husks of people after the Bluddites had drained them. That would be him soon, and his family.

But if Davids *did* know about Bluddites, did that mean that some secret Security Force was already on it?

This wasn't the time to sit back hoping someone else would finish the job. He wasn't going to be powerless. He was going to hunt that Bluddite, so first he needed something to defend himself with.

Wyatt looked to the bright orange, foam-dart aqua blaster

leaned against the media unit. That wasn't going to cut it, even if it was modelled right out of the games down to the blue wave patterns on the sides and an electronic recording of the same *SHWOOP!* sound. It looked too cartoonish. Funnily enough, that was the reason his mom let him get *Fathom Fall* in the first place.

"I don't want you playing war games," she'd told him, trying to walk away from the display at the mall. They were supposed to be buying him new gym shoes, but he'd decided he wasn't walking away until his parents used their Hydrexo IDs to buy *Fathom Fall* on presale. "You're thirteen—you already have more than enough hormones running around in your head without a dopamine hit every time you put a bullet in a person. No thank you."

Obviously he could tell the difference between pixels and real life, but he'd known he needed a better argument. "You're not shooting people! They're like aliens. They make cartoon sounds like a little kid game," he'd explained, trying to pull her attention to the video screen's looping game footage. "The guns shoot lasers—"

"It looks like a Super Soaker," his dad had added, grinning at the cardboard cutout of a huge avatar holding the cartoonish blaster. Even so many months later, Wyatt remembered how his dad's voice had gone a bit softer as he watched the footage, smile falling just slightly while it reflected in his glasses. "Wow. When was the last time you saw a water gun?"

They'd caved; he'd gotten *Fathom Fall* a few weeks later

for his birthday, all because the "violent" parts seemed too silly to be realistic. The aqua blasters were just big water guns, and the mini-blasters just water pistols, and even the hurricades seemed more like lawn sprinklers. There was barely any blood, just little spurts.

But now as Wyatt looked at that fake aqua blaster, he realized he was going to need something truly lethal. He slipped down from his stool, strode toward the knife block on the counter, and pulled out the biggest blade. It shone against the kitchen lights, the steel winking cold and silver. He turned it, not knowing what to feel. One slip, and he could cut flesh: a Bluddite's *maybe*, but his own too if he wasn't careful. These weren't toys.

Luckily, some spare bit of true crime knowledge piped up to remind him that he couldn't do any stabbing with a knife handle this smooth—that was a one-way ticket to slicing his palm open. He cringed at the idea, shook it off and scraped his lips on his braces, and instead picked up the honing steel his mom used to keep all the knives in proper carving condition. The dull steel rod was almost the length of his forearm. When he turned it in the light by its black plastic handle, the pointed end looked sharp enough to go through an eye right to the brain. He'd have to be more exact than with a knife, but it would do.

He grabbed his wallet, and magnetically snapped a pair of tinted lenses over his glasses. The darkness made him think of putting on his Goggles, the blackness of the loading screen, the distant memory of waking up to Leo trying to cut him free of his seat belt. His spine prickled. His hands tightened reflexively, though they closed into slack fists rather than around controllers.

Wyatt blinked, shaking off the strange impulse. But he didn't shake off the feeling of being battle ready and lethal. He'd need that to finish this.

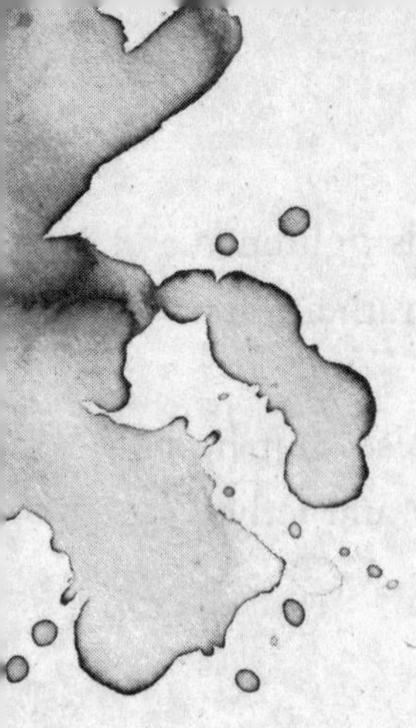

LEVEL 10

WYATT UNLATCHED THE HEAVY-DUTY locks, opened the living room window, and looked down at the sill. The police had done the same when they investigated the "break-in," but they'd been looking for a person. A proper target might give Wyatt better results. He slipped onto the fire escape.

The autumn weather wasn't too hot that day, overcast enough that Wyatt's concussion-sensitive eyes didn't sting behind his sunglasses. The fire escape had one soil-filled pot and one white plastic chair stained brown from smoggy rain, but nothing else of note. Wyatt climbed down the ladder.

From there, he could head out to Jarvis, but that was too open and loud for a Bluddite. Instead, he turned to look down the alleyway, toward the parking garage. Bluddites liked the dark and the damp, and with no nearby sewer grates opened, that was either where it had come from, or where it had gone. Wyatt marched off with the honing steel hidden up his sleeve.

As he walked, something tickled at the back of his neck. He touched there nervously. The fuzz at the base of his squared-off hair was standing up. The sensation crawled over his arms. It felt like he was being watched. Wyatt slowed and looked around, scanning the windows all the way to the penthouse, even if it was impossible to tell if anyone was watching from up there. But it was an empty alley early in the morning when everyone his age was at school and most adults were at work. Maybe his alert hairs were sensing rain? They weren't supposed to get any, but he'd learned long ago that Toronto weather wasn't exactly predictable.

He walked faster, keeping his arms tight to his sides and his steps quick but silent. But when he turned to the garage, expecting the usual crossbar, he was instead faced with the new chain-link partition that opened with a car-key pass. He'd forgotten that they'd installed that a month or two ago to stop robberies and trespassing. Wyatt narrowed his eyes. That Bluddite had been small, probably a juvenile, but even still, it couldn't walk right through a fence. Wyatt looked to the top edge, where he noted that the gate rattled out like a shower curtain. He scanned his eyes down—the gate wasn't fixed to anything at the bottom. In fact, there was a gap. It was too small for an adult to slip under, so he doubted the police checked it, but it was big enough for Wyatt, and for that smaller-than-average Bluddite. Beyond the gate, the ramp tilted downward into the dark, with only one amber bulb visible before a sharp corner.

Wyatt could picture a den in there, with a brood mother over its clutch of eggs and the others swarming around to protect it. He doubted that was *actually* in there, considering his parents drove the Jeep in and out of there every day, but it was a good enough visual to convince him he was heading in the right direction.

Wyatt took one quick look around the alley, then dropped down to his stomach in an army crawl.

He'd overestimated how small he was, which would normally be a nice reminder that he was in fact getting taller, but in that moment it just meant that the gate's sharp bottom edge dug into the side of his head as he tried to weasel under. His still-bruised cheek ground against the gravel-scattered pavement. He crammed his arms past, planted each forearm, and dragged himself out. Once his head was through and he wriggled his hood off the gate's prongs so it would stop choking him, he didn't have much trouble. He pulled his torso and legs past to stand up in the dark parking garage.

In just one moment, the alley felt a thousand miles away, like he'd gone into another level and couldn't back out now. The air smelled like dry stone and car exhaust. He was nervous, but he'd planned for this.

Wyatt crept down the ramp, following the painted arrows leading him into the gloom. He flicked his sunglasses up for better visibility, but the change was minimal. Still, Wyatt knew his formations: he pressed his back to the cold corner, let the honing steel drop into his waiting hand, and took a quick look up, which any good soldier should do when things were suspiciously quiet. The ceiling was only rusted pipes and old wires, all socketed safely.

All right. Good so far. Wyatt took a breath, adjusted his

grip around the clammy plastic handle, and slowly peeked his head around the corner.

The floor of the parking garage sprawled out, still with quite a few cars in it. The problem was that there were only lights around the walls—the middle of the garage faded into shadows under the hazy glints of chrome. There were so many hiding places between those aisles . . . and considering the faint slope of the cement floor, he knew the sewer grate would be smack dab in the middle.

Wyatt swallowed, quieting his heartbeat with a few deep, slow breaths. He stepped forward into the first aisle at a low crouch, scanning under all the tires as far back as he could. He didn't see anything moving, didn't hear anything either, but it didn't make him feel any calmer. It was like that moment with the black screen, where he knew something was going to jump out, but he didn't know when. He stalked forward with his back aching from the stiff crouch, but he held his nerve. He'd know what to do if an enemy came at him.

Wyatt heard a faint dripping echoing around the garage. He crept farther from the light of the walls, wading toward the gloomy middle. He turned a careful, roving arc with the steel pointed ahead like a sword, his other hand in a ready fist. His chest ached despite several long, slow nose breaths. That prickly, watched feeling still burned on the back of his neck. The closer he got to the grate, the more details he could discern even in the darkness. He was becoming a night thing, like a Bluddite. He was going to think like the enemy to catch the enemy.

He slipped through the cars and stayed crouched to press his shoulder into the cold metal of a sedan's back bumper, one hand braced on the rough ground, the other holding his weapon steady. Everything was gray, like the color was switched off in that area.

There it was, just ahead, the sewer grate.

Unfortunately, it looked exactly the same as every time Wyatt hopped out of the Jeep with his parents and never thought twice about monsters. He had wanted it to be open, or for there to be blood around it, or any sign. He maybe even wanted to see the Bluddite again. But there was no evidence.

Even still, it could have lifted the grate with its humanlike hands, slipped in, and pulled the cap shut. It could be down there still, waiting.

Wyatt also had human hands. He knew what his avatar would do if it meant raising his kill count.

Wyatt was just about to ease forward to hook his fingers in that small gap when he heard movement behind him. It was only the slightest crunch of pavement, barely enough to trip a volume sensor.

Adrenaline shot through Wyatt's every nerve. It was time to fight.

He tightened his grip on the steel and whipped around, dodging left into the other car just as a shadow tore past him. He gritted his teeth and thrust the honing steel out, but the shadow dove nimbly over it and swung up onto the hood of the car next to him, so catlike the alarm didn't even go off. Wyatt knew Bluddites could be agile, but they were still heavy—this shadow seemed like it was clipping through the world rather than weighing into it. It crouched with one foot on the car's hood, one foot on the windshield, and then leapt for him again.

Wyatt stabbed the steel upward, but the shadow's leap became a sweeping kick. Something boot-hard smashed into Wyatt's soft fingers. He let out a sound between a snarl and a gasp. The steel flew from his grip, clanked across the pavement, rolled across the sewer grate with an innocent *tink-tink-tink*, and then flipped vertical like a capsizing boat. It fell straight down into the water far below.

There was no time to wonder how he would explain that to his parents: two very *human* hands closed on Wyatt's shoulders. They swung him out from between the parked cars, tossed him back toward a better-lit aisle and away from the grate. Wyatt hit the ground and slid along his side, bruising his skin through the thick fabric of his hoodie. His brain cringed and whined in his skull. He tried to recover. There was a strange buzzing sound.

When he managed to scramble backward and sit up against a car's front bumper, there was a neon-orange mini-blaster barrel pointed between his eyes. He didn't even have time to wonder if it was a toy: blue-white light burned down the muzzle, too bright to be fake. There was a laser in there, ready to kill him.

He'd thought aqua blasters weren't real, or frightening, and was wrong on both counts.

LEVEL 11

WYATT HAD SEEN AQUA blasters in *Fathom Fall*. He'd seen glossy renders in his handbook. He'd seen toy models. But seeing a mini-blaster in real life, watching that spark in the middle that told him it wasn't some fake kid's toy, that it *could* shoot some sort of laser energy to burn right through him?

It was like his body forgot how to be a body and defaulted to goo, slack and useless. In video games, you had just enough time to mash the right keys and disarm the shooter; otherwise it was totally unfair. In movies, the gun jammed, or else the story would be pretty short.

But there were no miraculous fake-outs in real life.

As far as Wyatt was aware, the only thing that saved his life was getting a good look at the person behind the mini-blaster, which meant she had a good look at him. She was short, with a long nose and brown skin, wearing rough black pants, Zip-Go Gaming Goggles turned on to Standby Mode and adjusted to their green "high-res night vision" setting, as well as a thin, aqua-blue jacket. The jacket had the "Operation Hostile" logo across the chest, the Hydrexo sponsorship symbol below it. Up one arm, it read, "COMPETITOR," and up the other . . . "ALPHA_TEST."

Wyatt's eyes widened. Still, Ava Maraj spoke before he could.

"Oh, it's just *you*," she said. She tapped the safety back on her mini-blaster and put it on her belt, alongside a knife Wyatt recognized. Not just from *Fathom Fall*: B_Townz had been flashing that same blade all over the forums and Twitch and Instagram, and that same style of jacket.

A walkie-talkie buzzed on the other side of Ava's belt. "Wagwan?" a voice asked.

Ava unhooked the walkie and held it up to her mouth. Her usual bored voice smoothed, swinging into some other language entirely, or at least every other word sounded like it. Wyatt wondered if his concussion was worse than he thought. He kept thinking he *almost* understood what she was saying: he caught "garage," "Bluddite," and the incredibly condescending combination of "Docherty" followed by "wasteyute." Only then did he realize she was speaking Patois, which he hadn't known she could do. Frankly he knew next to nothing about her, and felt he knew even less now, besides suspecting that she was *intentionally* trying to ice him out.

Fortunately, the person on the other end replied in English. "You kidding me? You told me you were just going to drop the pack off. Nize it with the patrolling before I get in trouble too," the other voice said, sounding more exhausted than upset. It also sounded familiar, or maybe just young. Wyatt strained to understand through his still-ringing ears. "At least you found the guy you're looking for. Be nice. Remember those social skills, eh?"

She breathed out heavy through her nose, slipping one strap of her backpack off. "Nize yourself," she muttered, and clicked the call off halfway through the other person's cackling laugh.

Silence.

The two of them stared at each other. Wyatt didn't know what to say because there were a lot of things *to* say. The fact she had jumped at him like a ninja, the fact she had *a real mini-blaster*, the fact she was "patrolling," and that there were apparently more people in on it. Clearly she'd been looking for the Bluddites too, but she was far better prepared.

And she'd been looking for him? Why was Ava Maraj looking for *him*?

Still, Wyatt couldn't take his eyes off her competitor's jacket, and the name written on the sleeve:

Alpha_Test

That player everyone thought was a bot, with an astounding 99.9 score. And then he was being his usual, awkward, bad-at-talking-to-people self, but couldn't stop it before he asked, "Is that your brother's jacket?"

More heavy, stone-smelling silence. He knew he should apologize, but didn't know how to say it.

Her eyes narrowed behind her Goggles. For a moment, he thought she was going to pull the mini-blaster back out and shoot him dead, and he thought about how he could probably kick her hand away now that he saw it coming, but instead she was shrugging off her backpack and pulling out a blue bundle.

"For the record," Ava said, while Wyatt sat speechless, "I didn't want it to be you. I said you won't take it seriously, 'cause you're a spoiled Water Baby, so I'm pretty sure sending me to give this to you is some sort of punishment."

What was she talking about? Wasn't he in the garage because he wasn't just a spoiled Water Baby sitting at home? He got ready to leap forward, his fists tight. "Hey—"

But before he could argue, she'd thrown the package at him and he was forced to catch it. It was soft, but heavy. There was a postage label smacked across the front, with the shimmering *Fathom Fall* logo watermarked behind it.

DELIVER TO

Wyatt "DoctorDoctor" Docherty

TOP SECRET "OPERATION HOSTILE" RECRUITMENT PACKAGE

Your draft number has been pulled for the Toronto-Area Fathom Fall Championship

By the time Wyatt looked up in surprise, Ava had already stalked up the ramp and toward the exit.

"Wait!" Wyatt shouted. He rushed to his feet, holding the package under his arm. "Ava! Hey!" She'd been sent to deliver his recruitment package, and she was competing too, and "patrolling" with a *real* mini-blaster! Whatever was going on here, it was bigger than a random Bluddite. He felt so close to getting all the answers. He just needed her to slow down and tell him how this was all connected. "Ava, I'm sorry I said—"

He turned the corner and saw the gate was shutting behind her, as if she'd unlocked and opened it. He raced up to the gate.

"Bluddites," Wyatt said, staring at her through the metal links.

She stood in the sunshine, looking at him like he was a gross piece of gum she just scraped off her shoe.

"Bluddites are real, they're in Toronto, and Hydrexo knows." Was this part of the competition? Was Wyatt getting a real mini-blaster soon? "And you're hunting them, right?"

She sucked her teeth, nice and loud like she *really* wanted him to hear that she didn't think much of him.

She'd caught him by surprise, and he'd been an ass, but he was better than this. He was trying to help . . . He'd just let his Wyatt-ness get in the way.

"I'm not supposed to, *yet*," she said. "But when I wipe the floor with you tomorrow and finally get the green light, then those monsters better start running."

So the competition was about more than just video games? Wyatt's face pinched up. "That doesn't explain anything," he snapped, but already she was turning away from him. He bashed his hands into the gate, but it didn't move. All he could do was watch her stride down the alley, adjusting her competitor's jacket over her weapons so they wouldn't show.

It was effortless. Whatever was going on, Ava knew *exactly* what she was doing.

"Ava!" Wyatt shouted. She was already gone. "*Crap*," Wyatt breathed, then punched the gate again for good measure. It scraped his knuckles. He couldn't believe he'd let her walk away still thinking he was deadweight, but more than that, he couldn't believe he'd let her walk away without telling him anything. He knew Bluddites were real, he'd gotten that far, but now he knew that there really was some bigger plan happening around him.

Whatever it was, the competition was part of it. He got the sense that they were heading toward some final move, but not what or why or how, or who.

Something might have moved behind him. Wyatt looked frantically back toward the single amber light before the corner, clutching his recruitment package and waiting for a shadow to appear on the wall.

It never did, but still Wyatt dropped to his stomach and wiggled out of the garage as fast as he could. Running around alone was a one-way ticket to game over. He knew Ava was long gone, taking any answers with her, but there was something big brewing.

If Wyatt wanted to figure it out, he knew he had to get to the Hydrexo Centre tomorrow morning, even if his parents tried to keep him away.

LEVEL 12

WYATT ARRIVED BACK AT his building with the package wedged under his arm, holding a sandwich in one hand and sipping on an Iced Capp from the other, with a box of Timbits hanging from his wrist. Despite the steep price of an iced drink, it was a successful Timmies run; he needed the brain fuel to figure out how to get to that competition, and maybe even to make some guesses about what the heck the competition actually *was*.

He'd gotten a confirmation email on his phone not five minutes after Ava left, which meant she wasn't pulling some elaborate prank on him. No, Ava Maraj was connected with Operation Hostile, seemingly as more than just some video game player. She'd said that she'd get to hunt real Bluddites after she won. If Wyatt won, would *he* be hunting Bluddites? With a real mini-blaster? Was the General real too, and ready to ask dorky little Wyatt if he had what it would take to stop the fall of humanity?

The idea seemed too ludicrous to even consider how he felt about it. All he knew was that Ava Maraj had answers, and since he couldn't count on running into her in the building, but knew she'd be at the competition, he'd go too. Maybe he'd meet that other person on the walkie-talkie connection as well.

He was so caught up in all of this thinking that he didn't even see the person standing next to his building's revolving doors until they spoke: "H-hey, Wyatt."

Wyatt flinched.

Under the shadowed overhang of the building, Zav Silva looked small and sorry, not unusual except the fact that he wasn't in school at noon on a Thursday. He was wearing his typical faded clothes, a Toronto Raptors ball cap pulled low, and carried Leo's old tote bag. He pulled a file folder out and thrust it toward Wyatt.

"I tried to go in, but the doorman said I had to wait outside," he said. He wasn't looking at Wyatt's face; he was looking at the Iced Capp.

Wyatt felt that usual pang of guilt. He numbly took the folder to wedge under his arm with the recruitment pack, keeping his lips smashed shut before he could say something awkward and terrible.

Zav blinked and looked to the parched pavement. "I heard you got a concussion so I—so I collected all your homework and—"

Wyatt's heart jolted. "You didn't have to," he started to say. The thought of water-starving Zav doing anything for Water Baby Wyatt seemed wrong, and cruel. They'd barely spoken all year, and not at all before that. So why was Zav trying to reach out now?

Zav turned his head, just barely, like shaking it all the way would hurt too much. "I just thought—well you'd been talking about playing video games after school and I-I didn't know how to ask so I . . ."

Wyatt's stomach was dipping and spinning. Here it was, the great big post-friendship breakup awkwardness. The moment when they had to remember growing up like brothers, and playing video games on Wyatt's fire escape, and climbing the brackets together even though they were weird because they just understood each other. Zav too quiet, Wyatt too loud, and they just *fit*. But one of them had stayed a Water Baby, and the other hadn't. And while Wyatt was *still* playing his video games, complaining about teasing, taking long showers, Zav wasn't. But what could Wyatt have done to stop it? Nothing, he thought, but wasn't sure about that. And that was even worse, that he could have helped and hadn't, and now any sort of attempt to fix that would mean thinking about it.

"I get it," he said, trying to smile. It felt forced. Zav was the one rambling, and so he had to be the one to try to find a way to put that into something coherent. He'd never been good at that, but tried anyway. "It's . . . it's weird. Everything, now."

Zav stopped. His chapped lips pressed together. Wyatt wondered if he'd messed this up and just made everything worse.

"I'm sorry," Zav said. As if he had anything to apologize for. "That I didn't try to reach out instead of—"

"Me too," Wyatt added, as fast as he could, like saying it

quick would somehow make up for a year of silence. He flexed his fists, trying to take this slow. "I guess I just felt . . ." The world was full of monsters, actual real-life scaly creatures, and yet being honest was just as terrifying. "I felt like you wouldn't like me anymore," Wyatt admitted. Yes, Zav made him feel a bit guilty, but he'd always known that Zav couldn't control that feeling in him. "Like I'd make you feel bad."

Zav nodded, and rubbed at his eyes. They were looking puffy. Wyatt thought he was just going to leave it there, no obligation to correct Wyatt if it was true.

"Me too," Zav said.

Neither said anything else, because there wasn't much else to say. Even if they were honest, it had still been so long. And yet, despite how the world could be falling apart, Wyatt didn't want to turn away. Even the awkward, tense silence here was more human connection than he'd had in a long time. Maybe for Zav too.

"So about *Fathom Fall*," Zav started. He seemed to chew on the thought. "Maybe we can play together?"

After two years of nothing in common, there might be this. "Leo bought it for you?" Wyatt asked.

Zav put his hands in his pockets. "The community center had a raffle last week—just filled out a form and won it. Lucky, I guess," he said. There was a bit more brightness in his dark eyes, like he actually believed that. "I've been playing after school. Maybe we can play a game tonight? I could come over?"

Wyatt's stomach sank. He might have to spend the whole

night convincing his parents to let him compete, or planning how to sneak out. He couldn't give Zav the truth, even if he wanted to just cough it all up, messy and awkward and terrible, until it formed one mega beast between the two of them that they could fight together. Still, he didn't want to burden Zav, yet didn't want to make him feel pitied. He could only be so honest.

"Maybe," he said. "Concussion."

Zav's posture crumpled worse. "Um, right," he said. He swayed like he might be dizzy. "I gotta get back before my lunch—my lunch—lunch period ends, but my profile number's the same and I put my number on a sticky note in the folder—it just goes to the front desk, but you can leave a message."

"Okay," Wyatt said. He prepared to turn back for his building, and yet couldn't.

The Bluddite problem was so huge and complicated that helping one person, especially Zav who had been like a brother, seemed easier than it ever had. And Zav had given him some help too, even if he didn't know that homework was the last thing on Wyatt's mind.

"Do you want my Iced Capp?" Wyatt asked. Did this look like pity? Cheap charity? He didn't know what the rules were here: he just wanted to help. "Transactional, as a thanks for the homework?"

"Oh, gosh—gosh, I couldn't," Zav tried to say, but his eyebrows were furrowing together, and his round nose was crinkling. He kept blinking, hard. "I mean you paid for it and—"

"Here," Wyatt said. He fumbled to flip the straw upside down (that was a good gesture, right?), swapped the Iced Capp and the Timbits box into one hand, and held them both out.

Zav seemed to decide that manners had gone out the window; he snatched them both from Wyatt's hands, hugging them close to his chest. "Thanks," he said. "J-j-just give me a call if you want to play."

Wyatt nodded. "Gotcha. And, um, stay away from the sewers," Wyatt added, before turning through the revolving door before Zav could ask what the heck that meant.

When Wyatt stepped into the cool AC of the lobby, he turned back to look through the plate glass. Zav had chucked the Iced Capp straw and lid away and was tipping half of it back into his mouth. Wyatt watched some of it miss to drip down Zav's cheeks. He thought of the Bluddite over the sink. Zav swiped his arm over his face and then went tearing into the Timbits box.

Wyatt wanted an easy, no-one-feeling-guilty world where he could play video games with Zav again. He wanted to see Leo too, and for his parents not to be so stressed out and annoying, and for water to be as easy to drink as a turn of a tap. And so, before he could get the future he wanted, he had to make sure the present didn't dive-bomb into destruction.

He had to get to that competition to find answers, which meant he had to find a way around his parents.

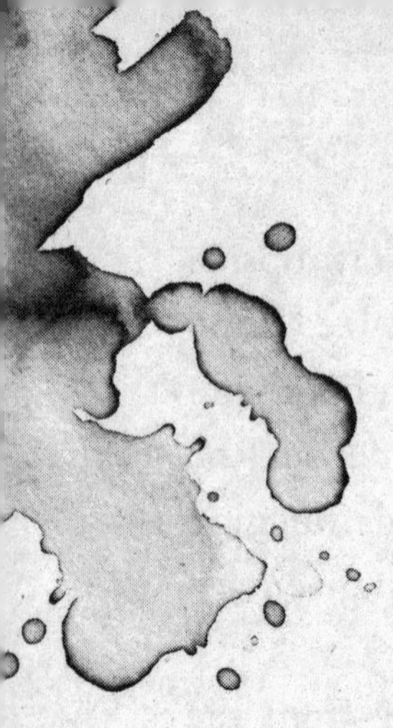

LEVEL 13

WYATT SAT IN HIS room, reading his handbook over and over. He was wearing his jacket, thin and blue with the logos and sponsorships and his username down the sleeve. The official invitation with all the location info was sitting nearby, along with print copies of the waivers his parents had signed when he submitted his application, and his commemorative knife. It was like the ones in *Fathom Fall*, though smaller—he'd have to put some force behind it to do real damage. He figured there'd be no harm if his parents caught him with it.

There *would* be harm if his parents caught him with competitor's merch and knew he'd do anything to get to the Hydrexo Centre. He'd decided that there would be no way to convince them why this mattered. Last night had proven that they'd rather control him than listen. So, he'd cut them from the equation: tomorrow, they'd leave for work, and then he'd sneak out and head off for the competition without their permission. He could ask for forgiveness after.

After. Ava had said she'd be shooting Bluddites after she won, but was Wyatt supposed to believe that this competition was some sort of . . . *recruitment*? Why run a championship for kids under sixteen? Yeah, the game was most popular with teenagers, but surely there were adults who played? Why give Ava a mini-blaster in the first place, instead of some big army veteran like the game's version of the Hydrexo Private Security Force? He just couldn't believe that any adult would trust her enough, or him. He was missing something here.

Whatever it was, it had to be important. It had to mean *something* in the fight against the Bluddites. He refused to believe that there was no bigger plot, or that there was no way for him to help.

He chewed on that and kept studying up through the afternoon and evening (his teachers would be thrilled if he had this sort of attention span for school, but his grades would never be as important as the fall of humanity), until he realized he was hungry. He looked up from his studying and the glow of his desk lamp out the dark window. Past the alley below, the Hydrexo Outpost logo shone neon blue in the night. The price had climbed to $4.38 thanks to all those open hydrants, and though that wasn't great and he knew they had to get a handle on the Bluddites to stop it, what was stranger was that the clock said it was 7:59. His parents still weren't home.

Wyatt frowned and reached for his phone. He'd set it to Silent to focus, but saw that some texts had come in from his mom.

5:16 : Staying late. Should be done by 6. Love you.

6:32 : It's looking more like 7. There's a frozen pizza in the freezer.

Wyatt looked from the messages back to the time on his phone, then walked out to the living room.

It was entirely silent. Everything was black and gray and quiet, besides the glowing time on the stove. Definitely eerie.

Wyatt knew he'd need strength for tomorrow, so he turned on the oven (unsure if this was a "bake" or "convection bake" situation, since he rarely had to do anything more than heat up leftovers), opened the fridge-freezer in a rush of cold light to locate that pizza, and then decided he should call. He almost tapped his mom's contact, but was frankly still a bit sour about her taking away his *Fathom Fall* gear. Maybe it was petty, but he tapped his dad's contact instead.

It rang until it went to voicemail. Wyatt huffed. He told himself he was just annoyed with them, but it wasn't entirely true. His parents *did* work at the biggest remaining water refinery that had already been blown up once, presumably by the very same monsters that were only getting stronger out there.

Wyatt stopped that thought. "Don't go freaking out now," he muttered, maybe just to hear a sound other than the humming fridge in all the quiet darkness. He flipped on the kitchen lights so it wasn't just him and the glow of the oven, but the bright white against the cold chrome and marble didn't make him feel any better. He called his dad again, to the same ringing and voicemail message. Wyatt shifted his lips against his braces.

"He's standing in the pump room," he told himself. He

was probably working with all the chugging machinery, so he couldn't hear his phone going off. It happened all the time. Wyatt forced himself to stop being a petulant little child. He was trying to prove to her that he was mature, so he tapped his mom's contact. The call rang, and rang, and rang.

"Rebecca Docherty," he heard her say. He'd be lying if he said it didn't calm him down juuuuust a bit.

"Hey, Mom," Wyatt said. He threw the pizza onto a baking sheet and sat back on the stool by the island while the oven preheated. "I'm making that pizza."

The machinery rattling on her end faded as she moved to somewhere quieter. "That's good, sweetie," she said, voice clipped. "We might still be a while."

"Okay," he said. But then his eyes caught the blank spot in the knife block, where he'd taken and lost the honing steel. He thought about how it had all started before: something strange with the boilers. His stomach tightened. "What's going on? Is the machinery being funny?"

"Oh, it's nothing like that," she said. There was an uncomfortable pause, like she was debating telling him or not. "Don't worry—how's your concussion? You're not straining yourself too much, right?"

He rolled his eyes. "No," he said, which was almost a lie. His head hadn't stopped pulsing since Ava threw him, but he'd taken some Advil and would get through it.

"That's good. Try to stay away from the TV, all right?" she said. "And I told Mr. Greene to check on you."

A fire-hot feeling struck through Wyatt to curl in his knuckles. "Mom, it's fine," he said, his voice growing sharper. "I don't need a babysitter."

She sighed. "Don't start with me, Wyatt—"

"No, I will start with you," Wyatt snapped, swiping the remote off the island and standing. Maybe it was because she wasn't in front of him, so he didn't have to look at her when he told her off, or it was because he knew something terrible was happening right under everyone's noses and they could all *die*—either way, he wasn't going to take all this coddling. "First you say I'm lying—you say I'm crazy—"

"Going to therapy doesn't make you crazy," she tried, in that soft, sympathetic way that he was starting to hate. He knew she was right, but it just made him more frustrated. Sure he'd used the wrong words, but why couldn't she just understand what he was *trying* to say?

"You said I hallucinated," he tried. He was already turning on the TV, muting it so she wouldn't hear anything, then raking through the channels toward CBC. He knew something was going on; that's why she didn't want him watching TV. He wasn't a dumb kid. "And then you take away my video games 'cause, what? You think I can't handle it? That I'm a baby?"

"You are still a *child*, Wyatt," she said, a little louder, less exhausted and more angry. His mom rarely snapped at him. He was getting under her skin. Good. "I don't like this tone."

"I don't like yours," he said, just as sharp. "You're treating me like a kid, but I'm grown up enough for you to tell me things and not do that 'you'll understand when you're older' crap. *You're* the one who isn't understanding."

He heard the door open on her end and a voice that sounded like his father.

"Yes, all right," she called, and then turned louder back into the phone. "We'll discuss this later, young man," she said. He knew she didn't actually see him as a young man at all, just a whining baby. He wanted to throw his phone across the room so it broke into a million pieces. "If you want to be treated like an adult, then start acting like one."

He was! Why couldn't anyone see how much he was doing!

"You don't get to just hang up," Wyatt said, louder now, almost shouting. "I want to discuss this right now! Why don't you care what I wan—"

The line clicked off, just as Wyatt reached CBC, and he lost all his fighting spirit. There was an overhead shot of the refinery, but something was so very wrong. Bright helicopter lights flooded down into the streets, catching rainbows shimmering out from every fire hydrant in the vicinity. They'd all been opened.

And all along the fence that circled Hydrexo, there were kelpy-finned *things*.

Wyatt's heart jolted.

He unmuted the TV.

"—hostile gathering outside Hydrexo's Lake Ontario refinery," a reporter's voice-over said. The image switched to a cell phone camera through the fence. Wyatt was sure he was going to see blue-and-orange Bluddite faces as they charged.

The things against the fence *were* bug-eyed and strange-faced, but when Wyatt blinked, he saw they weren't Bluddites at all, but people dressed like them, or at least similarly. Some of them wore goggles like big round eyes, had helmets to make the tops of their heads bulbous and skull-like. Others had gas masks that split their mouths into circles with the two filter holes on the sides where they'd spit out the blood solids, or big scarves that made them look like they had ruffled gills. Some of their clothes were tattered, like kelpy fins.

They weren't Bluddites. They were protestors. The similarities were a bit uncanny, but clearly coincidental. As the hydrants poured water down onto them, they kept their arms linked right up against the fence, a dense crowd with painted fabric banners held at the front, or signs raised high. Wyatt saw a few actual Bluddite faces painted on posters, including a grisly cartoon of one biting the neck of someone who looked a lot like the Hydrexo CEO. The phone cameras zoomed.

Game over: prices down NOW!

Hydrexo is a climate criminal

What's yours is mine! Enough to go around

Water is Life! 100+ Indig communities
still unsupplied!

Cut the Corporate Breaks—People Over Profits

"While protestors have declined to speak with media," the voice-over continued, "social media posts have called this the Water Raid, an indefinite protest calling on Hydrexo to lower the cost of water, eliminate breaks for corporations or stock investors, expand its waterlines further into remote and low-income neighborhoods, and to address its alleged stock ties with weapons manufacturers and natural gas companies."

Wyatt moved slowly around to the front of the kitchen island. He couldn't do anything but stare at the TV, even with his pulsing headache. The reporter said that the protest had built up slowly, first as laborers looking for work, like always, but then more and more people joined, pulling out signs and pulling on gear. Security cameras in the area had been knocked down, or blinded by laser pointers. By the time anyone knew what was happening, Hydrexo had fallen under the siege of a thousands-deep crowd.

"Anonymous social media posts also suggest that there may be some Hydrexo employees at the protest," the reporter went on to say. Wyatt cringed. Why would Hydrexo employees protest the company that paid them, housed them, gave them everything? "One anonymous post reads, 'As long as Hydrexo can rely on cheap labor, our safety protocols and pay won't change. Solve the water crisis NOW!'"

As if it was so easy.

The camera feed switched again. Hydrexo CEO Peter Davids sat at what looked like a boardroom table, wearing his usual wire glasses. He was still smiling, yet there was something just a bit more distant about it.

"We're not panicking," he said into what was obviously his laptop webcam. Behind him, a window looked down on the floor of the plant, where the pumps were all still churning. Wyatt squinted, trying to spot his parents among the distant, blurry people marching through the aisles and catwalks. "We're working to meet with representatives from the protest to create a committee addressing these concerns. All protests end, even indefinite ones. To be honest, we've been expecting something like this."

Wyatt had felt the powder keg lighting up as well. He knew every word out of Mr. Davids's mouth before it came: they'd been saying the same thing for over a year, ever since the explosion, even as nothing seemed to change.

"We aim to meet these demands, but currently, without the Lake Superior refinery, there just isn't enough water. We're doing the best we can to give everyone what they need, and we're doing it alone, which means we face the brunt of people's fear," Davids said calmly.

The camera switched back to the protestors. Someone raised a smoke bomb high, flooding blue clouds through the lights that rolled like waves across the protestors. Their masked faces looked like Bluddites rising from the lake. The footage switched to the security gate, where protestors were shouting at the cameras behind the closed chain-link. They surged against it, threatening to break the gate off its hinges. What then? How would breaking in solve anything?

"To those continuing to support us, we thank you—your gratitude and investment mean the world to us. Together, we can rebuild the Lake Superior refinery as the first step to supplying everyone as necessary."

"Mr. Davids," a voice said. The feed switched back to Davids in a split screen with a reporter alongside. "Several signs and protest posters have been using the image of the Bluddites from the Hydrexo-sponsored game *Fathom Fall*, with many claiming that the game is propaganda and a distraction from the current crisis. What do you have to say about these claims?"

Davids nodded slowly. "*Fathom Fall* is about the importance of humanity banding together to protect our natural resources," he said. He didn't say it was fictional. He didn't say Bluddites weren't real. He looked harder at the camera. For some reason, Wyatt was sure he was looking right at him, or at least at anyone who knew *Fathom Fall* was more than a game. "Anyone who plays will tell you that the Bluddites aren't sympathetic. They aren't noble. They're hostile creatures trying to tear us apart physically and socially. I'd hate to think the people of our city would replicate that by opening hydrants on purpose."

Why choose to act like the monsters that sucked your blood right out of your body? Monsters that targeted humanity's last remaining water and would steal it all until they had no more? Wyatt couldn't understand. Even in desperation, why were people fighting against the one place trying to help them? There was a much bigger threat!

But if they knew, would humanity band together to fight together, or would they just be angry that Hydrexo had kept the secret for so long? The longer the problem went on, the worse it was. And this anger in the streets clearly didn't need any more panic added to it.

"We'll do what we can to keep the plant running at top performance, despite the threat," Davids said, with a sure nod. Again Wyatt didn't think he was talking about the protest, but something larger that swam under all of them. Only certain people could be trusted with the truth, Wyatt realized. He wanted to be one of those people, even if Ava just thought he was a spoiled Water Baby. "Because we can*not* afford for the Lake Ontario plant to shut down. There isn't enough water to fill quotas, and if we lose this plant or aren't smart with how the water is distributed, we'll be in some serious trouble. I know that sounds frightening—"

Wyatt *was* scared, but he was ready. The same ready feeling he always had before a game, where the thrill outweighed the fear.

"—but it's the truth," Davids said.

The camera flicked back to the usual reporter sitting at his CBC desk. He was touching at his earpiece like he was getting breaking news.

"This just in," he said, which Wyatt usually found funny because it was cliché, but couldn't that night. "The Toronto police have arrived to peacefully disperse the protest and identify organizers, in order to allow working vehicles through and reach a solution." Wyatt leaned forward, waiting for the footage. There was none. But the police would find the people who organized this so they could join that working group Davids was talking about. Then it would all be resolved, peacefully. "Contacts inside Hydrexo say they'll remain in soft lockdown until sunrise, but it appears that tonight's performance will draw to a quick close."

In the bottom right, where commercials streamed by, the *Fathom Fall* General asked if *you* would fight the fall of humanity, and announced the championship would be commencing at 9:00 a.m. Eastern Standard Time, where ten lucky soldiers would fight for three title spots. He needed to be there tomorrow. He'd planned to sneak out after his parents left for work . . .

But if Hydrexo was going into soft lockdown until sunrise? He didn't know when his parents might come home in the morning. And considering his argument with his mom, she'd want to talk to him.

That would complicate his plan to sneak out, but he wasn't going to be stopped by some adults thinking he was still a child.

Wyatt aimed the remote like an aqua blaster and hit the power button. The TV snapped to black. It was just him in his half-lit kitchen, the oven humming.

Think, *Wyatt*. He narrowed his eyes, staring at the blank TV across the room and pretending it was the loading screen. What could he do to escape the problem? How would he fix this? They couldn't afford to lose the last plant they had.

They had to fight back. He looked down at the homework folder sitting on the island. Wyatt didn't know what the competition was, but he knew he had to get there.

LEVEL 14

STEP ONE: WYATT COOKED and ate the pizza, because he did need energy.

Step two: he called the front desk and told Mr. Greene that he might head to bed soon, making a big deal about how he was going to sleep in for "concussion healing." With any luck, Mr. Greene would relay that to his parents in the morning and give him some extra time, but just in case . . .

Step three: Wyatt used the oldest trick in the book: he arranged various blankets and spare pillows under his covers to look like a sleeping Wyatt was curled up under there, complete with an old Toronto Zoo orangutan stuffed animal where his head should be—the resemblance to his own choppy orange hair was uncanny. He switched to his spare glasses (even bigger and dorkier, unfortunately) to lay his usual set on the bedside table next to his half-empty water bottle.

When he stepped back, it looked more like a dead Wyatt under the covers; it was too still, and too quiet. It was freaky, actually. Wyatt flexed his hands to keep a level head, asking himself what a real soldier would do. He had to be resourceful.

So he grabbed the old night-light in his closet to plug it in on top of his dresser. He was *way* too old for it, but once the steady white noise started up, and the revolving cover spun shadows and lights of stars and moons all around the room, the pillow-Wyatt seemed like it could be breathing. His mom already thought he was a stupid kid, so hey, why not work with what he had?

Step four: his recruitment letter said to bring his jacket *and* his Goggles, so he dragged a chair over to fish his Goggles off the top of his parents' wardrobe (the same place they hid everything), perched them in his hair, zipped on his jacket, and looked to the empty spot on the knife block where the honing steel used to be. He was going to leave the apartment at night, alone, so he needed to be smart. Good thing he had a proper weapon now—he hooked the commemorative knife in its hard-shell carrying case onto his belt, then covered it with his jacket.

Step five: Wyatt opened his homework file, found the sticky note, and reverse-searched the number. The address for Zav and Leo's building popped up. It was only a short ride away from his building, would give him some good cover until morning with the only people he trusted not to rat him out (and frankly, the only people he knew, which was even then pushing it), and then he'd hop another transit line to the Hydrexo Centre.

Wyatt packed a bag, left out the fire escape, and shut the window tight behind him.

Just because his parents thought he was a dumb kid didn't mean he had to act like one.

LEVEL 15

THE RIDE TO ZAV'S place was a straight shot on the 501 streetcar. Wyatt trooped out to the stop and waited on a bench, shifting uncomfortably to keep the bars from bruising his tailbone. He didn't understand why they couldn't just make normal benches—well, he understood *why*, that it would let people sleep on them, and apparently letting people sleep on benches was bad.

After the streetcar arrived, he tapped his metro card, then sat down on the red seat, staring out the window as they puttered west. Some businesses were beginning to close for the night, switching off their bright signs, pulling grates shut across their windows and doorways. They passed Trinity Bellwoods Park just as a city worker locked the gates shut, watched over by the two night-guard police officers who would ensure no one would try to sneak in overnight. That always felt a bit weird to Wyatt—it was a *public* park, right?—but his dad had said there were rules in place to make sure everyone was using public space fairly. When they stopped at the next light, Wyatt saw a shadowy figure curled up under the awning of a closed store, sitting on an old sleeping bag and leaning against the rough bricks. He figured it wouldn't hurt anyone if they got to sleep on soft grass instead, maybe even in a tent like on the sidewalks or in the little park near Hydrexo, especially when no one else was using Trinity Bellwoods anyway.

The streetcar trundled on, past pockets of modern condos rising taller every day. The street was bright as they neared Zav and Leo's neighborhood; there were posters on streetlamps announcing DIY concerts and community theaters and other artsy things, reminders of why he'd always thought Leo and Zav were enjoying it out here. But when the streetcar stopped to exchange some passengers, he spotted three dark shadows spilling from a side street, of two cops speaking with a swaying man in worn-down clothes while their curbed car sparkled with siren lights. He wondered if that man was going to be escorted to one of the shelters in Toronto, but had heard they were full, so he figured somewhere farther than that. He didn't know how far you had to go before there was room, but water was even more expensive out of Toronto, so folks just came right back to what they knew. A Hydrexo Outpost seemed to stare from the street corner, the price glaring down on the pedestrians wading through the city lights.

When water went up, rent payments fell short, evictions got worse, and more people were left sleeping in alleys. "Way of the world," Wyatt muttered, because his dad always said that. He didn't think that was true, or that it had to be, but he understood why it was easier to pretend. Otherwise, you had to think about how useless you felt. In an alley, a huge graffiti Bluddite screeched with blood on its face and gills. If the Bluddites won, then humanity wouldn't just have to worry about water competition with each other, but also with terrifying monsters.

But if someone did something, they could save the Lake Ontario refinery, and maybe even bring back the one at Lake Superior.

There were answers to all of this, every bad feeling and strange disaster. Soon, Wyatt would understand it. And then he'd fix it too, for everyone.

The streetcar stopped at Queen and Sudbury, where he exited with a small crowd. On the sidewalk, the other passengers peeled away in their own directions. Wyatt took a moment to get his bearings, blinking in the harsh neon off the HOTEL sign standing tall above him. He rarely came so far west, and never alone. The streetcar rolled on, ducking into the shadows of a high train bridge along with a few other late-night cars. But still, as Wyatt tried to orient himself, he realized he was the only one on the sidewalk. A distant siren called from somewhere farther out. Condo windows gleamed down. Wyatt knew there were hundreds of people alive on this block, and yet couldn't see or know them specifically, the same way he didn't really know anyone in his building. He figured it was the sort of alone-in-a-crowd feeling you could only have in a big city like this. If he suddenly disappeared into the dusty pavement beneath his feet, who would know?

Wyatt scraped his lips against his braces. He focused on Sudbury Street ahead, which curved south off the main strip into quieter darkness, following the GO train tracks. He smacked the button on the crosswalk. A poster stared at him from above it:

WHATS YOURS IS MINE
DROP PRICES NOW

He was trying.

He crossed and stepped into the gloom of Sudbury Street. The dull rumble of Queen Street fell away, until the electrical buzz of the streetlamps grew louder than the distant tires far behind. Wyatt kept his eyes on the sewer grates as he passed alongside them. Even though they were closed, the flickering white lights off the train tracks made him unsure. He bundled into his jacket and walked at a careful pace. Not suspicious, but ready to run if he had to.

Something shifted ahead. Wyatt stiffened. Past a corner of construction scaffolding bracketing up a new skyscraper, a woman was leaning in the alley, wearing a faded denim jacket and fraying toque. She looked up at Wyatt with her sunken eyes, fingertips working a greasy knot into the hem of her T-shirt. Despite the swarm of feelings in his stomach (guilt, worry, shame, so many things that were his fault more than hers), Wyatt offered a flat pedestrian smile as he passed.

Her fidgeting hands reminded him of scraping his braces against his lips. "Any cigarettes?" she asked him.

Wyatt swallowed. "No," he said. Leo used to carry some on her, even though she didn't smoke. "Sorry."

She squinted at him, or in his vague direction, perhaps recognizing his age now in the low streetlamp light. He couldn't tell how old she was, younger than his parents, he thought, but old enough to give him the drug talk apparently: "Good," she said, nodding. Her words were dry and stilted, like Zav's. "Nasty habit. Don't start on that."

Wyatt wanted to roll his eyes, but maybe it was kind for some random adult to care about his lung health. "I-I have water?" he offered, holding his backpack straps tight. "If you want some." He wondered if that was the wrong thing to say, too eager to help or maybe even a bad spot to put himself in, but held his ground.

She shook her head. "S'fine," she said. She kicked a bag at her feet, where Wyatt noticed a semi-crunched plastic water bottle in the side pocket, mostly full. "You have a good night now."

"You too," he said. And for good measure, even if he didn't know how to give a proper warning without freaking people out: "Stay safe." He carried on past her down the sidewalk. He was three steps away when her voice rang after him.

"You stay back from the sewers," she said. It sent ripples riding down Wyatt's spine, making the hair on his arms prickle up against the thin-smooth fabric of his jacket. "Trouble down there tonight."

Wyatt was surprised, and yet, hadn't he said that the

Bluddites would target people alone at night? He just hadn't suspected that they'd live to give warnings.

Wyatt looked back over his shoulder to ask her more, but she'd already gone off down the alley. It felt rude to follow. Still, whatever this Bluddite problem was, it was getting big enough for word to catch on. Pretty soon, maybe everyone would know. Ahead, a poster pasted onto the lamppost had a drawing of a writhing Bluddite, with the blocky words "GAME OVER, WATER MONSTERS" slammed around it. Wyatt wondered if the artist knew about the Bluddite infestation, or if this was related to the Hydrexo protest.

People were already so angry. If monster-word got out, there'd be even more chaos. This needed to be fixed soon.

Wyatt made his way down the street, passing a few other buildings. Finally, his target location appeared around the bend: a tall brick-and-glass apartment complex that actually didn't look too bad for Zav and Leo, all things considered. At least it was still in Toronto. Wyatt's stomach tightened with both apprehension and excitement. After all this time, he was going to see Leo again—he wondered if her hair was still pink, or if she'd gotten any new piercings, or what she'd been doing this whole while. And really, if there was anyone to mention Bluddites to, wouldn't it be her? She was grounded and practical. And Zav had always come up with such great plans to distill Wyatt's thoughts down into smooth logic.

Sure, the whole world couldn't know about Bluddites, but maybe Zav and Leo could. And then Wyatt wouldn't be so alone with this. The three of them could make a plan even before he got more answers from Ava.

But to get to the front doors, Wyatt would have to walk past the apartment building's adjoining courtyard. It spilled out along the sidewalk, a deep gouge with no lights on, the streetlamps only catching the faintest gray outlines of some bike racks on the edges. Wyatt swallowed, leaning forward as if he'd step past the neighboring building. But that courtyard had too many hiding places, and he'd just heard that there was trouble around. He wished he had night vision.

He did have his Goggles sitting on his head. *Fathom Fall* to the rescue yet again.

Wyatt pulled his Goggles down over his glasses and ears and turned them on to their Standby Mode setting. The world blurred for a moment, static and glitch lines fizzing at his vision like a video game powering up. Finally it calmed to the utilities symbols circling the real world ahead, just as dark and quiet.

Wyatt spun the dial on the side and watched as the sidewalk ahead of him changed colors. Blue, then yellow anti-glare, then infrared colors that Wyatt knew weren't *actually* infrared. He landed on high-res green.

Even if it looked like the world had been dunked in green slime, the courtyard was a bit clearer. There was a tidy rock garden just off the sidewalk that had probably replaced a fountain, then a skate park in the middle, and brick paths on either side filled up with bike racks stretching off toward the distant alleys. Too many hidden corners.

Wyatt scraped his lips on his braces and toggled at his settings again, this time selecting the volume. He crept it higher and higher until even his own breathing sounded monstrously loud. He'd hear anything coming at him. And, just to be sure, he pulled out his knife. It was as light as the right-hand controller.

With that, he crept slowly down the sidewalk, swinging his aim between the shadows and dips of the courtyard, but also the grates on the street. He wondered if he was being a bit paranoid.

Nope.

His volume sensor spiked to a warning yellow—through the amplifying in his earpieces, he heard movement from the skate park, past the cement planters and rock garden. He recognized it immediately.

A scrabble of claws on pavement.

Wyatt turned, gripping his knife and darting his eyes over the lip of the skating bowl. He couldn't see into it, but he did see a hand rise up, five-fingered and scaly. It splayed out against the pavement, shortly followed by a second. Wyatt watched with red-hot lungs as the two hands hauled up two kelpy-finned forearms, then the smooth dome of a fishy head, two bulbous eyes shining white in his night vision, and a round mouth filled with tiny teeth.

Wyatt's first instinct was to sprint for better cover than the planters, hope he could outrun it. In the corner of his vision, his volume sensor lit up suddenly orange, then *red*—an oncoming train whistle screeched through Wyatt's raised volume. White light washed blindingly across his night vision. His concussion *screamed.*

The Bluddite leapt up from the skate bowl. Wyatt yelped and raked his Goggles from his eyes. They fell to the pavement. Wyatt dove behind the nearest planter, falling to a crouch and pressing his back to the cement, knife clutched in his sweaty hand . . . and Goggles lying forgotten where he'd stood, out of reach.

Crap! His head was ringing and pressurized, and his vision was all frantic images of toxic spit landing in his eyes and turning them milky and blind. Forget night vision: he could see the sidewalk and road ahead of him just fine under the streetlamps, and if he could draw the Bluddite out toward him, then maybe it'd be a fair fight? At least if he could count on his chunky glasses to block its spit? Was it worth it to chance going back for his Goggles? Should he abandon the mission and try to run? He was wearing a backpack, but it wasn't as heavy as security gear, so maybe he could still sprint?

Before he could make a decision, footsteps rushed toward him. They didn't sound quite as slimy as a Bluddite, but he didn't have time to second-guess this. A dead monster couldn't spit.

Wyatt took a deep breath, staring out at the weedy train tracks across the road. He adjusted the grip on his knife. He made his face like a blank mask.

The footsteps slowed just behind him. Wyatt held the knife underhand so he could plunge it down over and over. He'd tackle the monster and stab it into the pavement—

"Wyatt?"

He almost jumped out, knife raised, when he looked up to see Zav Silva staring down at him with his nose crinkled in confusion. In the low light, his face looked like a sunken skull. "Oh man, that's—that's a knife. Why do you have a knife?"

Wyatt had no time to answer. He jolted his head out from behind the planter to scan the courtyard again.

Nothing, besides him and Zav, and the distant creak of something metallic from down one of the alleys.

Whatever he'd just seen, it had been scared off by the train, or maybe by Zav.

They were safe, for now

LEVEL 16

"DO YOU WANT TO tell me—tell me why you're here and why you have a knife?" Zav said, swaying beside Wyatt while he stalked through the courtyard pace by pace, scanning every crevice with his knife at the ready and his Goggles back in his hair. Now that he had Zav with him, he was a little bolder. Plus Zav knew where to wave his hands to turn on the motion lights, so Wyatt didn't need his night vision.

"I thought I saw something," Wyatt said, unsure if now was a good time to explain everything. By then they had swept most of the courtyard and there was no sign of any Bluddites, besides a sewer grate down one of the alleys. The cover was slightly crooked, which was good evidence, but Wyatt wanted to be absolutely sure.

"Why d'you have a knife in the—in the first place?" Zav asked him, trying to get a good look at it. "Is that the competitor knife? Did you get picked?"

The courtyard was clear, or at least *looked* clear? Wyatt debated another sweep, but decided he would have to trust his instincts. "Yeah," he said. He put the knife back in its holder, but didn't close the safety strap just yet. He wouldn't do that until they were both inside, when he could talk to Leo.

There were far more frightening things out there than this question: "Can I sleep over tonight?" Wyatt asked. "I dunno if you saw the news, but my parents aren't home and . . ." *And I told them I'm staying with a friend*, he almost said, but didn't want to lie to Zav.

Zav's shoulders tensed. "And so you came here," he said slowly. They were under one of the motion lights, where Wyatt could see every detail of Zav's face down to the flecks of skin on his chapped lips, and the dry, itchy redness of his squinting eyes. Wyatt wasn't sure how he'd expected Zav to react, and yet wasn't comforted by the way he looked back over his shoulder, as if he'd rather be somewhere else. "Without calling."

Wyatt's throat felt dry. "Well, you said we could play *Fathom Fall* together," he tried, even though he *knew* that hadn't been the request.

"At *your* house," Zav said, louder now and forced out through his teeth. For the first time, Wyatt noticed that Zav's voice had gotten deeper since they were twelve. "Leo isn't—isn't home right now."

Wyatt wanted to melt, but he had to keep his nerve. "I just need a place to crash," he said, voice pitching toward something desperate. "I don't care if it's on the floor or whatever—"

"I've gotta be up—gotta be up early tomorrow."

"Me too," Wyatt told him. "I'll be gone early, I promise."

Zav took a slow breath through his nose. He didn't sway,

but he looked exhausted. "You should have called," he said again, more stern than nervous. The corner of his mouth twitched—was he angry? "You can't—you can't just show up and not call and expect me to—"

"I know," Wyatt squeaked. Dammit. He blinked, trying not to let on how tight his ribs felt. There was so much on the line. He couldn't afford for his parents to keep him home, and he couldn't afford to sleep outside tonight when there were bloodthirsty monsters out there. "I really need this favor, Zav. I know we don't hang out anymore—I've been thinking about that, and I'm sorry, like . . ." He tried to think of anything good to say, but he was still Wyatt, so painfully awkward. He needed help, but where had he been when Zav needed him? How was he making up for it? "Like . . . like super sorry," Wyatt decided on. But because he knew it wasn't enough, he started pulling off his backpack. He dropped it between them, crouched to open the zipper, and showed five water bottles inside. Zav's eyes stayed narrowed, like he might kick the whole backpack away. Or maybe like he'd kick Wyatt.

"You can have them whether or not you let me stay," Wyatt said while he looked up at his old friend, maybe his *only* friend. "But I'd appreciate it, Zav. Like . . ."

"Like *super* appreciate," Zav said. Wyatt swallowed dryly, but the corner of Zav's mouth twitched into what was almost a smile. It was flat, maybe even bitter, but at least he had the humor to mock Wyatt while his eyes stayed dim. He reached down and picked up the bag, hugging it to his chest like he had the Iced Capp and Timbits.

It wasn't a permanent fix, to anything, but hopefully it was the first step.

"Fine," Zav said, looking at Wyatt's shoes when he stood up. "Only 'cause Leo would—Leo would be mad if I didn't give someone a place to crash when they needed it."

Wyatt finally exhaled, only then realizing how tense he'd been, perhaps even since sneaking out of his apartment. He could explain once they were inside. Surely Zav would want to know, and help, right?

Without a word, Zav turned back for his building's side door. Wyatt took one neck-craning look into the skate park to see that the bowl was empty. He was still ready to pull out the knife if he had to.

He followed after Zav, who tapped his keycard to the reader to let them into a dimly lit hallway. There was a wall of mailboxes, and a corkboard filled with job postings and some mental health resources. Another doorway led to a long hallway of numbered doors with a stairwell sign at the end. Wyatt opened his mouth to say that the building looked nice, actually—he'd expected worse. But before he could say that and then realize it was rude, Zav turned to shove instead through a dark, metal door with a No Unauthorized Entry sign. Inside, a flickering light shone greasy shadows that smelled like wet rock and gasoline.

Wyatt pressed his lips to his braces, but followed in after Zav anyway. They stepped into a cement stairwell. Pipes and wires ran along the rough walls and ceilings, like they were heading toward a garage instead of a warm apartment.

Wyatt had eased his nervous gait since stepping inside, but now it was Zav who was looking around, peering over the banister before they descended. It smelled awful down there, the gasoline reek mixing with something more sewer-y. Wyatt noticed a fair amount of cigarette butts collected in the stagnant puddles. A plastic No Smoking—No Drugs sign was bolted into the wall, with information about the nearest safe-injection site. They'd closed that, Wyatt remembered, something about it attracting too much trouble.

Ahead, there was just one door, labelled as a maintenance room. Zav knocked. The sound rang out. Maybe he had to clear visitors with the maintenance team, instead of a security guard?

But when there came no answer besides the shadows shifting with every flicker of the lights, and Zav pressed his ear to the metal door, Wyatt began to doubt that. Some part of him understood what was happening, and yet he didn't want to say it. If it was true, it would mean so many other awful things.

He caught Zav's eye. "Hey," he started, but Zav just pressed his lips together and shouldered through the open door. Wyatt could do nothing but follow.

The maintenance room smelled like a dusty old mop, all chemical and thick and wet. A few cobwebbed fluorescents spattered light over a rusty boiler, a collection of metal cabinets with hazardous labels, and thick pipes running up the concrete walls to twist along the ceiling. Wyatt thought to snap his Goggles on and grab his knife, do a good scan, but the drain in the middle of the floor was too small to let anything through, and frankly, it was Zav who stopped him.

"I guess we can go to—go to the Hydrexo Centre together tomorrow," he said. His voice was quiet, detached. He'd walked to the back of the room, to a dull ladder leaned against the wall. He scooted it sideways. Wyatt stepped around the boiler, in time to see Zav rock the ladder over to a cluster of pipes along the ceiling. Above them, there was a small, dark gap. When the ladder clunked into the pipes, a blue sleeve fell out like a tongue, aqua blue with the entire username easy to read:

Z_Lion_Z

That rookie, who'd played for the first time the day Wyatt was attacked. He'd thought the nickname was some sort of "the lion sleeps tonight" joke, but it was probably a mix of Zav and Leo. Was that Leo's competitor jacket? No. She'd be way too old. Wyatt might have been one of the only kids who knew Bluddites were real, and suspected that competition was more than just a sporting event, but he knew he wasn't the only person given a chance to compete. Someone must have reached out to Zav too. Wyatt didn't know how good Zav's scores were, but he was sure he knew why Zav was happy to compete in a game he'd just started playing.

If he looked closely, he could see Zav's tote bag and schoolbooks hidden up there, as well as his *Fathom Fall* gear.

But what he couldn't see there, or anywhere in this maintenance room, was any sign of Leo Silva.

"Make yourself comfortable," Zav muttered. His expression was hard to read. He pulled himself up into his hidden "room" that was just a sheet of wood balanced on the pipes, threw Wyatt's backpack against the wall, then used a hockey stick to knock the ladder back to where it had been. If Wyatt didn't know to look for him up there, he would never have seen him. Zav opened Wyatt's backpack and started downing the first bottle of water with that same parched desperation from before.

Wyatt looked around at the boiler room with his stomach tight, like when he saw tent encampments and felt so upset that it was like fear, or maybe like guilt. Zav stared down at him, mouth still wet and eyes a little wild from under his greasy hair and sun-bleached Raptors cap, but Wyatt knew his old friend was no Water Baby anymore. It was hard to think of Zav as that same kid who sketched Zip-Monsters in Wyatt's room, putting a vision to whatever strategic dream Wyatt was barking on about. They used to understand everything about the other. He'd thought he knew how bad things had gotten, but apparently not.

Wyatt pulled himself up onto the top of the boiler. He was still a foot lower than Zav, but it felt better, like he was closer.

"Zav," he started. He was scared that he already knew the answer, but had to just say it all. Say the uncomfortable, awkward truths, and hope they could figure it out together. "Leo isn't here."

Zav made a quiet sound, like "yeah, obviously." He stared down into the water bottle. He'd already drank two-thirds.

"Is she . . . ?" Wyatt started. His eyes felt dry too, skin tightening uncomfortably. He had to keep saying it. "Is she supposed to be coming back, or . . . ?"

Zav tilted his head, as if he couldn't find the energy to shake it all the way. "It's been a while," he said, then sniffed just once, no tears. He could afford to waste the water now, but Wyatt figured he'd gotten good at saving. "We were living here—living here in an actual room after she quit Hydrexo, but then she went out—she was always going out for work . . ." He trailed off, still staring down. He sniffed again, shoulders beginning to shake.

"I get it," Wyatt said. He realized too late that it might sound like he was pretending to understand what Zav was going through, not that he just meant "I understand what you're getting at." But this was Zav, who understood Wyatt's poorly placed words, and so Wyatt carried on. "She didn't come home."

Zav just sat there. "I w-was working a bit, but I couldn't pay the rent. I knew—knew they'd call someone, take me away even if she did show up again. So I hid here until . . ." He swallowed, as if he might only now be realizing the next part. "I don't think she's coming back," Zav whispered. But he couldn't have possibly guessed what Wyatt suspected: that this could have been more than some hit-and-run, or being jumped in an alley.

Leo had been out alone, in a city full of monsters. The

image of claws and blood and reaching hands made Wyatt's stomach plummet straight down.

Leo was gone. That was it. No coming back for a second round, just gone. He hadn't talked to her in more than a year, but he had at least thought that he *could*, believing that Leo Silva would continue to be one of those lives behind a glowing apartment window, still there even when he didn't check in. The snapshot of Leo reaching up to cut him loose of the car wreck wouldn't move aside for the nicer memories. He could picture the blood in her hair, the way it dried against her tanned skin, her trembling fingers and her backpack spilled across the ceiling-turned-floor of the upside-down Jeep. And still, she'd been telling him "it's okay." And it wasn't. She'd gone off to live somewhere else, get a fresh start, but she didn't. Because nothing was working. Things were only getting worse, and now it was Leo who paid for it, and Zav who waited for her after school. Surely he knew she wasn't coming back, but what could be done at that point besides pretend it wasn't so bad?

It was. All of it was.

Wyatt swallowed stiffly. He wouldn't cry. That was for dumb kids; that was baby crap. And yet he knew that more people would die. He wondered if that woman from the alley had a safe place to go to, and if she'd made it there. Or that man the cops were talking with. There were hundreds of people out there in the city, maybe thousands, who could just disappear. And who probably did, while the people who knew them didn't even realize it.

Wyatt pushed down the tears. He was going to fix this tomorrow, somehow. Somehow there would be answers and a solution, because there *had* to be. The idea of sitting here powerless and accepting every horrible hurt and every big mean thing out there was impossible. If anything, now he had backup in Zav—the two of them were going to the competition, so all the more reason to let him in on the truth, right?

Zav sniffed. Wyatt watched one single tear shine down his cheek before he angrily swiped his arm across his eyes, wrenching himself away from Wyatt and shaking his head. "I don't wanna talk about this anymore," he forced out. He took another quick sip, then capped the bottle, fingers stiff. "I have to focus, for tomorrow. I'm gonna make the top three."

Wyatt didn't know if his score was good enough to even try, but Zav's eyes were fierce, the same look that scared Wyatt a bit when he was chucking back that Iced Capp. A look that said there was no "trying" to win, because there wasn't any other option.

"Ten *thousand dollars*, and all the water—all the water I can drink forever," Zav said. "Maybe I can even get a sponsorship. I can stream or . . . I can make this into a job."

Zav didn't have time to worry about the world ending, not when he was on the edge of ending too. Wyatt flexed his hands out, trying to stretch the tension from his fingers. Once it had been him picturing his face on cereal boxes, believing that if he wanted something bad enough, obviously he could get it, because he'd gotten everything else. But he knew it wasn't because he was special, or lucky, or particularly talented . . . He just had a stronger start than other kids. He could spend all his time practicing, while Zav had spent all his time hiding and trying to figure out where the water would come from next.

Zav was right: Wyatt couldn't distract him. He'd had a week to process Bluddites being real. Zav didn't have the space to mull that one over, come to terms with his sister's gory death, and prepare to save the world. But Wyatt did.

Sure, it would have been nice to be less alone with all the bad things, but that was what going to the competition was for. He'd figure out the rest tomorrow. And in all that, Zav could still win that prize for a future more permanent than some water bottles from Wyatt's bag. They could both walk away from this better.

For now?

"You're gonna win," Wyatt said. He wasn't certain what the competition would involve, even just in the gameplay let alone the wider plan, but he knew *Fathom Fall*, and Zav knew Wyatt. "It's about strategy. If you plan it right, then—"

"Like *Zip-Monsters*," Zav said, almost a whisper, like he hadn't thought about this in years. "Make the right team."

Yes. "We can make a strategy," Wyatt said. Just like *Zip-Monsters*, or even like being the only two Water Babies in their grade. Together, they could get through this. Zav was already pulling his notebook from his backpack. "I don't totally know how they're running this 'Operation Hostile' thing but—"

"Don't care," Zav said. Already, his voice wasn't so dry. Perhaps by tomorrow he wouldn't sway either, or wince through his words. Things could get better, and they would. "Tell me what you—what you do know. We'll go from there."

Whatever tomorrow's test would be, they'd win, and set a path toward fixing everything.

LEVEL 17

THEY'D STAYED UP PAST midnight planning. Wyatt rambled, and Zav wrote notes, until they decided it was better to be well rested and start again in the morning. They were getting a plan together to win, because this was bigger than a game for both of them. Wyatt didn't know all the details about why Hydrexo was bringing so many *Fathom Fall* players together, or about Ava's cryptic threat about hunting Bluddites after she won, but he knew that he was going to help defeat the monsters *and* get Zav up on that podium.

They woke up, bought a box of pastries and two large sodas from the Portuguese bakery on the corner, then set up a study spot at the back seats of the streetcar. Despite how every bump and rattle made his bones ache (the cement floor hadn't exactly been a nice bed, even with the blanket Zav tossed him), Wyatt reviewed the basics: don't go near open sewers unless you're ready for what might come out, keep moving because the Bluddites can hear your blaster going off, don't walk on silos or water towers because there's *always* some sort of trapdoor that'll drop you down to drown in water or grain or cement—all the general things.

Zav nodded along, looking more awake than he usually did. Even if his jeans were still too big, his shoelaces were fraying, and he had a weird half-faded bruise stamped in the middle of his forehead, his competitor jacket was bright. Plus, he'd gotten to tidy up in the bakery's sink once he said he was with Wyatt, a paying customer. Now his longish black hair was pulled into a tiny, stiff ponytail at the back so it wouldn't get in his face, and he didn't smell like dry shampoo and Axe, but like that pink restroom soap. His sway and headachy squint seemed to have backed off a bit, but he still had that foggy, careful way of speaking.

"Are we starting—starting in the same place?" he asked, holding his notebook in one hand and using his other thumb to pick pastry flakes out of the nearly empty box. "That one time we played together, we all started in the truck."

"I don't know. Some maps you're together, and some you're separate," Wyatt said. Zav's pages were fluffed up with notes, full of speculations and plans for "what if," but they didn't know what any of the ifs were. "I guess if we're all racking up our own scores—"

"We don't know that," Zav added. "What if it's still a group score?"

Wyatt didn't think that was a very good way to find a winner, but he didn't have an answer. There'd been no news about how Operation Hostile would be different from regular *Fathom Fall*.

Zav clicked his tongue. He looked at the last egg tart, took it when Wyatt nodded for him to go on, then flipped through rough sketches of various game maps, each with a star scribbled in. "We have meeting spots," he reminded them both, nodding more to himself than Wyatt. Wyatt could find those spots easy enough, but Zav wasn't familiar with all the maps just yet. If he was too focused on following the game map in his utility screen, he'd be an easy target. And if it was a *new* map they hadn't planned for?

"Just . . . don't rush to it," Wyatt decided. If they died on the way to each other, and with bad scores, that'd be it. "We still need to get kills in. Take your time. Be . . ." He waved his hand around, trying to find the word.

"Methodical," Zav said. "Make sure we're clearing buildings and checking that the coast is clear as we move."

Wyatt snapped his fingers to agree.

"I'm still confused about the scoring," Zav said, squinting at the notebook as if that might clarify it all. He took a huge crunch of the last tart, speaking through a mushy mouthful. "Your score sets when you die, but why isn't it just 'last man standing'?"

Wyatt took a second to answer. He'd never thought that hard about it. "Then people could just hide. Wait out the clock," Wyatt reasoned. "The scores have to matter."

Zav nodded and wrote out *scores set when you die*. "What about if there's—there's two people left and they have the highest scores already? Does it just end?"

Wyatt sipped his soda. Zav was kind of killing him with all

the questions, but he supposed he'd never bothered to think this hard about a plan beyond "shoot and win and look cool doing it." He'd planned to get to the competition, but hadn't actually put much thought to a strategy once it started.

"They have to die too to set their scores," Wyatt said. "'Cause like . . . what if they got disqualified or something?" Zav opened his mouth—Wyatt knew the next question. "Leaving the game early puts your score down to zero, so no rage quitting. *Or* you can get your score halved by friendly firing someone."

"Yeesh," Zav muttered. He crumpled the tart's aluminum wrapper and slumped down further, scribbling it all in. "People really try to shoot other players?"

Wyatt shrugged. "I figure we're going to be a bit more careful about it when there's ten K on the line."

"No kidding," Zav said, and began gently dragging his pencil through the Northern Highway map, twisting toward the meeting spot with his eyebrows pressed in tight with focus. It was a lot to memorize so quickly, but Zav had the good sense to ask questions, and Wyatt had the answers.

Hopefully it was enough. The streetcar passed a Hydrexo Outpost—someone had spray-painted "WHATS YOURS IS MINE" across the door, and a splattery Bluddite. In the streetcar window's reflection, Wyatt saw Zav watching it too, or maybe he was focused on the price inching ever higher.

"We'll just have to be smart," Wyatt decided, which seemed like a mature thing to say. "Be logical about getting to the spot, and stay calm."

Zav snorted, almost a laugh. "Says you," he said as the streetcar lurched to a stop. "Don't pull a knife on me this time, and keep your feet to yourself."

Wyatt was still a bit embarrassed about last night's knife mishap, but mostly he was confused about the feet thing. He opened his mouth as the streetcar doors slid open on the first wave of *Fathom Fall* fans rolling in to fill the seats. Then he was distracted.

Every fan who joined them on the streetcar heading east to the Hydrexo Centre was dressed in their game merch—hoodies like Wyatt's at home, some with chevrons and even one with a star from the top twenty-five. There were people with graphic tees of the General, or with their faces painted in camo, and a few kids with real military fatigues that they must have bought from the army surplus stores, or they were Cadets (which Wyatt had always thought of as "Boy Scouts, but military") wearing the smaller, kiddie versions. Some were dressed like Bluddites, in kelpy "ghillie suits" and goggles, looking suspiciously like those water-desperate protestors. There were a few adults, mostly confused commuters or chaperones, but the oldest fans were barely past their high school years.

And, Wyatt noted, the majority of them kept giving him and Zav careful looks, because they were the ones in the aqua-blue jackets with "Competitor" down the sleeve and their Goggles in their hair. Was Ava getting the same looks, wherever she was? Or Loop? Or B? Wyatt realized, perhaps for the first time, that he really was going to the competition he'd been dreaming about for *months*. He felt far more serious about it now, but it didn't stop the subtle excitement. Down the aisle, some younger boys were staring at him. One of them had big glasses and choppy hair, not the sort of "hero" you'd expect, so Wyatt waved, and the boy grinned and talked excitedly with his friends while the streetcar rolled between all the tall downtown buildings.

"I feel famous," Zav said.

"Not famous," Wyatt said. He noticed a few people in the same merch shirt: a Bluddite spitting with its gills all fanned out, the words "GAME OVER" written under it. "We're important, Zav."

Zav hummed like he didn't quite agree, scribbling restless doodles in the notebook's margins. Ahead, two boys with three chevrons each were staring down the usernames on Wyatt's and Zav's arms. They turned to the guy sitting beside them, who was wearing a blue jacket too—Wyatt also saw brightly colored gaming headphones around the boy's neck, and orange-and-aqua sneakers so clean that even the treads were sparkling white. The boy's dark hair was spiked up like a flame, cool enough to be in a Red Bull commercial.

Kevin "B_Townz" Park, a broad-shouldered East Asian boy who was probably almost too old to compete, sat staring at Wyatt and Zav. A week ago, Wyatt would have been starstruck and worried about fumbling, but instead he just waved cordially to flash his username. B nodded at him, like, "I know *you*, DoctorDoctor," but then tilted his head to signal Zav.

"Show your username," Wyatt said. Zav lifted his arm

awkwardly, like he was holding up a shield against a dragon. B and his friends seemed to read it a few times, think hard and realize they had no idea who he was, and then reconverged into a circle of muttering. That was B's team, Wyatt reasoned.

Zav deflated, tucking his notebook away and sipping on the straw of his mostly empty soda so it gurgled. This was Wyatt's team.

"I only recognize four competitors by their usernames," Wyatt offered, hoping to be helpful.

"What's his score?" Zav asked. The energy in his eyes was dying out. He looked so serious, as grim as Wyatt felt. Zav probably didn't care about being a nobody so much as he cared about being low on practice.

"Doesn't matter what his score is," Wyatt said. He shoved his shoulder into Zav's, unsure if that was awkward or comforting, but trying anyway. "I said I'd watch your back, and we made a good plan. We'll win this."

Zav nodded, but both he and Wyatt still sat in calculating quiet. Wyatt kept catching his eyes on the snarling Bluddite graphics in the crowd.

There was so much on the line.

LEVEL 18

THE CANNED TRANSIT ANNOUNCER voice called out, "Bremner Boulevard," the streetcar stopped, and the doors opened. The people holding the overhead railings funneled out first. Zav and Wyatt hopped off last, tossed the pastry box into a recycling bin, and joined the river of fans flowing down Blue Jays Way. Steel-and-glass buildings rose above them, still miniscule against the CN Tower looming so high up it seemed to bend against the pristine blue sky. The chatter of the crowd grew louder and louder, mixing with drum-and-bugle music coming from unseen speakers in the distance.

Just ahead, the domed Hydrexo Centre stadium waited for them, in the middle of a courtyard so crowded it looked like a rippling ocean of merch hats and sun-struck hair, cresting up into islands of vendor carts, swirling with spinning currents. As they crossed the street into the flood, Wyatt spotted a covered army vehicle painted to look like a Hydrexo Private Security Force truck, where real Canadian Armed Forces soldiers were letting fans try on the heavy body armor or helmets and handing out pamphlets to the oldest ones. People shoved past, dragging siblings by the hand, clutching branded popcorn cups. It was all so loud Wyatt thought he'd have to shout for Zav to hear him, but he had nothing to say anyway. He was filled up with a dull roaring in his chest, excitement and nerves and just a hint of fear.

Wyatt and Zav had to do some elbowing, but they finally made their way to the doors, and then into the concrete stadium entryway where everything echoed and smelled like hot popcorn and spilled soda and crisp new T-shirts. It was just as crowded with kids of all ages. Wyatt noted that there were way more girls than he'd expected, especially considering that Ava was the only girl competing. He wondered if she felt like she had something to prove too.

At the turnstiles, they showed their jackets and waivers and were allowed past the slow trickle of people heading through the metal detectors—Wyatt hadn't even thought of getting the knife through that, and was glad to luck out. He felt trusted, which was a new and good feeling.

The wide hallway around the main stadium was cramped with people running every way and trying to shove up into the stairwells for the upper levels. Wyatt had been to the Hydrexo Centre for Blue Jays games (with Zav, actually, when both their families got tickets on behalf of Hydrexo), but this was even more hectic. They said there were no fans like baseball fans, but Wyatt disagreed. There were no fans like gaming fans.

"Look," Zav shouted, grabbing Wyatt's shoulder. Wyatt

turned to where he was pointing: a hanging electronic sign above one of the arches leading to the stadium floor.

COMPETITORS, PLEASE FOLLOW THE ARROWS TO YOUR WAITING ROOM ⟶

"Good eye," Wyatt said. He and Zav made their way around the circular hallway. A Hydrexo worker in a blue hardhat and Hydrexo Cares shirt was handing out free water bottles—they both took one, accepting a "Good luck, boys" as well. At the reminder of his parents, Wyatt realized they were probably already home and waiting for him to wake up. He switched his phone to Do Not Disturb. Once they realized he wasn't actually asleep, they'd know where he'd gone.

Through the stadium archways, Wyatt saw chairs stretching across the floor of the arena, blinking and strobing in the sweeping lights while music pulsed. Up on the stage, a screen was divided into ten angles, each of them showing different audience members shaking signs or waving their hands. That wasn't unusual for a gaming competition: when they started playing, that would stream all the competitors' game feeds.

But where other gaming competitions usually had ten fancy stations set up for the players, with ten high-tech gaming chairs and sleek controllers, this stage was completely empty besides a podium in the middle, probably for a commentator of some sort. Well, this *was Fathom Fall*, where you needed good range of motion with your arms—they'd probably just stand up there in their Goggles, ten players locked into the virtual reality of whatever Operation Hostile was. Considering what Ava said, Wyatt was certain that this competition's gameplay would be different than the usual rounds, but still didn't know how.

He just had to stay sharp, find answers. Prove he had what it took to be let in on it all, because he did.

Finally, he and Zav reached a set of metal doors, where a *huge* guard was dressed in real-looking Security Force fatigues. He had a walkie-talkie on his shoulder, and a taser on his belt. Zav drew back a bit, but the sign above the door had an arrow pointing down, so Wyatt went on ahead. They had every right to be here.

"Hi," Wyatt said, and popped the front of his jacket. Zav stayed a half step behind him. "We're competing."

The guard looked them both over, tilting his head like he was judging if they were competitors or had just found a way to forge the jackets. He looked longer at Wyatt, and then turned into his walkie.

"Docherty is here, sir," he said. Wyatt paused. The guard stepped aside for them, opening the door and holding it with one broad hand. Wyatt waited for him to add "and Silva" . . . he didn't.

"Let him get settled," the radio said. Wyatt's pulse stopped. He *knew* that voice, especially when it was rustling with static, just like every command in the game. "And tell him I'll speak with him soon."

Wyatt didn't need to be told twice. Without having a face to put it to, Wyatt recognized the voice of the General, right from the games. If there was someone who had answers about what today was all about, it would be that guy. This was all going exactly as he'd hoped.

"Why just you?" Zav asked, pausing in the doorway.

Wyatt pressed his lips together. "Maybe it's something with my waiver," he lied. "Don't worry about it."

And even though Zav narrowed his eyes like he *was* worried about it, and maybe like he didn't trust Wyatt all the way, the two of them walked into the competitors' waiting room together with only half an hour until game time.

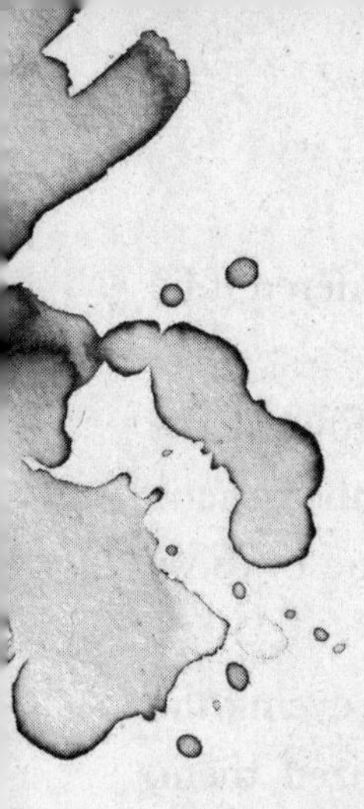

LEVEL 19

WYATT AND ZAV ENTERED a long rectangular room covered in aqua-blue and orange-gold *Fathom Fall* merch. There were posters on every wall, and streamers on the tables. It looked like the sort of birthday party Wyatt would request if he was five years old. There was a table full of shirts, hats, sunglasses, phone cases, lanyards, and anything else anyone could get a logo on. Across from it was a selection of every snack or drink that had ever put a *Fathom Fall* character on its packaging, which was quite a lot. There were no listed prices, just signs with a max limit per competitor.

They must have been the last two to arrive; eight other kids were milling around to have their picture taken next to the gold trophy they *might* win, or filling up *Fathom Fall*–printed plastic bags with all the free stuff. Wyatt didn't think they all needed six new T-shirts, but if it was being offered anyway, they might as well stock up. Somehow, B had already beaten them there, and was letting the excited, fully uniformed Cadet take a selfie with him. He smiled without teeth, chin up, looking casual and confident. Wyatt wondered if he could ever replicate that.

It didn't matter—Wyatt was on a mission. Toward the back of the room, there was a semicircle of beanbag chairs shaped like curled-up Bluddites. And sitting in one of those chairs with her feet on another was Ava Maraj.

Zav was already easing toward the food table, eyeing the two boys standing there. Wyatt sort of recognized them, thought they might have been streamers too. From the sounds of their conversation and the way they held up their phones, Wyatt guessed they were comparing game footage. He knew Zav didn't even have a cell phone.

"I gotta talk to someone," Wyatt said over the game music from the speakers just near them. "Are you good until we start?"

Zav looked to him, nodded slowly, and took a deep breath. "I'm good," he said, voice still slow but with new confidence. Wyatt wondered if the sorry and small way Zav used to walk was from dehydration too; his posture was easy as he strode toward the table. He gave the other boys a nod before he started grabbing some cheese puffs.

As for Wyatt, he marched across the room, right toward those beanbag chairs and Ava.

She wasn't being very social, which he might have expected from someone so . . . *intense*. Instead, she leaned back with her hair falling around her face in the usual veil, her thumbs plunking into her phone screen. Her feet were on the chair next to her, but so was another boy. While Ava was playing the antisocial video game addict, the boy she was all close with was chatting away with some other competitor Wyatt didn't recognize.

"It was a total roast," the boy said.

Wyatt knew that voice: Ava had been speaking to him yesterday. The boy was just a bit older than Wyatt, or maybe just taller, with sharp cheeks and a broad nose and one dangling earring. There were three chevrons shaved into the side of his fade-up, which was popular fashion with the other Black boys at Wyatt's school, at least the ones who played *Fathom Fall*.

"I'll do the same thing today," he said, moving his arms in some little idle dance.

Wyatt recognized that too, or at least the way the boy never stopped moving. Before Wyatt could say anything, the boy noticed him standing there. Wyatt didn't know what reaction he was expecting, and even so was surprised when the boy's dark eyes widened, and his mouth stretched into a grin.

"Doc!" he said, throwing his arms wide like he expected Wyatt to dive in for a hug. "Wagwan, man? Damn, you look *exactly* like I thought you would."

Wyatt had never imagined "Loop_D_Round" as anything other than his avatar, six-foot-seven in a neon vest with a Bluddite tattoo. He blinked, darting his eyes from Loop to Ava sitting next to him; she was still looking at her phone, thumbs blurring over some rhythm game at a frankly inhuman speed. Loop seemed to notice.

"Easy, fam," he offered the other kid, who gave him a goodbye nod and then moved on to trail after B. With that guy gone, Loop held a loose palm out toward Wyatt. "Luther Derond," he said. He had a rainbow thread bracelet on his wrist, the sort of thing you'd get at a Pride parade. "But Loop's good by me. Ava told me about what happened yesterday, so I'm guessing you got questions about it all."

Right. That was the whole reason he was here: answers.

Wyatt sized Loop up, trying to figure out what his game was. He wasn't decked out like B, didn't have a video game star smile. He was just, well, a person. Just another boy, one who surely knew that real monsters were out there, and yet sat all casual. Wyatt didn't know what to think about it, but at least knew Loop to be friendly.

"Good to see you, Loop," he decided, reaching to shake Loop's hand.

"Sure. Hopefully you play better than last time," Loop said. It was clearly a joke, but the embarrassment of that final *Fathom Fall* game still struck through Wyatt's stomach. All too late, he realized that Loop had been looking for a dap—their hands fumbled into a very weak little shake. Wyatt's cheeks burned, perhaps even more so when the corner of Loop's mouth twitched up.

Wyatt looked *exactly* like Loop expected, and Wyatt knew he didn't look like much. So had that been an insult? He thought he and Loop were on good terms, but what if that wasn't true?

"Yeah, I have questions," Wyatt said, lurching his hand

back and resisting the urge to shake the feeling away. "I was hoping I could get answers from Ava."

Loop shrugged. His hand landed easily on her shin, where he gave her a friendly little shake. Perhaps as expected, she kicked him off instead of looking up, but it wasn't as hard as Wyatt figured he'd have been kicked. Clearly they were close—well they *were* coworkers, of a sort, it seemed. Did Loop have a mini-blaster too? Would he also be able to shoot Bluddites if he won today?

"She's not a big talker," Loop said, and then motioned to himself like, "but clearly I am." Wyatt *still* didn't know what to make of him, which was only shortening his fuse.

"How come I've never met you before?" Wyatt asked. He set his feet apart, trying to puff his chest to look a bit taller. "I see Ava at Hydrexo events all the time, and around the offices."

"Not my scene. Go to some corporate party and hang out with the admin nerds?" Loop started, pointing both open palms at nothing. He swiped them to another invisible option. "Or stay up in the penthouse with all the strawberry energy drinks a man could want? Easy choice, ahlie?"

Sure. Wyatt said nothing, mostly because he was realizing that Loop also lived in his building. Of course, Wyatt scuttled through the halls as fast as possible to avoid all social interaction, so he wasn't exactly surprised he'd missed out on meeting Loop, just disappointed in himself. Then again, he surely would have botched any chance of friendship the second they interacted off-line, so maybe it was for the best that they were only meeting now under these serious terms.

Loop was still talking: "Besides, they want their eyes on Ava more than me anyway."

"Loop," she said, even without looking up. Wyatt had known Ava was impressive, but now it sounded like she really did have Hydrexo's favor. Could he actually beat her? Did he have to, if there were three spots? Was he even playing at the same game as her? Maybe *she* would get a chance to fight Bluddites if she won, but what about him? Then why bring him anyway? But why bring her and Loop?

Wyatt flexed his fists against his sides, trying to be subtle about it. "You've been in on this for a while, huh?" he asked, keeping his voice low. "Why?"

"Loop," Ava said again, but Loop didn't seem to care about secrecy as much as she did. He rolled his eyes and held up a hand beside his mouth, like he was telling a secret.

"Early recruits," he said, in a voice not much quieter than before. "Ava got brought in for the Alpha tests, and I got brought in on the Bravo tests. Us two got the highest scores so . . ." He patted his chest. Wyatt realized what he meant:

Ava and Loop weren't just *Fathom Fall* players, but play *testers*, training in whatever penthouse Loop had mentioned. How long had Hydrexo been developing *Fathom Fall*? And, perhaps more importantly, how long had Ava and Loop been practicing for this moment?

"So why am I here?" Wyatt asked, quieter. He took a

quick look over his shoulder. Most of the other contestants were a ways off, but Zav seemed just about done loading up on merch. "If I win, then . . ." He trailed off, looking for any sort of confirmation.

Loop raised an eyebrow and leaned back in the seat. "If you win, then," he said, like that was an answer. "Yeah, man. It's what you're thinking."

"You don't know what I'm thinking," Wyatt said.

Loop raised an eyebrow. "This whole thing"—his finger spun through the air, indicating the room or maybe the whole Hydrexo Centre—"this is the Charlie test. Winners move on. We'll be hunting them Bluddites."

Ava shuffled her feet. Wyatt wondered what that look was, but Loop held confident eye contact, enough to tell Wyatt he'd been right about this: whoever won today would be fighting Bluddites *for real*.

"So you wanna team up?" Loop asked easily. Monsters were real; this was a recruitment mission, yet Loop still seemed so casual. Wyatt wondered if he'd just had time to get used to it all, or if that was just who Loop was. "We might be seeing a lot of each other at the end of all this, so best get to knowing you IRL, you get me?"

"You wanna team up," Wyatt restated, just to see if Ava would react. Was she in on that plan, or was Loop just putting out invitations? "You, Ava, and me."

"Yeah! Ava's got a killer score, and I've got a bunch of medic badges," Loop said. He pantomimed two little guns with his hands, rattling them off in Wyatt's direction. He was as fidgety in real life as in the game . . . Wyatt wondered if he had ADHD too. Maybe that was why he'd always liked Loop, not that it mattered now.

"I already have a team," Wyatt said. His skin was beginning to crawl, more so when he saw Loop shift his jaw uneasily. "Zav Silva—Z_Lion_Z—he's a friend of mine," he said, for the first time in over a year. His skin crawled worse.

"Well, only three of us are moving on up," Loop said. He jerked a thumb to Ava, then himself. He was still smiling, though Wyatt liked it less and less. "And not to sound cocky or nothing, but us've been at this longer than you."

Wyatt wasn't going to let that get to him. "If you're so good," he said, squaring his shoulders, "why are they making you compete?"

Loop's smile widened. He shook a finger at Wyatt. "I told you he'd be a bad one," he said to Ava; it appeared to be a compliment more than an insult. Her flat expression hadn't changed. Maybe he'd impressed Loop, but not Ava. "That's fine though—bring Lion too. We can all patrol together and just let the scores go up however they do. We're all on the same team, really: us against the monsters, right?"

Wyatt had never thought of it that way. And yet, when Ava looked down her nose at him, he suspected she hadn't either, and wouldn't. Wyatt still didn't know how today's competition would differ from the usual *Fathom Fall* game. But no matter what it brought, only three of them would win.

Wyatt looked over his shoulder; Zav was wandering over with a paper plateful of nacho chips and three slices of pizza.

Several bags hung off his arm, holding what looked like an entire six-pack of *Fathom Fall* energy drinks, along with half the clothing. If he wasn't leaving with the prize pack, he'd make a killing on resales. But that sort of money couldn't last forever, not the way 10K could, or perhaps even whatever stable job this "monster hunting team" could be.

But before Wyatt could say anything, Ava stood up.

"I'll take him to the General," she sighed, like it was a great big chore. Wyatt resented being treated like laundry, but this was still good: he was going to speak with the General. Loop had given him some good answers, but he still wasn't wholly sure what Operation Hostile was, or why *he* and these other kids were being asked to hunt Bluddites.

Ava didn't even bother to check if Wyatt was following when she started walking toward a door at the back of the room. Zav sauntered up, kicking his shoe into Wyatt's like a silent greeting. He already had his chin lifted, clearly trying to size up Loop. This was Wyatt's team.

He leaned sideways to whisper to Zav. "This is Loop_D_Round. He wants to make a team of four. Figure out if it's worth it—I gotta deal with the waiver thing."

"Lion!" Loop smiled. He happily held out his hand. "Did Doc teach you everything you gotta know or do you still need some tips before we go on in there?"

Zav easily dapped him up and fell back into the beanbag chair. He popped an energy drink open. "Tips are good," he said. "What's this about a team?"

Loop grinned. Wyatt reminded himself that Zav was still

his friend first, and that neither Zav nor Loop seemed underhanded enough to leave him out of the mix. With that, he scuttled away to follow Ava out of the waiting room.

They'd entered a long cement hallway with a few dull lights that made her look like just a silhouette. The door to the waiting room closed behind, leaving them in almost complete silence, besides a dull reverberation of music. He thought they might be behind the stage.

She didn't say anything, even when he caught up to her. The hallway was too long to walk in silence.

"So . . . " Wyatt started. She stared dead ahead. He was committed to getting better at socializing. "I didn't know you're Caribbean." No response. His mouth kept going. "It's cool you speak Patois. I wish I could speak another language. I only got a B in French."

She said nothing, but he saw her jaw tighten, like he was annoying her.

"Are your parents from there?" he asked, realized that wasn't quite clear, and then fumbled out a very awkward, "The Caribbean? Are they from the Caribbean, I mean."

"*Were* from Guyana," she said quietly.

"Yeah, obviously," he said, because he figured they *were* from there, and *now* were here, working at Hydrexo. He wished his parents were cool enough to let him sign up for something involving mini-blasters and training in a top secret penthouse. "Are they gonna watch the—"

"They're dead," she said so easily Wyatt thought he might trip. He waited for her face to change, but it didn't. "So they *were* from Guyana, and then they worked at Hydrexo, and now they're dead."

Wyatt's hands went cold. Admittedly, that made a bit more sense than parents willingly putting a mini-blaster in her hands, but it just meant he was *still* screwing up talking to her. His posture was better, he felt slightly more sure of himself, but he still couldn't crush words together right.

"Oh," he said. He didn't know what else to offer, but wanted to try anyway. "My, uh . . . Zav lost his parents too, when that all happened, so if you wanna, like . . . talk to someone who—"

"I have Loop," she said, as if she hadn't been basically ignoring him before. Then again, he and Zav used to just sit on the fire escape playing their own games, not saying anything, and weren't those some of his best memories? "We live in the penthouse, and the General pays us to train for killing what killed my parents, and I get to go to Hydrexo meetings and build *Fathom Fall* and talk to investors about it. It's a job. There's nothing to cry about."

It did sound cool, when she put it like that. Swept up into the care of that tough, military-adjacent guy in aviator sunglasses, trusted to tag along to all sorts of important places, given a fancy penthouse with a secret gaming/training facility in a hidden room behind a vault or a bookcase. Or, well, maybe Wyatt had read too many comic books, surely it was a bit more realistic than that, but she was basically an orphan superhero now.

Still, her parents had died. Wyatt hated his parents

sometimes, wished they'd stop treating him like a toddler, but if they *died*? He knew he'd be devastated. And lost. He wanted to think that a blank poker face was good for soldiering, but seeing Ava's in profile felt not just creepy, but kind of sad too. He figured no all right person could look like that, even if they did have a fancy Hydrexo penthouse and top secret job.

"So if you've been training since then, why *are* you still competing?" Wyatt asked.

"Confirmation," she said simply.

He supposed that made sense? Except not fully—her score was practically perfect. What more was there to confirm? "Well, I'd be happy to team up with you, like Loop said," Wyatt offered. "If you need more help."

She froze. Wyatt's shoes squeaked as he stopped.

"I don't need a team. It's insulting that I'm even competing with people like you," Ava hissed, almost like a threat. One hand hovered near her hip—he saw a tiny sliver of her knife's hardshell holster. So she'd brought it too. They were a lot alike. "You're all playing a game, even Loop. I'm not."

"I know what this is," Wyatt said, refusing to back down. But so did Loop? Why was she so special? "We're on the same team, like Loop said."

Her eyes hardened. "Loop's sweet," she said, not like a compliment. Loop was lounging back playing video games all day, but it was Ava who attended all the meetings. Wyatt wondered how much more Ava knew. He got the strange impression that even Loop was a step behind her, no matter how close they seemed to be. "He still thinks we can all be friends, that we're doing this to help each other out. That what you think too?"

Well . . . yeah. "We're trying to save the world," he said. "We're changing something, to make it all better. I don't think that's *sweet*. It's brave."

Ava didn't say anything for a moment. Wyatt's neck prickled. He wanted to flex out his hands, or scrape his lips against his braces, but forced himself not to move.

"Loop and I are gonna win here today, I'll make sure, but this isn't about *saving the world* or whatever," she said. It was cynical, almost disappointing. Maybe he'd overestimated her. "There's just doing what we need to today, moving to the next phase, and getting even with what killed my parents."

It was one thing to just let the scores fall as they did, like Loop said, but why did this sound like Ava was willing to tip the scales? Well, wasn't Wyatt willing to do that for Zav too?

He opened his mouth, then closed it. There were four of them, and three spots. His math wasn't phenomenal, but he knew that left four options of who they'd leave behind.

Loop, because he wasn't serious enough?

Ava, because she was *too* serious?

Zav, perhaps, because he didn't know what this was all about?

Wyatt. No, not Wyatt. He refused. But if Ava was an orphan, and so was Zav, and perhaps Loop was in some strange spot too considering he lived with Ava in that penthouse, did they need this opportunity more than he did?

He wondered, but didn't know. No one had prepared him for something like this.

Ava turned. Only then did he notice the door beside them, recessed into the cement wall. She rapped her knuckles against it in three perfect knocks.

"General," she said, chin up and face blank, "I brought you DoctorDoctor."

Wyatt had no time to keep pressing at her: the voice inside the office made him freeze. "Roger. Come on in for your briefing, Docherty."

Oh man, Wyatt thought. *This is really happening*. He turned toward the door, breath caught up in his chest. Finally, he was going to get answers about everything weird going on, and how it all had to do with *Fathom Fall*, and with him.

"Guess we're not teaming up," Wyatt said, decided. "Good luck out there."

"Luck's for Water Babies," she said. "I know what this looks like once the Goggles come off."

Wyatt had no idea what that meant, and didn't like the coldness behind her eyes, but he couldn't let her mind games bother him. He had the skills, and soon he'd have the answers to know what to do with them. Wyatt pushed the door open and went to meet the General.

LEVEL 20

WYATT HAD EXPECTATIONS FOR walking into that dressing room. He wasn't surprised that it was just a small cement room with a table and chairs on one side, a mirror on the wall, and a briefcase and suitcase sitting abandoned. And maybe he didn't think the General would be dressed up with all his cool Hydrexo Private Security Force medals. But he'd expected, at least, that the General would be the same hulking man with the same cool moustache.

Instead, the guy smoothing his Hydrexo T-shirt in front of the mirror was white and wiry, sort of short, with scrappy hair that he seemed to have given up on keeping in line. He turned to see Wyatt come in. Looking at him head-on, Wyatt realized he knew who this was, even if it wasn't who he was expecting.

Peter Davids, CEO of Hydrexo, held out his hand with a warm smile. Wyatt was too stunned to move. He'd seen Mr. Davids plenty of times before, in passing at Hydrexo galas and luncheons, and obviously on TV. But here and now, despite logically understanding why the CEO was at a competition for the video game he sponsored, and then why Ava addressed him as a "general," Wyatt felt like he was seeing a teacher out in public where they weren't supposed to be.

Mr. Davids smiled from under his wire glasses. Despite his thin build, and his T-shirt and khakis and Zip-Go–patterned Converse shoes that made him look fantastically *normal* for such an important person, his posture was bold and proper.

"I bet you were expecting someone a lot bigger," he said. Now the voices matched up almost exactly—it had just been a bit too ludicrous before, to even consider that the tough, heroic General was voiced by the very ordinary-looking CEO. "But I doubt your avatar looks much like you either."

In the mirror, Wyatt saw himself reflected next to Mr. Davids. Just as ordinary.

And yet he'd seen a Bluddite, and was going to find out how to stop them. And this was the man who didn't say there *weren't* monsters in Toronto. The guy who hired Ava and Loop to test and train, and who surely had a hand in organizing this competition to recruit more help.

Despite how they both looked, they were heroes in their own rights, or could be.

Wyatt stepped up and clapped his palm into Mr. Davids's, shaking firm like his parents had taught him. "Are you General Davids or Mr. Davids then?" Wyatt asked in a voice as sturdy as his posture.

"Let's go with just Davids," he said. This close, Wyatt could see the faintest shadows beneath Davids's eyes, a loud contrast against his bright skin and teeth. He let go of Wyatt's hand and motioned to the table, where Wyatt noticed an empty Smoke's poutine container, and a tablet waiting on a stand. "And I'll just call you Docherty."

Wyatt's shoulders tightened. "Those are my parents," he said as he sat down in the chair. "Wyatt's fine."

"Your parents are important people," Davids offered as he sat too. "More important than ever. Being a Docherty seems pretty cool to me."

This wasn't the time to be insecure. "I know," Wyatt said. "But I'd like to do something important *myself*. In my own way."

"I felt the same way," Davids said, because he'd taken on Hydrexo from his parents too. There was only one Water Baby bigger than Wyatt, and he was right here in this cramped little room that smelled like stone and fry grease. Despite what it all looked like, this was real.

Davids leaned in over the table, hands clasped. Wyatt held his breath.

"So, Wyatt," Davids said, quieter beneath the bright white fluorescent bearing down on them, "Maraj told me you saw a Bluddite."

Wyatt's heart gave a sudden pang. "Yes!" Wyatt said, like a gun finally going off. "Two, actually, now. The first time I was in a game, and then something triggered my volume sensor—that's why my score went so low; I'm usually better than a seventy-eight percent, but the Bluddite attacked me and—" It had stared at him, croaking out a clatter that sounded like his name. The memory squealed down Wyatt's spine. "Then

I kicked it." And then he fell, and lay concussed on the floor. The dreamscape of fighting to stay awake, when he felt like he was swimming in Bluddites, feeling their strange bodies crush in on him. Leo flickered through that space, her trembling fingers as his parents hung unconscious.

"So you know how serious this is," Davids said, low like he was reassuring himself more than Wyatt. Davids reached for the tablet, but he didn't type anything in. His fingers trembled, once. "It's not a game, Wyatt—"

"Of course not," Wyatt said, almost offended. He recognized the hesitance. "I'm ready to fight them, all of them. So you can show me whatever you're thinking about showing me."

Davids's lips smooshed together, almost the way Wyatt's looked when he was fidgeting them against his braces, or trying to decide what to say. "If this information spread—" Davids started.

Wyatt knew. "There'd be mass panic. People would fight. Prices could skyrocket. I *know* this." He resisted the urge to sound like a whining child. He didn't come here to cry, and he'd prove it. "Show me. I won't tell anyone."

Davids breathed out slowly through his nose. "All right," he said, rattling in the tablet's password. "I trust you, Wyatt."

Trusted. Finally.

Davids unlocked the tablet and pulled up a video.

In it, an entire swarm of Bluddites slammed themselves against a chain-link fence. It was dark, but someone had set up floodlights on the camera's side, turning the swarm of creatures into a white-struck mix of blue-and-orange-and-kelp-green bodies. Wyatt couldn't look away from them, those horrible teeth, the ragged, kelpy fins like moth-eaten clothing. It looked as real as the two Wyatt had seen. A forest stood behind them, huge, toothy pine trees with gnarled roots clinging to shield rock—clearly this wasn't Toronto. He knew this level, actually; you had to hold down the perimeter around the infested Lake Superior plant. Except this wasn't a video game screengrab: there was a speck of blood on the camera. The Bluddites had red all down their faces and flecked in their gills, which didn't happen in *Fathom Fall* where the blood just sort of splattered out and then disappeared. The person taking the video cursed under their breath, words that Wyatt's mom would call "crude."

This was gruesome, R-rated, the kind of thing any other adult might hesitate to show Wyatt even if it was fictional, and this wasn't.

"Bluddites are real," Davids said quietly, while Wyatt watched the proof. "And you need to be afraid of them." It was an odd thing to say, and yet Wyatt felt somehow reassured by it. "If they can spread here, they'll open every hydrant they can. They'll drink us dry before our investors can even get a drop, and then they'll move on to people instead. They've already done horrible damage to the water prices."

"I know," Wyatt said. He thought of Zav, how he'd already begun to bounce back after just a few bottles. And then he thought of the street folk who drifted around Hydrexo.

There wasn't much he could do to help them. The protest last night said people were getting more and more hostile—there could be human riots before a monster infestation even began. He'd never seen the water prices get over five dollars a liter, but now they might. What about Zav then? What about *anyone* then?

The video played on: the fence came crashing down, letting the Bluddites storm forward with their funny cartoon sounds. And yet, even though the sounds might have been comical alone, there were grown people screaming, and wet splattering noises as blood flew. Those monstrous faces closed in over the cameraman who fell backward until the lens saw nothing but teeth and fins and not a bit of night sky. The video ended there, on all those horrible eyes.

The silence felt louder now.

A sick feeling sat low in Wyatt's stomach, a mix of shame, as if he'd been caught playing with matches or doing something else he knew he wasn't supposed to, and curdling disgust for the blood-soaked faces of the Bluddites.

"Our Hydrexo Private Security Force is real," Davids said, voice quiet and serious. Wyatt just stared at the screen, at all that blood. "We knew there was something out there before the explosions; our output numbers, especially at Lake Superior, were falling behind more and more, and we couldn't tell why. There were safety mishaps, people disappearing on shifts—our staff were starting to refuse work. That's when we created the Security Force, to make them feel safer. And then . . ."

Then the explosions. Davids touched at his glasses again, shaking his head.

"Then we learned just what we were up against, what they were capable of doing. Of course we told the military. We managed to keep everything safe in Toronto. Lake Superior was already swarmed. We tried everything short of dropping bombs, but with the fresh water so close, and all the lakes connected, we just couldn't risk ruining the product—the *water*—like that. It would need to be tactical, like in the games, but no one could get past the front lines. The people we send just don't come back."

Wyatt's stomach churned. Real people, real death. "The Bluddites kill them," he said, blunt.

Davids's mouth crinkled. "Yes, but we're also losing them to retreat too. These are grown people, but they're scared, Wyatt. I'm sure you can understand why."

Because this wasn't human. Those protestors last night, Wyatt knew why *they* were rushing the gates, could even empathize with them. But the Bluddites? There wasn't anything to reason with or understand. There was only a thing that had to be killed before it killed first, and man were Bluddites good at killing. He'd learned just how they did it, the way they could work together to overpower you, or entice you into corners. And when the teeth came out, there was no amount of begging for mercy that would save you, because these weren't people like him.

They were monsters. Yet when that Bluddite in the bathroom had come at him, Wyatt knew *exactly* what to do.

Because he'd played *Fathom Fall*, had made it into common sense. He'd beat the Lake Superior level a dozen times.

"That's why you made *Fathom Fall*," Wyatt said. Davids blinked and seemed to look at him more closely, as if surprised that he'd made that jump himself. But Wyatt wasn't stupid. "As a training simulation, to prepare force troops for what they were actually up against."

Davids sat back a bit in his chair, eyes tired but still bright. "Exactly. But if that's all it would take to keep people alive or stop them from abandoning the front line, we wouldn't have a monster problem."

Right . . .

Davids leaned in again. He took a deep breath and let it out slowly through his nose, as if trying to find the words. "This might be hard to understand," he started.

"Don't," Wyatt said, almost sharp. "Your adult troops aren't working, I'm clearly here for a reason, so don't talk to me like I'm some stupid kid."

He'd expected Davids to frown, or even end the conversation right there. Instead, for perhaps the first time, Davids's smile looked wholly real. Not forced, not for cameras, but something genuinely relieved.

"*Exactly*," he said again, with even more enthusiasm. "Our usual troops, they think they know everything there is to know about the world. They're rooted in their realities—Bluddites terrify them because they're monsters, of course, but they're also terrifying because it forces them to admit how horrible the world truly is. But you kids, you're quicker to adjust to something new like this. There's something to be said about psychological elasticity—you kids are desensitized early to this sort of violence—but more than that, I think you realize the gravity of this."

Davids tapped a finger against the table, as if stabbing a battle map. But his eyes didn't leave Wyatt's, and Wyatt wouldn't look away either.

"Adults can pretend that things will go back to how they used to be," Davids said, "but for you, the world has *always* been frightening. I can promise you that the water crisis won't get any better unless you stop it, but I'm sure you already know that."

He did. And yet his mom had stood over his bed, reaching for his face, telling him that it would all be okay. Did she think this was just one bad spot in history? That it would all swing back sooner or later, regardless of what they did? It wouldn't. Even if she knew that, she couldn't admit it, not to him and maybe not to herself. If Toronto died out tomorrow, she and his dad could go down still clutching all those nice memories of Super Soaker water guns and winters with pearly white snow. And what would Wyatt have? Fourteen years of knowing the world was awful? Of feeling guilty, and terrified, and angry? It wasn't enough.

"Bluddites don't scare me as much as losing all our water does," Wyatt said. It came out sort of small, and he despised how young he sounded, but maybe that was the entire point. "If we fix it, soon, then I can spend most of my life in a better situation."

Ava had said they weren't heading for that, but she was also . . . *intense*. Depressed too, probably—she'd dealt with so much. But Wyatt still had hope. He had to.

"So you started recruiting kids," Wyatt said quietly. It still sounded ridiculous. Maybe he didn't have fortyish years of hearing that monsters weren't real, maybe *that* was easier to wrap his head around than an adult, but he had experienced fourteen years of being told he was small, and useless, and would have to wait until he was an adult to understand. "That's how you found Ava and Loop."

Davids tapped the tablet again. The screen changed to a split-screen picture. On one side stood a girl, with brown skin and long black hair, holding what appeared to be a crudely made, plastic aqua blaster that looked more like a kid's pop gun. The first version of *Fathom Fall*. Even while she was wearing Zip-Go Gaming Goggles, he recognized Ava Maraj. The date above it was three months after the explosion.

"Maraj was part of our Alpha tests, from a pool of Hydrexo orphans. She was the only one willing to keep up with the program when we told her the truth," Davids explained. But Loop had said she'd stayed because she had the best score? Wyatt became more convinced that Loop didn't know the whole truth here. But Wyatt did, or was about to. The second half of the screen had a screengrab of "FATHOM FALL: ALPHA TEST" (according to the label). Despite the low-poly graphics, Wyatt recognized the nose of the cartoonish aqua blaster and the shape of a Bluddite. The background wasn't a *Fathom Fall* map, but what appeared to be the same room Ava was standing in, with Bluddites digitally transposed into her vision. It was augmented reality, he realized. He understood why she knew all her ninja tricks: Ava had been trained on a much more physical simulation.

"And then Derond came in with our Bravo pool," Davids continued. "It's a nice story, really. He was living in a Hydrexo Cares youth shelter; I believe his mother is alive, but there was something going on at home—anyway, he really took to the simulation."

The picture rotated out. Wyatt leaned in closer. The next split screen showed a boy, eyes sunken with the beginnings of dehydration, holding chunkier versions of the modern *Fathom Fall* controllers. It took Wyatt a second to recognize Loop: he wasn't smiling or dancing. He looked thinner, wearing a Hydrexo Cares shirt in bright contrast to the dehydrated gray of his skin. Wyatt remembered what Loop had said about them all being on the same team . . . "Team Hydrexo" had clearly pulled him out of a bad spot, so was he just trying to pass on that goodwill? Maybe he *was* as nice as he seemed, no strings attached. The graphics of his gameplay were smoother, still on an AR background of the same room.

"We released to public," Davids started to say.

"Three months later," Wyatt said, noting the date of Loop's test run. Three months before Wyatt begged his parents to buy the new, fun, totally not realistic game with fake monsters and fake guns and fake everything. And yet, it had accurate maps of Toronto, of the sewers and the Hydrexo zone, and even inside the plant. Keeping your Goggles on to keep the spit out of your eyes wasn't just immersive gameplay—it was actual monster-fighting advice. "You were running out of time for those small test groups. You needed something bigger."

Just as he said it, more pictures rotated in: B streaming his games, those two others from the snack table. A photo of the Cadet he'd seen taking selfies, but he was at some field training camp, shooting an air rifle in the hot sun. A school picture of a kid in a *Panda Parade* T-shirt who looked barely older than ten. The science fair kid with his gold medal. There was Zav, his school photo from this year, where Leo was already gone, and his eyes were beginning to dull.

And then Wyatt's photo. He was a scrawny kid in a hoodie, with choppy orange hair, big glasses, and braces shining in his "smile for the camera, buddy" grimace. But with a high score, Wyatt knew.

As with Loop and Ava, each photo was split to one screenshot of gameplay. Along the bottom of each read four words.

CHARLIE TEST: "OPERATION HOSTILE"

Wyatt and Zav, Loop and Ava, and B and all the rest—they were the next test group. Three of them would win, and then they would infiltrate Lake Superior to take out the Bluddite nest, the first step toward saving their water.

And yet Wyatt's throat prickled. It was the same reservation he'd been feeling this whole time, the one thing keeping him from truly believing that the winners would hunt Bluddites. "But why make Ava and Loop compete?" he asked. "If they're already trained?"

Davids nodded slowly, as if to stall. He seemed to weigh if he should say, but before Wyatt could repeat that he ought to be taken seriously in all this, Davids relented. "We have some doubts," he said simply. "Derond isn't always a team player," he decided to say, which didn't quite sound like Loop. "We're not sure if he's quite mature enough—sometimes he seems more interested in making friends than doing what needs to be done."

That sounded like Loop. "And Ava?" Wyatt asked. He debated saying that Ava had really socked him in that garage, but she was still his competition. "She seems pretty good at what she does."

"She is," Davids said. "Maraj is—" He stopped, looking behind Wyatt, and swallowed.

Wyatt turned to look over his shoulder. There was a very thin line of light under the door, just thick enough to see a shadow blocking it. Wyatt remembered the mouth of the mini-blaster poised between his eyes, and Loop's comment about keeping an eye on Ava.

He'd thought she was favored to win. Maybe Davids was hoping she wouldn't.

Davids lowered his voice. "The Alpha tests were, well, *messy*. Rushed," Davids said. "Maraj was very eager, wanted to train as much as possible and know everything, and we encouraged it. But now we wonder if it was the wrong decision."

So that was what Ava's stone-cold "I don't care about

anything" pessimism was: she'd pushed too far too fast, and the pressure had cracked her. Wyatt began to understand why Ava was at all the events while Loop was trusted to stay home alone. They weren't keeping an eye on her because she was some phenomenal player, but perhaps because they were worried about what she'd do when they turned their backs on her.

"You're scared she'll crack," Wyatt said quietly. "That she won't be able to finish this."

Davids swallowed. "The opposite," he said. "We're worried she'll do whatever it takes."

She wasn't supposed to be hunting him in that garage, and had done it anyway. Wyatt understood that Ava was being given one last chance to show she could play the game properly. And if not?

Where do you send fourteen-year-old, veteran monster hunters?

From the stadium floor, there came a loud crash of applause and cheering. They must be starting soon. Davids reached for the tablet.

"But why do you want *me*?" Wyatt asked, without meaning to. But now it was out, hovering thick as smog.

Davids carefully closed the tablet, tucking it under his arm. "Why not?"

This felt cruel, to make Wyatt name all the reasons he didn't feel good enough. "I . . . I have braces," he fumbled out. Davids raised an eyebrow. Wyatt felt even more frustrated by himself, but tried to explain further. "I just mean I'm . . . I'm five-foot, and I have bad posture and don't know how to make my hair look good." His throat prickled worse. Was he going to cry? *No.* "I just don't look like anything impressive—and I know looks aren't everything and everyone says I'll understand when I'm older, but you want me *now* when I'm just . . ."

"Just fourteen?" Davids said. Wyatt thought it was terrible to make him say it all, but it was worse to hear it: "Too small to make a difference?" Yes. "Too awkward to know what to say?" *Exactly.* "Too spoiled to do anything but wait for someone to save you?"

Wyatt swallowed hard. "Yeah," he breathed.

Davids stood and reached across the table to put his hand on Wyatt's arm. Wyatt stared back, eyes burning. Maybe Davids had made a mistake and just now realized.

"Wyatt," he started. "What if I told you that all of that—every reason you feel like you can't make a difference—what if I said that those reasons are *exactly* why you're here today?"

Then Wyatt would call him a liar. But he didn't seem like one, not when his hand was firm on Wyatt's arm, holding hard enough nearly to hurt yet just enough to stop him from babbling. "I don't get it," Wyatt said.

Davids let go, still holding that close, careful eye contact. "You've grown up being told that only certain people can make a difference," he said. "That's a lie. I just told you that you kids are antidote. All that frustration you feel, all your drive to prove everyone wrong about kids like you, *that's* what we need."

"Whoever wins today," Wyatt started, never taking

his eyes from Davids's despite the glare across his glasses, "you're recruiting them for active field duty. Right now, no waiting."

"More or less," Davids said. "There'll be a choice to be made. I can give more information then."

A heating fan kicked on above them. Davids flinched, but Wyatt slid up to his feet. He hoped none of the winners would say no: there was too much on the line. But that was what the competition was for—they'd weed out the kids who didn't have the chops. Wyatt was certain that, whoever it was, the three winners would be ready.

Davids stepped around the table. "But between you and me," he offered, "if even one Bluddite gets away, it's too many. So I'm hoping you say yes."

He was already insinuating that Wyatt would win. A few days ago, Wyatt would have been surprised, and thrilled. But as Wyatt stepped back toward the door, he only felt determined to prove Davids right. Wyatt had gone up against a Bluddite already, that was a *huge* leg up, and he knew *Fathom Fall*. Maybe he was small and awkward, but he'd let that drive him. He'd prove everyone wrong, be a hero, and fix everything so no one else had to hurt.

There wasn't a choice.

Davids flinched at a sharp knock at the door. "Sir," Ava called. "They need the competitors on their marks."

Davids swallowed. "Yes. Thank you, Maraj." Wyatt swore he saw fear go through the man's eyes. Maybe fear of the competition, of the looming threat they had one last chance to fix. But maybe of Ava Maraj. Chills crawled under Wyatt's jacket.

But now he knew even more information than Loop, surely just as much as Ava. He was on her level, ready to compete.

"Thank you, sir," Wyatt said as Davids stepped up. "I'll prove myself out there, I swear." He realized only then that he *still* didn't know what this competition would entail. How was this test different from the regular games? It didn't matter. Whatever it was, he'd be ready.

And with that, he slipped out into the hallway to where Ava was waiting against the wall, arms crossed and chin up. He didn't care if she'd heard what they were saying. And maybe he felt a bit sorry for her.

"You better hope we *both* win," Wyatt told her, his face as hard as hers. He found it strange to smile now that he realized how truly terrifying the world was out there, and that the results of this competition were the only thing stopping it. He wondered if that was why she didn't smile either. "Because I'm leading the charge whether you like it or not."

She narrowed her eyes at him, sucked her teeth, but said nothing. He figured they'd be going head-to-head, but the big question was if it would be Loop or Zav or even B in the final spot. Wyatt knew that both he and Ava had people they wanted on their teams.

He wondered briefly if he should play favorites when the end of the world was at hand, but didn't have time to think on it for very long.

LEVEL 21

IN THE WAITING ROOM, Wyatt strode back to Zav just as another security guard gathered them all up, gave a very official "competitors walking" report into his radio, and then led them off down a series of twisting, dark hallways. Wyatt breathed slowly in through his nose and out through his mouth, in and out, in and out. His heart kept trying to thud faster, but he wouldn't let it. He couldn't afford shaky aim, not when only three people would be recruited past the competition to finish the Bluddites once and for all, and he'd be picking up Zav's slack. The nearby crowd reverberated through the concrete. They seemed to be getting quieter as Wyatt walked.

"We're walking away from the stage," Zav whispered. He'd changed out of his faded jeans and sneakers and into a pair of *Fathom Fall* track pants and branded Air Jordans. A new set of blue-and-orange gaming headphones hung around his neck. "Do you know where we're going?"

"No," Wyatt said simply. Ahead of him, Loop had leaned a bit lower to speak with Ava. They were definitely talking strategy. "Did he say anything? Loop?"

Zav eyed Loop too. "He was nice," he said. "Said we could team up if we see each other."

Wyatt shifted his lips against his braces. Okay, he believed that from Loop, but Ava? Would she sabotage him or Zav if she thought it would help her kill more Bluddites? "Let's try to steer clear of them," Wyatt said. "Just focus on getting your score up and moving to the meeting spot."

Zav didn't nod, but did try to practice his breathing; it kept shaking through his nose or spluttering from his lips. Wyatt took a hesitant look over his shoulder to the rest of the competitors streaming behind. A lot of the other kids looked younger, and a few of them more nervous, so Wyatt figured Zav could beat half the pack.

And the rest? Sabotaging anyone to help Zav win would mean a pretty sorry recruitment for Davids.

This is so much bigger than me, Wyatt thought as the security guard herded them all into the next room. He wondered if that meant letting things just happen, even if Zav went home with nothing but a swag bag. Wyatt could give him the prize pack—it wasn't like he needed it. But even 10K could be used up, and water was only a small part of survival. Charity didn't last forever. What Zav needed was a future; if he joined the new task force, he'd have support as long as they were killing every last Bluddite, and surely long after when the world praised them for their service.

That was why Zav had to win: not the prizes or even the chance of a sponsorship, but because he could have all the care and support of a Water Baby again. It wasn't a terrible thing to be.

They turned into a room that looked more like a garage than a stage platform. The metal door was thrown open on a quiet backlot, where that fake Hydrexo Private Security Force truck waited amid a small flock of idling soldiers dressed in force fatigues . . . or maybe that actually was a real Security Force van, and those soldiers were Security Force members.

"Competitors, on your markers," someone said. Wyatt turned to see a woman standing near a control booth with a few other guards. She was dressed in the same blue fatigues, her blond hair pulled into a tight bun that made her nose look beak-sharp and her face coldly severe. She waved them toward a line of changing-room-like stalls against the back wall, each with a competitor's name on the door.

"You think we're getting more clothes?" Zav asked, but Wyatt suspected it was more than that.

"I think we're getting upgrades," Wyatt said.

Zav narrowed his eyes. He looked back over his shoulder, toward the door they'd come in through. Wyatt wasn't sure why, but Zav eventually shrugged. He bumped a fist against the back of Wyatt's shoulder, a bit awkward but still friendly, and then both of them stepped onto the low stage and peeled off for their stalls. Wyatt walked in and shut the door behind him.

There was complete silence then; the stall was even closed off at the top, with just a small slit to let light come in. It fell on the wall ahead of Wyatt, where a sheet of instructions was pinned beside a full-body polyester suit at eye level. The elastic limbs hung like a sad, deflated ghost. Wyatt noted the little white circles on all the joints—this was a motion-capture suit, like what video game actors wore in behind-the-scenes footage.

Operation Hostile was about to be a full-body simulation. This was going to be as close as possible to the real thing. Were there little treadmills on the stage so they could run and jump in place while they piloted avatars on the big screens? Wyatt was glad he'd gotten better at using his legs to fight.

He took a glance at the instructions, stripped to nothing but his underpants, and pulled the suit on. It was cold and slimy-smooth. The circles glowed along his arms and legs and feet and even the knuckles on each finger. The suit also happened to suck right in like a morphsuit, which he didn't find flattering at all on his bony legs and arms, and *especially* around his boxers bunching up like a diaper. He thought about Leo's classmate who got called Pampers for twelve years . . . There was too much on the line for *that* to be today's takeaway.

Luckily, he found a pair of gym shorts and a Sponsored by Hydrexo, Your Number One Source T-shirt folded on the little bench. He tugged them on over the top, put his glasses back on and set his Goggles in his hair, and then sat back to slip into his shoes again.

The knife stared at him from the waistband of his discarded jeans. He didn't know what the guards would do with the rest of his clothes. Would he be in trouble if someone saw that he'd brought a knife into the Hydrexo Centre? He knew

Ava had hers, but had also been given a real mini-blaster, so the rules might be a bit different for her. But if he was training to be a soldier, shouldn't he be allowed to carry a concealed weapon?

There was a knock on his dressing room door. Without time to think further, Wyatt swept the knife up, holstered it to the inside of his shorts, and pulled his T-shirt down over it. Once he quickly confirmed that it was impossible to see under all that flowy fabric, he opened the door back to the startling light of the garage.

In the frame, the woman in fatigues was holding a large box. "Your helmet," she said.

Inside was in fact a helmet. The rough plastic shell was a muted steel blue, identical to the Security Force helmets in the game. Wyatt pulled his turned-off Goggles into position, then sunk the helmet down over his choppy orange hair. The helmet and Goggles slotted together perfectly, no gaps, with the band closed in snuggly over his ears to muffle sound. He put his clothes and phone into the box; then the woman shut the door again. He stood there in the muffled quiet, waiting.

His pulse was starting to speed up, despite his slow breathing.

Get it together, he reminded himself. There was no backing out now. He had so much to prove today, and so much to fix. Finally, the future wasn't just a terrifying monster closing in on him, but something he had some say in.

Maybe he was small, and awkward, and weird, but he wasn't powerless.

Suddenly, all the walls of Wyatt's dressing room turned clear. He flinched; the other competitors lined up on either side of him flinched too. The woman was standing ahead of them while the other guards marched the boxes of their belongings out of the room.

"Goggles on," the woman said. Wyatt took a steadying breath and tapped the power button over his ear.

Game on.

"Audio-visual-scent re-creation calibrating," the woman's voice said, even though the actual woman's mouth hadn't moved. There came a whirring sound from somewhere in the helmet, or in the entire suit as it hummed against Wyatt's skin, a click, a gentle *whoosh*, and then a metallic and sharp scent, as if someone sprayed an air freshener of wet metal. That was blood, Wyatt realized. They really were about to have a full-body experience.

A figure suddenly appeared in front of Wyatt, standing right where the glass wall was. But Wyatt knew the glass was real, and it was just the figure who wasn't. And yet, the General standing in front of Wyatt looked realer than real, with all his medals and his clean white gloves. Wyatt wondered if they'd actually gotten an actor to do this bit; the graphics were movie-worthy, or maybe it was just all the more convincing when Wyatt could step sideways to see a slightly new angle. The General's face turned to follow him, even if his eyes were hidden behind shiny aviator sunglasses.

Augmented reality was trippy; Wyatt was impressed where he wasn't drop-dead serious.

"Are you ready to fight the fall of humanity like never before?" the General asked. His lips and moustache moved around every word. His chest expanded with each breath. "Through auditory, visual, and scent re-creation, as well as state-of-the-art digital skeleton and sensation mapping, you'll be digitally transported from your world into the territory of the Bluddites. Everything you are about to experience is a simulation: you cannot be harmed by the Bluddites in this game."

Yet, Wyatt thought. Being digitally transferred made sense to him: even with just the usual Goggles and audio-visual trickery, it could feel like you really were in another world. So they'd walk to the stage, turn the Goggles on, and then be right in the game? That made sense, but he didn't quite understand what the General meant by "digital skeleton" and "sensation mapping."

"Your game ends when you do," the General said. *When we* die, Wyatt clarified, trying not to sugarcoat this for himself. "The three highest scores will win."

Wyatt looked sideways, hoping to lock eyes with Zav, but he was too many stalls away. They'd blocked out their strategy as much as they could, but there were still so many variables. Wyatt wished they'd been given more information about this game, wished he could have had a bit more time to know what to expect from all this, but perhaps that was the entire point. The world was running out of time, and Hydrexo needed recruits who could adapt under that sort of pressure.

"If at any point the game is too intense, you have three ways of retreating," the General continued. Wyatt could practically feel the other competitors shift. He knew he was supposed to be scared of a Bluddite swarm, but he was also supposed to be brave enough to finish this. The two thoughts were hard to balance out. The General held up a military sign: thumb across palm, then fingers curling down. "Signal distress, remove your Goggles, or say 'AWOL.' Players who retreat will be disqualified." The General gave Wyatt a scan. Wyatt knew that every other player was probably getting the same look down, but it seemed too much like Davids to feel generic. "If you win today, you'll do it through honor, bravery, and good old grit."

Someone whooped. Wyatt suspected it was Loop, but didn't care.

"Audio-visual-scent re-creation calibrated," the woman confirmed. "Digital skeleton calibrating."

The General reached forward and grabbed Wyatt's wrist. There was no sensation, but his arm was suddenly lifted into the air—he hadn't asked it to do that. He looked sideways through the glass and saw a row of other competitors in their gear, no General in front of them, each with their arm raised. Wyatt watched, dumbfounded, as the General turned Wyatt's hand left and right. He stiffened his muscles to stop it.

There was resistance, but too much pressure to fight against. His arm kept turning in the General's digital grip. Trippy.

Wyatt understood: if a digital Bluddite grabbed him, it could *actually* move him. Not just his vision, but his body too, like a little puppet on the stage. He'd stumble back, or even fall. He wasn't afraid of that. If anything, it meant the audience could truly see how hard he was fighting.

"Digital skeleton calibrated," the woman confirmed. "Sensation mapping calibrating."

Without warning, the General shifted his grip to grab Wyatt's shoulder roughly. Wyatt's digital skeleton jostled him, but it was more than that: Wyatt really *felt* that grip, especially when the gloved fingers closed tight against his skin, sinking pressure into the meat and bone. The General stared at him, mouth slightly crooked at the corner like Davids's. This was Davids's grip, bracing and steady.

"Hey! Let go," Wyatt heard a voice through the glass. The *Panda Parade*–shirt kid was in the booth next to him, a head shorter than Wyatt with his face painted in camo colors. "That hurts. Miss, hey, miss—this thing hurts."

Then tap out, Wyatt thought, and yet he wondered how high the pain threshold was allowed to climb. They were meant to play until death. This was just pressure, but was the suit detailed enough to replicate individual teeth? Wyatt's skin crawled. If they killed him in the fake world, he'd know exactly what he was fighting against. And if the pain and sensation were real, then that was all the more reason to shoot well and run fast.

"Sensation mapping calibrated," the woman's voice said.

The General smiled, like he was impressed. "Press to start,

soldier," he said. Suddenly, two words were floating ahead of Wyatt.

Operation Hostile

Wyatt did as he was told: when he lifted his arm, the suit tightened around him, heavy like body armor. Wyatt heard the crowd cheering through the bands of his Goggles. He looked at the medals on the General's chest. They were just a digital illusion. When Wyatt got his own medals, they'd be from shooting the enemy.

He was going to help save the world, whatever it took, because it had to be done. And he would be the one to do it.

He tapped the words. There was a sound like an aqua blaster. His vision flooded bright white. The red Zip-Go logo faded in, and Go-Go the alien popped his head up from behind.

Every pore of Wyatt's body suddenly lit up hot as if he'd been pumped with acid and—wait, wait, wait, that *hurt*!

"Zip Go-Go!" Go-Go the alien cheered, and winked in a shimmer of stars.

. . . LOADING . . .

WHEN THE CALIBRATION PAIN ended (how long had it been? Seconds? Minutes? Days?), Wyatt was staring at a spinning water droplet logo. There was only darkness behind it, stretching on and on forever. He was in the loading screen, emphasis on *in*. Wyatt turned his head frantically, but only saw the loading symbol. Had the digital skeleton held him still, or were his Goggles set to only this image no matter where he looked? He tried to pinch himself and felt nothing.

He hadn't loaded yet.

Far off in the distance, as if through the vents, David's voice echoed.

"Are you ready for the competition of a lifetime?" he shouted, with all the enthusiasm and charisma of a video game announcer. The crowd cheered back. Wyatt thought he could feel himself moving. A thousand ideas flickered through his head: his glass fish tank stall was being transported to the stage through some lift system; he was being carried by one of the big security guards; he was walking to his mark all by himself, digital skeleton marching his captive body. Wyatt found all those scenarios creepy, but he wasn't even sure that was happening, so there was no sense being bothered about it. All he could see was the logo spinning, spinning, loading, loading.

"Ten competitors, one hunt, three winners."

Wyatt tried to scan for the edge of his Goggles, but they fit seamlessly into the helmet, too close to his face and too wide to see the bottom. He moved his arms to test them. They were heavy, as if he was wearing thick, military-tough fatigues under heavy-duty body armor. He noticed the same weight everywhere, and a subtle ache in his feet as if they were pressing against the arched sole of a stiff combat boot. But when he looked down to find his body, it wasn't there.

Wyatt wasn't sure he liked this feeling, or how long it lasted. But he needed to press on. Discomfort could be ignored.

"The objective is simple," the woman's voice said. Wyatt heard the crowd screaming. They were on the stage now, he was sure, and everyone was looking at them—those screens he saw earlier were showing their loading feeds. The crowd would see everything, including if he messed up. But he wouldn't—*they* wouldn't. Wyatt was going to help Zav. They were going to be a team on that winner's podium. "Take down as many Bluddites as you can, and die trying. Scores will be marked at the time of death. Top three scores win."

Even if Wyatt played defensively, he'd get taken out eventually, maybe sooner than he'd like. And if he went on the offensive? At least he'd be meeting death straight on. He wasn't sure what was best—he and Zav would have to figure it out once they truly knew what they were dealing with.

Right now, it was time to focus.

"The fall of humanity is at hand," said the woman's voice, echoing from somewhere strange. "All forces deploy in three . . ."

Wyatt rolled his neck, laced his invisible fingers together, and pushed them out. Tension rippled up his arms, growing stronger by the second. He wasn't a very strong person, or athletic, but he knew *Fathom Fall*.

"Two . . ."

He knew how to fight Bluddites. He'd gone head-to-head with two. That gave him an edge.

"One . . ."

The loading symbol snapped away. The cheering went silent.

"We're counting on you, soldier," the woman's voice said. "Mission a-go."

Wyatt heard his own breathing, and his heartbeat, each echoing loud. Suddenly, there was something heavy in his hand. He looked down.

An aqua blaster hung in his hands, tethered to him by a sling around his torso. The orange plastic felt rough under his pleather tactical gloves, rough as a real thing. All right, he knew it wasn't actually real, but it was real *here*, in the Goggle world of Operation Hostile. He peered closely at every groove and seam where the bulbous parts locked together. He'd seen close-ups of the blasters in the game, and in his handbook, and even his stupid toy at home and the quick look at Ava's own mini-blaster. But none of that compared to the resistance of the spring-loaded magazine ejector, to knowing that he'd have to reload properly at some point, and that he'd need to click that tiny safety button off each time he shot, and back on each time he needed to run. And that the trigger right there, gleaming under the tiny white light from the side of his helmet . . . pulling that would send off a lethal shot.

Something icy sloshed up to Wyatt's ankles. He still couldn't see beyond the blaster in his hands lit up in that circle of light, but knew he was standing in water. It dripped all around him in the blackness.

He was standing in the Brotherhood Mode loading screen. And he knew what came next.

He didn't have time to remember Leo or the car wreck. Wyatt, breathless now, hearing his heart and knowing this was battle practice, lifted the blaster up to his eye. It was much heavier than he'd expected, even with the sling around his torso taking most of the weight off. He hoisted it up until he could look through the crosshair sights.

There was a terrible shriek, so loud Wyatt swore he felt it grind through his eardrums and turn his skull to powder. He turned for the sound—the blaster was too heavy off his torso, forcing him to lurch in an awkward semicircle while the sights dropped from his eye.

And then, from the darkness, Wyatt saw it.

Kelpy fins and wide eyes, gills fanning out as it reached for him with long fingers. It was as real as it had been in his bathroom, in the skate park, smelling of rot and sweat with blood dripping all down its front and smeared across its scaly face.

Wyatt jerked to pull the trigger before he could aim properly. The blaster spasmed in his arms, firing a shot off into the water beyond. You *never* missed on the loading screen, never ever, even if you aimed totally wrong!

But this was a new game. They needed to adapt, and fast.

The Bluddite kept coming at him. "*Gra-ha-ha-ha*," it said, sort of like a laugh.

"Oh man, oh man," Wyatt heard himself muttering. Was he really going to die in *the loading screen*? When he managed to bring the crosshairs to his eye, to pull the blaster tighter into his shoulder and settle his limbs around it, his aim was still swaying in delirious figure eights. His breathing puffed fast and shallow. The Bluddite was only a few steps from him now. Its claws and teeth were high-definition real.

Prove them wrong.

Wyatt pretended this was the final kill, the last Bluddite between him and a hydrated future. The crosshairs fell right between its fishy eyes. Wyatt pulled the trigger.

"Noooo—"

SHWOOP!

The blaster recoiled into Wyatt's shoulder, hard enough to bruise. Even still, the shot tore through the Bluddite's head in a splatter of comically blue blood. Wyatt saw a fleck land against his tough black glove. It smelled like phosphates and nitrates and toxic water. The Bluddite body dropped, and disappeared.

"First blood," the woman's voice said. There was a *plink!* as a **Ø1** appeared top center of Wyatt's vision. As the other utilities popped in, he caught a quick glimpse of 10 competitors remaining, and the moment that it solemnly rolled down.

9

Someone had already left the competition. Were they killed in the loading screen, or did they yank their Goggles off the second they saw the too-real monster? Wyatt took his blaster away from his eye and aching shoulder. Even if the Bluddite corpse was gone, the blood still stank on his hand. He could feel sweat building under his clothing.

This was just the start. But that wasn't terrifying, because he realized he could do this.

"Game on," Wyatt said. He thought he heard the crowd cheer, but it faded quickly. Words appeared ahead of Wyatt.

Remember: Bluddite saliva is potent, acidic, and blinding.
Keep your Goggles on at all times, and get ready
to save humanity.

The game map finally loaded, and the real deal began.

LEVEL 22

WYATT WAS STANDING ALONE in a room. He didn't remember arriving in the room, or blinking and being in the room—it was like he'd just zoned out for a moment and then come back. His utilities were ready for him: a water bar was across the top of his vision, his volume sensor beside it, the time (9:30 AM) on the bottom right. But there was no map on the bottom left—that put a wrench in the plans, especially for Zav making his way to the meeting spot.

The window to his right had no glass in it, just boards. Light crept through the cracks and caught the dust in the air. The room was familiar, and yet it all seemed a foot taller than he was used to. He was just Wyatt here, not his avatar. Even his usual gear had been replaced by the default vest and tactical belt and fatigues, all steel blue. Still, he knew exactly where this was: that chug-chug-chugging in the ground was unmistakable. It wasn't just coming through his headset, but echoing up through his feet, into his bones. The air smelled like heavy dust, with reeking lake water beneath it.

"Four-D experience," Wyatt whispered to himself, enough

to spike his volume sensor to yellow. That reminded him that there was a blaster in his hands, and a knife on his hip (sitting on the opposite side of his actual knife), and his goal wasn't just to stand here.

He had to start finding his way to Zav. Luckily, this might be the one area Zav could navigate without a map.

They'd been digitally zapped to the map near the Lake Ontario refinery, in the industrial zone around Hydrexo that Zav and Wyatt had both been to dozens of times in their childhood. More specifically, Wyatt had been dropped in one of the two empty apartments on Munition Street. He'd have to make his way to their decided meeting spot, but had to be *methodical* about it too, especially when his counter was only sitting at Ø1 kill. Getting to Zav wouldn't mean anything if he died on the way, especially with a score like *that*.

Wyatt stepped forward in his stiff combat boots and heavy gear. An ajar door showed a sliver of dim hallway, but Wyatt moved instead to the window, to make sure the coast was clear out there before he went tearing forward. There was a convenient break between the boards, just enough to aim the muzzle of his blaster through and peer down the sights.

In the street a few stories below, wind sent a discarded chip bag and other litter bits swirling across the dusty pavement. Everything else was eerily quiet. Wyatt scanned the roofs of the empty shop buildings across the way, and then the pylons lining the road that sectioned off a dark hole down into an open sewer pipe. It was the perfect place for Bluddites to disappear into . . . or appear out of.

Wyatt felt shivers move slowly through him, making all of his hair point up against his thick clothes.

Something (or rather three somethings) had come creeping up the side of the shop buildings and slithering out onto the flat roofs. Each was bright blue and orange with kelp-green mats of fins along its torso. Bluddites, stalking carefully toward the access door that led down into the buildings. Wyatt gathered his breath and aimed, following the one in front. It lumbered up to the door, reared onto its hind legs, and dropped a clawed hand onto the handle to give it a rattle. When it didn't open, the second Bluddite began to chew at the doorjamb, trying to gnaw its way to the latched lock.

Wyatt didn't give it a chance to get through. He pulled the trigger.

The kickback was still powerful, but he was more prepared for the sudden lurch. A shot of white-blue energy splayed the first Bluddite out dead with a splatter of blood streaking across the door. *Plink!* A comforting, familiar sound. 02, said Wyatt's kill count. He imagined the crowd roaring with cheers, while some intense military guy in a room full of screens scribbled notes. He'd give them even more to write about.

The other Bluddites' gills expanded while they screeched out a warning call and looked around—Wyatt fired another shot. Both times, his volume sensor had spiked to red before settling back to green. He knew he had to fire quick and move on.

Plink! 03

The third was trying to run away, had already swung itself over the side of the roof and gone crawling down the windowsills, back toward the street.

"Nope," Wyatt said with a smile, and fired again. It missed, shattering the window. Wyatt's teeth gritted. The Bluddite zigzagged toward the gap in the road. Wyatt swung his aim to the sewer tunnel. The Bluddite dove into his sights. Wyatt pulled the trigger.

Plink! 04

Suckers. Wyatt was about to swing his blaster down and get away from there, when he again saw movement. This time, it came from inside the store, through the window he'd just shot. Wyatt prepared to aim again, before he noticed the steel-blue helmet and orange Goggle-visor of another competitor. He couldn't be sure who, maybe the Army Cadet? It was hard to tell from a distance, especially when they were all dressed in the same fatigues.

The boy leaned out the window, looked left and right to ensure the coast was clear, and then climbed out. He held his blaster at his chest, finger above the trigger, perfect form. Wyatt watched him move slowly toward the blue blood splatter near the sewer.

Wyatt panicked and wanted to scream at the kid to get the hell away from the sewer. Didn't he know that was where they came from?

But then he realized that anyone dumb enough to go near a hot spot like that probably wasn't war material. Was it better to let the deadweight fall away?

As soon as the Cadet leaned over the sewer, a slimy hand surged up, grabbed him by the front of his chest, and hauled him into the darkness. One scream echoed up through the street, then nothing.

8

Eight competitors left. Wyatt felt certain that Zav wasn't going around sticking his head in sewers, and that he'd been smart enough not to die in the loading screen, but it was still a good idea to start heading toward him.

Wyatt had just taken his blaster down from the sill and turned away when his volume sensor tinged yellow. There was a shrill, muffled squeal from somewhere deeper in the building: door hinges, he realized.

Dammit, Wyatt thought, crinkling his nose. He shouldn't have stayed to watch that kid get eaten. It was maybe even a bit gross of him—his stomach turned, as if he'd been caught putting a hamster in a microwave. Not just by one person, but by the whole Hydrexo Centre.

Well, all was fair in love and war, and this counted as war, right?

The wooden floor chug-chug-chugged under his feet, like a sluggish, watery heartbeat. Wyatt's volume sensor had settled to a comfortable green. The light through the window couldn't reach beyond the ajar door. Wyatt kept his blaster against his shoulder and his eye to the sights, reached out with his sturdy boot, and slowly peeled the door open.

The hallway ahead of him was empty for barely a breath.

Before Wyatt could even begin to step out, a Bluddite dropped from the ceiling. It landed on two legs, hulking in the doorway as it screamed with its gills splayed out. Four rows of teeth shone in its circular mouth. Toxic blue spit flew against Wyatt's Goggles.

Wyatt had been prepared for a jump scare: he pulled the trigger. A shot went right between its eyes. The Bluddite flew back, painting the wall with a splatter of bright blue blood before it disappeared.

Plink! 05

The bloodstain stayed, which was new. So was the bruising ache in the pit of Wyatt's shoulder. The blaster began to wobble in his hands. Still, Wyatt rushed into the hallway, spinning on his heels to face the dim kitchen. Another Bluddite was running at him. He dropped one knee into the hardwood with a *crack* of his knee guard and—*SHWOOP!*

Plink! 06

"Gotcha," Wyatt said. But there was still movement coming at him from behind, too close. He knew the code for the right move in *Fathom Fall*, but he wasn't sure how this worked with the digital skeleton and sensation mapping. What if he fumbled, in front of everyone? Game over for getting on the field team, and frankly game over for any social cred too. But if he didn't try, what then?

He remembered what Davids said. There was no option *not* to try. He wasn't going to let his fear outweigh his duty.

As the scuttling of wet claws was nearly on top of him, Wyatt pushed off with his kneeling leg, tucked his head to his knees and his blaster to his chest, and hurled himself forward into what he hoped was a shoulder-roll. He doubted he could do that in real life, so was the suit only simulating the hard impact of the floor against his shoulder, the pressure spinning down his spine, the tension in his legs while they followed until he caught his boots up under him?

Wyatt tumbled into the kitchen and popped back up to his feet. His lungs burned with exertion, and his joints were tense, but he was too thrilled to care. Maybe he could shoulder-roll all along, and just had to give himself the chance to prove it.

"Hell yeah!" Wyatt shouted. He flipped his blaster onto his back and turned around with his close-quarters knife in his hand, swinging for the neck.

The Bluddite was just behind him, a full-grown two-pointer for sure. Wyatt realized too late; the knife didn't hit its soft gills, but plunged only a few centimeters into the Bluddite's side before the blade stopped dead against the thick shell beneath its kelpy fins. The Bluddite screamed out a "*BLAH-OUCH!*" then tore sideways into the countertop in front of the boarded-over window, cutting tracks through the settled dust (wow those graphics were impressive) as it scrambled up on all fours. It spat and screeched.

Wyatt didn't have time to react before it leapt for him again. He dropped to a crouch and let it soar overhead and crash against a half wall between the kitchen and the living room. It cracked the plaster, but by the time it came galloping back, Wyatt had the knife firmly in his hand and knew exactly how to strike. He was only vaguely aware of his facial expression: it was halfway between a rigid sneer and an ecstatic grin.

The Bluddite tackled him, landing Wyatt flat on his back with a spine-bruising *smack*. His helmet saved him a good hit, even if his concussion sent faint stars across his vision. Last time he'd been laid flat by a Bluddite, he'd had to call for help.

"Not this time!" Wyatt roared, then stabbed his knife right into its neck. The Bluddite's bony mouth was permanently stuck in that little O shape, but Wyatt swore he saw surprise. He yanked the knife back out, the blade screeching against the Bluddite's rough gills.

"*Yowwwww*," the Bluddite croaked.

Wyatt expected a puff of blood and the body to disappear so he could pop back up to his feet and march out feeling proud.

Instead, as he watched the tip of his knife wink free, it was followed by a geyser gush of blue.

Wyatt had no way to escape as hot, slick blood speared out, splattering across the floor and then soaking down Wyatt's arm and washing over his grinning teeth. The Bluddite was too heavy to wriggle out from under. Wyatt spluttered and tossed his head while he was drenched under the world's worst waterpark dump bucket. Everything reeked like a nosebleed and fish guts and rotting flesh. Wyatt kept thinking the blood would stop, but it didn't.

Contrary to video game logic, a thing of that size actually had a lot of blood in it. And again, contrary to what he'd learned, a thing of that size had to be stabbed quite a few times to get it to actually lie down dead. The Bluddite screeched, shoulders tensing as it prepared to slash at him with its claws. Wyatt braced his other forearm up against its collarbone and slammed the knife back into its neck, pulled it out again, brought another geyser while his biceps burned and trembled and the Bluddite's claws scrabbled into the floorboards on either side of him. The blood kept coming, sinking hot beneath his helmet and past his Goggle-visor, soaking heavy down his arm as the Bluddite's limbs began to shake.

Wyatt's stomach churned awfully, like when he saw the R-rated footage. It was the feeling of doing something you weren't allowed to do, and couldn't be caught doing, because it was *wrong*. If his parents saw this, he was sure his mom would actually strangle Davids.

I'm not a baby, he thought, but was still panicking as the Bluddite struggled to claw him or sink close enough for its teeth to catch him, and he struggled to battle it back. What did this look like onstage? Was he just flailing on the floor while everyone else was striking intense stalking poses? Was Loop doing his stupid victory dance to cheers? Was Ava ninja kicking around? Was even Zav triumphant as he fought his way closer to their spot? And what was the *Water Baby* doing? Struggling, flinching, arms and legs churning at *nothing*. He was probably a meme already, an embarrassing GIF that would circulate forever.

This wasn't what heroes were supposed to look like. He stabbed again and again.

Plink! he finally heard, even through the screaming smell. His score rose by those promised two points, to 08. The weight finally disappeared from his chest, and surely the Bluddite's body with it, but Wyatt couldn't tell.

His Goggles were completely coated in blood.

Wyatt lay on the floor, head and arms soaked, the entire world chug-chug-chugging around him. His heart was pounding way too fast, his thoughts all colliding. *Blood, blood, so much blood.* Some had gotten in Wyatt's gasping mouth—he could feel it hot against his cheeks. He saw nothing but blue. His stomach convulsed. He tried to smear the blood off his visor, but it only swirled around and around, slick like motor oil. He thought to take the Goggles off, but as his fingers pressed at the seams, there was a warning beep. A pop-up smeared across his vision.

WARNING
Removing Goggles will end gameplay and result in disqualification

"Gameplay," Wyatt said. He felt his pulse stumble slightly slower, as if confused. What was more real: the unseen stage where his body was moving, or this world he was locked into?

It's not real, Wyatt reminded himself. He retracted his fingers—the message disappeared. *There isn't even blood in your mouth—it's all part of the immersion. It's not real, so stop being such a baby.*

Even though he *thought* he felt blood hot against his face, and he could smell wet metal and fish guts, he didn't actually *taste* anything besides sour spit. He only felt the blood under the surface of his helmet, and up to the top of his neck where his motion-capture suit ended, but not around his mouth where there was no special gear. None of it was real, at least for now.

Somehow, that settled him. Right now, this was still a simulation, so they had to be realistic about how much force it took to kill something, and how much blood would come pouring out. He better get used to it. Whatever would happen today, even if it could scare him, even if it could ache in his bones like that shoulder-roll and make his muscles burn and shake, it wasn't real. The knife he'd used was just a digital trick, holstered opposite the real-life one hidden under all the digital layers. The blaster was pixels too, and the monsters.

At least for now. All the more reason to be here: he could desensitize himself to this, take control of his body and mind, so he could do what had to be done.

He stood, sheathed his knife, then pulled his cuffed sleeve down just enough to scrape all the blood off his visor properly. That steadied him. He fixed his sleeve and pulled his blaster back to his front. He should say something cool, shouldn't he? Or at least funny? But he knew he wasn't good at that.

He was good at *Fathom Fall*. Time to move on and show it.

Wyatt shook himself off (the blood stayed, including a blue crust on the edges of his vision, but it was cooling against his skin) and walked toward the front door, ignoring the stiffness in his biceps as he held the blaster. He put his ear to the dingy wood, heard nothing and saw nothing on the volume sensor either, then stepped into the empty, dark hallway. The stairwell was right next to him. He didn't think much about it and walked over, put his hand on the stairwell door . . . but then he paused, narrowing his eyes.

If this were an objective level, like in Campaign Mode, he would run down the stairs and into the street, head up toward Hydrexo, and let the level end when he walked through the security gate. But this wasn't about getting from point A to point B, even if that point B was Zav; it was about racking up a score. It was practically an Easter egg hunt—it'd be reckless to leave this building without at least checking a few more rooms.

Wyatt remembered what Davids had said: if even one Bluddite got away, it was too many. He wasn't satisfied with leaving. And maybe part of him wanted to rewrite the very unheroic image of him flailing around.

He knew he shouldn't care about something like that, especially when Zav was surely on his way to the meeting spot, but he still did.

LEVEL 23

WYATT MOVED METHODICALLY, HOPING that Zav was hunting a bit too and not just hanging around waiting. He found nothing in the next apartment, and only two Bluddites in the second, but they were busy feasting on some other competitor (seven players now—it was going quick) and didn't notice him fire two shots from his close-range mini-blaster. Take that, Ava.

Plink! 09 *Plink!* 10

Once they were dead, the competitor's body disappeared too, so Wyatt didn't get a chance for a good look. It got him thinking that he might have to prepare for seeing that sort of stuff. The thought, sticky like melted gum, didn't leave him for a bit. Dead Bluddites were one thing, but dead people—dead kids like him—were another. It made him think of Leo, and how she might have gone. That only made him more determined to win. To *avoid* death. No looking away. He'd clear this building, then meet Zav.

Wyatt left the apartment, shutting the door behind him, and finally looked back toward the stairwell. Three rooms seemed like a good number. Maybe that two-pointer had been the big boss of the floor, or another competitor had killed an even bigger one already. Wyatt's score was 10, a nice even number to move on with.

But still . . .

"Just to be sure," Wyatt whispered, alone with only the chug-chug-chugging to hear him . . . and a stadium full of fans. "Be sure I got every last one."

And so, Wyatt opened the next door.

The apartment's entryway and living room looked the same as all the others, which didn't give Wyatt much hope that he'd find anything. He crept through into the empty kitchen, seeing and hearing nothing. He did, however, note a smell. It didn't bowl him over, wasn't a rancid rot that had him gagging and thinking about puking his guts out. It was the kind of reek that sat low in the subway tunnels on hot days, sewer-y and sweaty.

The smell of Bluddites, he now knew.

Wyatt turned to stalk down the hallway, blaster ready, breath and steps silent. He kept his heart rate steady; despite the sweat soaking through his hair and the strain in his arms, his barrel and sights stayed level. At the end of the hall, the door to the main bedroom was ajar. A dull chatter grew clearer, or as clear as it could when it was only garbled sounds and syllables that didn't quite match up into real words. He read once that parrots don't "speak"; they just blow air over a special valve in their throat. This sounded like that.

Not real speech, but parroting without thought behind it. There were Bluddites through that door—more than one.

Wyatt put his back to the wall next to the door, so close he could hear their claws scuttling around, and the wet slaps of some walking upright. There had to be *at least* three or four, maybe even a dozen if he'd found a proper nest.

This was a fitting Boss Fight.

Wyatt plucked a hurricade off his belt. It was about the size of a baseball, but definitely heavier. Luckily, he wouldn't have to throw it far. He'd finish this, and then he'd find Zav.

Wyatt pulled the pin—*five*— rolled the hurricade through the open door—*four*—then sprinted back through the kitchen and into the living room. He'd studied the handbook: he needed to be fifteen meters back. He'd learned to visualize the blast zone after one too many close calls in-game.

"Three," he said, pressing himself to the farthest wall. The Bluddite screeched, not loudly—*two*—more confused, possibly concerned about this contraption that had suddenly appeared.

"*Wuh?*" one seemed to ask.

Wyatt put his hands over the sides of his helmet, pushing them in against his ears so he could hear nothing but cushiony, muffled silence. He shut his eyes. "One."

"*Get back!*" a voice screeched. Wait, was that a person? Had he been mistaken? It sounded so human. Wyatt's eyes opened. His hands fell from his ears. He swayed forward, as if he could run to help—

BANG!

The light from the hall turned from overcast gray to red, orange, yellow, and then blinding white that seared his eyes. Wyatt winced, might have screamed. He wrenched his head away to squeeze his eyes tight. The flash burned into his vision, spattering stars against the dark. His eardrums protested as walls crumbled and cracked, and two-by-fours splintered. His brain felt like someone had hooked it up to a bicycle pump. This was *not* good for his concussion.

Even through the ringing in his ears, he could hear the shrieking. "*Hellllppp.*" It was a Bluddite's voice, *obviously*—he'd been so easily tricked. Just monsters. His head pounded, a painful reminder not to second-guess himself.

And then, as he blinked the last few sparkles out of his eyes, there was silence. A slight ringing overlaid it, but under that?

Nothing.

Wyatt blinked his burning eyes back through the kitchen and toward the hallway, where there was a long splatter of white dust and burnt clots of puffy pink insulation. It looked like brains. Wyatt's kill counter was still tallying up, rolling through numbers slowly and plinking happily: **13, 14, 15**.

It stopped there, but (just to be sure, and to *prove them wrong*) Wyatt crept back into the kitchen. The hurricade must have ripped the boards off the windows too—overcast light washed into the hallway ahead, through the remaining drywall and insulation and wiring held in the picture frames of the shattered bedroom wall. Wyatt sniffed through the pressure compounding in his sinuses and throat before stepping forward. Splinters and dust crackled under his boots.

Through the gaps, the room's empty floor and walls were splattered with blue. The corpses were already gone.

All except one huge body, curled up in the back corner. Was it just a frozen glitch? It didn't move, even with Wyatt's volume sensor shifting up to yellow with each step.

Wyatt stepped through the gap where a wall had been a minute ago (was that bad luck? Like stepping under a ladder?), when he realized that the last Bluddite wasn't dead. It was so still it might have been a statue, besides the subtle expanding and contracting of its flank. He thought perhaps he'd injured it, that it was *dying* on its way to dead. And yet, the black bear-sized Bluddite stared very attentively at him with its bulbous, pupil-less eyes and emotionless mouth, not even daring to screech or throw open its gills.

Against the curve of its scaly flank, there was a clutch of six soccer ball–sized eggs, translucent and neon blue like berry Jell-O. They looked far too vulnerable to have survived that blast. Through the slimy eggshell, little bug-eyed creatures floated serenely. That small, they were almost cute, like Level 1 Zip-Monsters. The sudden nostalgia made the blaster heavier in his hands.

But they would grow, and there would be more eggs, and this wouldn't end. Wyatt understood. The brood mother Bluddite wasn't glitching out.

This was a test.

Wyatt's stomach turned carefully. In the straining light catching all the dust and debris, against the subtle ringing still stalking beneath the silence, he crouched with his blaster and elbows rested on his knees. The Bluddite was only a few feet away from him, staring with its round mouth stuck always open, its round eyes stuck never blinking. It didn't even make its strange sounds of mimicked words. The hair on Wyatt's neck was standing, had been standing the entire time because he knew he was being watched.

Wyatt scraped his lips against his braces. "Every last one," he said to himself. And yet some part of him felt kind of slimy about squashing eggs or shooting a brood mother. He didn't know why, considering it was just pixels, and he'd done it plenty of times in *Fathom Fall*. And yet, still.

The Bluddite's tail twitched. It made the choice for him.

The brood mother snapped forward, scaly foot slamming down to crush one of the eggs like an oozy grape. Wyatt fell backward from his crouch—his tailbone and spine hit the floor hard. His muscles burned as he crunched his torso back up, tried to raise his blaster to his eye, but the sling was caught under his shoulder blade. The blaster would rise no higher than his chest. The brood mother lumbered at him, screeching and drawing back its hand to scrape for his face.

Wyatt pulled the trigger. The too-low shot slammed into the Bluddite's torso, where it only tore a few fins free from the shell. The hand kept coming. Wyatt kicked himself backward in time to watch those claws cut so close that he could see his visor-covered face reflected in them. Wyatt yanked the trigger a second time. The shot hit the shell again to send only a small puff of blood spurting out. Wyatt yanked his blaster, but the sling only bunched against his jacket. His mini-blaster was pinned under his side, impossible to reach when he was tangled like this.

"Come on!" he snarled. "Why now?"

Because anything can happen in the battlefield, Wyatt, he heard someone say. It might have been Davids at the announcing podium, or Wyatt just knew it to be true. He'd hesitated, and this was his punishment. Next time he wouldn't flinch. He tried reaching for his mini-blaster.

The Bluddite roared and slammed a hand down on Wyatt's ankle, along with what felt like all of its bear-sized weight. Wyatt screamed. Pain flashed up his leg, so sharp and bright that each chug-chug-chugging of the floor sent another ripple of fire through his limbs. Sweat poured down his greasy, feverish face.

It's just a game. It's just a game, he thought frantically, but the pain didn't stop. He couldn't even rationalize through it like when he realized the blood was fake, or when he could almost hear the stadium if he focused. It felt so real.

"*Craaaaccck*," the Bluddite croaked, and gave another heave. Wyatt swore he heard his bones grating. His muscles strained against the weight. Was the digital skeleton going to snap his leg? Or would the sensory map just make it *feel* like his leg was breaking? That wouldn't end the game; even if he survived this, he'd have to carry on with his leg burning and screaming for relief. Should he just hope the Bluddite killed him and set his score, or would that look pathetic?

How had it felt when those other players were killed?

Could they count the teeth in their necks? Did the people in the stadium know the players were actually hurting? Or were they just watching, like Wyatt had watched that Cadet die?

"Get off me," Wyatt heard himself saying, his voice tight and teary like a dumb little baby. The Bluddite stared at him with its expressionless face. Begging didn't work against monsters.

"*Evvverryyy,*" it started to say.

Distress. AWOL. Get the Goggles off. Each thought blitzed through his head, but he *wouldn't.*

"*Laaasstt. Onnnnne.*"

If this were real, he'd have no choice but to fight. There was no backing out.

Wyatt fired one last desperate shot. There was a sudden blast like a firework, the *CRACK!* of splitting bone. He swore it was his. He waited for his entire existence to be nothing but pain.

And yet . . .

"*YOWCHH!*" the Bluddite wailed, in that stupid cartoonish voice. It fell backward, landing on its side with a *thump* that shook the floor. He'd broken through its shell, *finally*. Wyatt's leg was freed, but the pain didn't stop.

He sat up as fast as he could, his eyes still stinging, his lip wrinkling, his ankle *burning*. He had no time to think about something cool to say. "Ow ow ow—crap, *ow*," he muttered to himself. Talking didn't ease the pain. In the regular game, his water level would drop from an injury, but here it had only eased down from the waves of sweat soaking through his clothes. The pain was its own warning. Wyatt's throat contorted; he hiccupped.

You're not gonna cry on national TV, Wyatt. You aren't.

He fumbled his gloved hands against his leg, probing along the hard bone of his shin, waiting to find a horrible break. He didn't. When he got to his ankle, his muscles were sore, but not sprained. He pried and poked his fingers against the leather of his combat boot, sure he'd awake some hidden disaster. Still, nothing.

He swallowed a mouthful of bile-tinged spit, closed his eyes, then pushed himself up onto his uninjured leg. Very slowly, he eased weight onto the other.

A sharp streak of pain shot through him, straight into his unhappy stomach. Wyatt blinked one tear down his cheek, but when he finally managed to even his weight out, the strained ache evaporated. He twisted his foot around until his ankle muscles stopped seizing.

The pain was still there, but it had quieted enough to go on. He took a deep breath.

He survived. He was fine. This was certainly getting way more intense, and yet? "It's gonna take way more than that," Wyatt muttered, his face numb and emotionless under drying sweat. He thought he might have heard a stadium of cheers. That was good.

A low gurgle bubbled up through the quiet, cresting into a pitiful whine. Wyatt looked over. The brood mother was on its side, breathing shallowly. Blood oozed slowly from between its ghillie fins to pool beneath it. He'd cracked its shell, hurt it badly, but it wasn't dead yet.

Wyatt pulled his mini-blaster from his belt to aim between the eyes. He pictured a rabid animal that he had to put down, for its sake and his. The five remaining eggs stared at him from the corner; he'd have to deal with those too. It had to be done. To save the water for the people, not the monsters.

"Game over," Wyatt said to the Bluddite, and then he really did hear cheering. Wild, *ecstatic* cheering. Because he was about to kill the five-point boss-monster for this building. He hadn't just outgunned, but outsmarted.

Wyatt, never forgetting that this was battle training for the real world, did what had to be done.

Building Cleared! You're on Fire, DoctorDoctor!
Current Score: 25
Item Acquired: Competitor Map

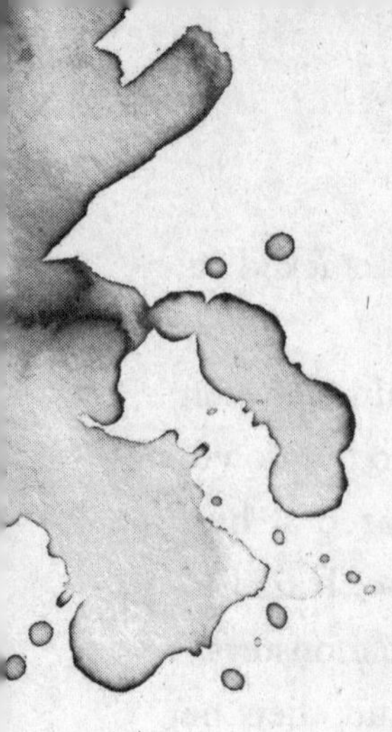

LEVEL 24

WYATT LEFT QUICKLY. NOW that the building was clear and his score was decent, he really needed to catch up on meeting Zav. He knew he couldn't get through the lobby's front doors (there was a construction blockade right through the middle, and the doorway needed a key that Wyatt didn't have), so he crossed the building and went out the fire escape of a second-story apartment to the east-most side. He descended quickly and tucked himself behind a dumpster where he kept his blaster to his eye. But he wasn't really looking down the sights; he was focused on the new map in the bottom left of his vision.

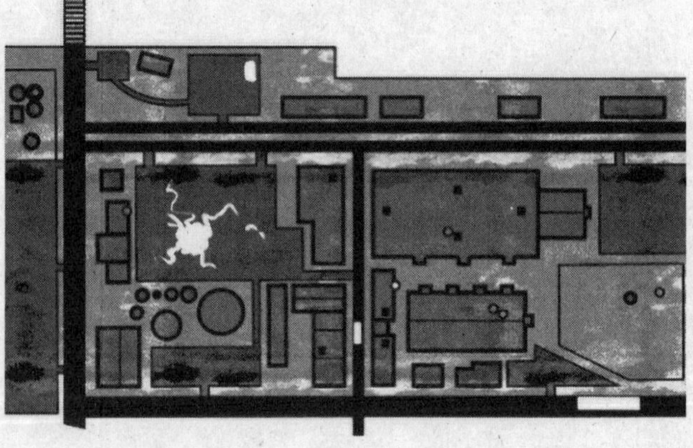

It looked exactly like the map in *Fathom Fall*, obviously, except there were six red dots on it—the other six competitors—and Wyatt's blue dot almost right in the middle. He scanned for the others.

There was someone on the big cement silo near the northern bridge—or they had fallen *into* it. Wyatt refused to think about how that would feel. The dot one street over was in a building Wyatt didn't know how to access, but maybe it was unlocked for Operation Hostile, or they were up on the roof. Most of the competitors seemed to be within Wyatt's block: one in the big warehouse to the north, two in the mechanic's garage to the south, and one in the tiny, depressing park stuck all the way at the end, the last place you could go before the fence into the scrapyard marked the edge of the map.

Wyatt nodded to himself. That was their meeting spot, which meant Zav had made it there safely. Part of Wyatt felt a bit crummy about taking so long—he hoped Zav hadn't rushed there, had been methodical enough to get some good kills in on the way. Wyatt would hurry.

As he thought it, the dot on the cement silo faded. Wyatt's competitor counter rocked down.

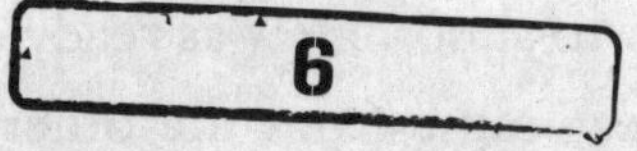

A gust of wind blew, fluttering the metal vent covers on the looming warehouse at Wyatt's ten o'clock, and the thrown-open loading bay doors of the garage at his three. Wyatt stood up and stared down the long stretch of cracked pavement between the two buildings. It was cluttered with wooden pallets and old garbage cans, parked cars, and fork-lifts. He could cut around the garage, to take the main road, but he'd already wasted enough time.

The sooner he got to the park, the better he'd feel about Zav's chances.

Wyatt eased forward with his blaster ready, ducking across the open back road and into the cold shadows between the warehouse and the garage. He kept a careful crouch, a roving aim, boots placed ever so carefully against the dirt as fast as he could manage silently. He scanned the pallets and parked vehicles, finding nothing. Under the garage's dark overhang, the loading bay doors yawned open on a maze of car parts and jacks shining in the diffused light from the warehouse windows. His map said the nearest players—probably Ava and Loop—were on the opposite end of the garage, surely working through the high shelves of parts on their way into the back room.

Then Wyatt swore he saw movement slithering across a disassembled engine. If it wasn't a competitor, then it had to be a Bluddite. He froze, lifting his blaster and aiming through the doors. If anything came running at him, he had the length of the loading bay to shoot. He was ready.

Instead, a threat came from the other side. Footsteps—heavy boots, not claws, spiking his volume sensor up to yellow.

Wyatt turned just in time to see a small shadow bust out of the warehouse door ahead of him, thundering down the two wooden steps and falling into the alley in a scramble of dirt and limbs. A metallic clatter sounded from above as a wave of Bluddites raced along the roof, silhouetted black against the sky.

Time to run. Wyatt hoped Zav at least had good cover while he waited.

He raced toward a parked truck as Bluddites screeched and thudded down onto the dirt. He didn't pause to wonder if he could pull it off: Wyatt dropped and slid like someone going in for home plate. He skidded into the shadows under the truck, wedging himself between the cover of its huge wheels and rolling onto his belly, mini-blaster drawn. His breath was hard and quick through his nose, burning in his lungs and coating his throat and mouth in sour bile.

He forced it to still.

The Bluddites were in the street now, a pack of six. They clicked to each other, made those small rumble-gurgles in their throats. Two of them were on their hind legs, the other four creeping outward, swinging their heads around. Their gills fluttered, listening. Wyatt held his breath. That garage door was open behind him up the wooden ramp. Was it better to try his luck with whatever was in there? Could he make it there in time before they pounced? He would have been *fine* if that other kid hadn't ruined his chances!

Wait . . . where did that other kid go? The map said he was still in the alley.

Wyatt leaned sideways in the shadows, enough to shift his vision around the tire. He spotted the other player, ducked behind a stack of pallets. He was small; it was the *Panda Parade* kid who complained that the General was holding him too hard. Wyatt wanted to scoff—if he died and Zav was left alone because this kid was careless, he'd be pissed. One of the Bluddites wandered closer to Wyatt's hiding spot. He could count every claw. If it lowered its head, it would see him for sure. He knew he wouldn't be able to get out from under the truck easily, not without making a sound and drawing attention.

Ahead, through the pallet slats, the other kid's shoulders jumped with every breath. The blaster was huge in his small, shaking hands, and he was crying. On national TV.

Wyatt's throat tightened. He felt for the kid; the entire stadium was probably booing him, or laughing. Could he hear it in his Goggles? Were the embarrassing GIFs already made? Even if he played at 100 percent, he'd still be the kid who cried from a video game. The crowd couldn't understand how intense this was. Wyatt could handle it, but that little kid, trying to lift his blaster despite his shaking as the Bluddite wandered closer? Wyatt didn't think it was fair.

And yet, if the Bluddite found that kid and tore him to bits in a bloody frenzy the kid could really feel, Wyatt would get his chance to run. That wasn't unfair. That was just the way the game worked. Was he expected to risk his neck to save another player? Would he look bad on TV if he didn't?

Why was he *still* worrying what other people thought? This was bigger than that. He needed to stop thinking about how good or bad things looked. He needed to focus on saving the world. If that meant letting one kid get axed (or making Zav wait longer?), well . . .

The Bluddite heading for the kid snuffled and turned its attention to a forklift instead. The one heading for Wyatt kept coming. Wyatt's held breath began to burn at the bottom of his stomach. His eyes prickled with dust. His muscles were still stiff.

Tears beaded off the bottom of the other kid's jaw. If he was gonna waste his water crying in a video game, then Wyatt doubted he could handle it in the real world. He'd buckle; he'd desert.

The Bluddite's too-sharp claws were getting closer. Wyatt's leg still ached. Hard choices needed to be made to make sure only the best won today. Even if those choices felt sick, and wrong, and Wyatt could feel guilty disgust creeping in his stomach.

This was *not* how he died.

As his eyes started to sting against the pressure in his lungs and the dust in the air, Wyatt planted his elbows against the hard ground, watching the kid's face above the iron sights of his mini-blaster. He needed to get out of here, and this was the only answer. Maybe it felt wrong, maybe no one would understand, but not every choice made sense in the moment.

As long as it meant victory, in the end, then everything in war was fair.

CRACK! Wyatt's shot splintered the side of the pallet.

The other boy screamed and dove sideways, right into the

open. It was over before he ran out of air—every Bluddite screeched and closed in on him. Wyatt took the opportunity to kick out from under the truck and raise his mini-blaster against his stiff bicep, aiming for the back of the Bluddites' heads.

They didn't even notice him standing back there, an executioner, in more than one way. Past their happily swinging tails, over their fanned-out gills, the kid's eyes were fading behind his Goggles all spattered in blood solids.

It's okay, Wyatt wanted to say. He really did believe it, despite the still-sick pressure in his stomach, and the knowledge that even digital teeth could hurt. His internal monologue sounded more like Leo, that day in the crushed clam of their car. *It's okay. It's gonna be okay.*

It hadn't been then. It would be now. He had to believe this would all turn out all right. It was the only way to keep moving.

Wyatt fired off six fast shots (*SH-SH-SH-SH-SH-SHWOOP!*) one by one into the back of the Bluddites' heads. They each squealed, then disappeared with that rewarding *plink!* Wyatt's score rose.

The kid stayed a second longer than they did, his wide eyes on Wyatt's, but every muscle limp.

Sometimes the small parts of the big picture felt sickening. There were going to be more moments like this, surely, where the right choice felt like the wrong one. Like having to stomp those little Zip-Monster eggs. Wyatt understood why so many soldiers were retreating from real-world Lake Superior, why they couldn't stand this. But he also understood that there would be no future if he couldn't be brave enough to fight for it.

All this pain, all this suffering, had to be worth something in the end.

He needed to clear the area. He needed to get to Zav. He needed so many things.

Wyatt holstered his mini-blaster and turned quickly from the scene, to run for the open door of the garage. The dead kid's eyes stared after him, maybe gone now or maybe burned in his memory. He'd buy that kid a soda or something after the game. Not to apologize, but to thank him for taking the out so Wyatt could keep going.

It would make sense to everyone, eventually.

Wyatt ran up to the loading bay doors, ribs tight and weary. Ahead, the floor and maze of parts was completely empty, no scales and no other players. There were only five of them left now—Wyatt could win this thing. He needed to stay ready on his way out to the park—he took a reload magazine off his belt, shuffling his blaster in his arms to reach the eject.

He'd stumbled into the middle of the room, halfway to an open door that could spit him back out to the main street, when he realized how quiet the garage was. On his map, Wyatt could see two dots in the garage's back room, unmoving. Considering they were the only two dots linked together, he assumed it was Ava and Loop.

Something had sent Ava Maraj, blank-faced and ninja-fierce, running for cover. Maybe she was breaking under the pressure, but Wyatt wasn't so sure.

The silence was broken by a curious "*Crrrk?*" Not from around him, but above.

Wyatt looked up into the warehouse rafters. Threaded among the steel lay a mat of Bluddites dozens and dozens and *dozens* wide. Eyes began to turn to him as they all stirred awake. For a moment, he thought of Zav's hideout, then felt even more guilty for reasons he couldn't quite pinpoint.

"*Eh?*" one said. It echoed in the unsure silence.

"Crap," Wyatt breathed. They were all at a standstill, the Bluddites beginning to wake, and Wyatt's blaster nearly empty.

Well . . . the world needed to keep turning. He had to keep moving toward the park. At least he could make that choice, even when he could feel his limbs going rubbery with exhaustion.

Very slowly, he thumbed at his blaster's magazine eject.

Click.

The first Bluddite braced.

Wyatt slammed a new round of ammo in just in time to gun the first Bluddite down as it leapt toward him from that impossible height. There was a horrible series of splats and thuds while the others fell like rain, and a bug-ish scuttling as more descended from the walls, blocking every exit. Perhaps he wouldn't make it to Zav after all.

Wyatt was almost grateful: there was no way to chase back

the ache in his stomach like a good old shootout. If he was going out, he'd take down as many as possible and show that he could be a hero even in his final moments.

Maybe the competitors were all lucky. Who else got to test run their own death?

LEVEL 25

WYATT KEPT FIRING AS his score tolled up up up, the *plink!plink!plink!* of the counter chasing back the lump in his throat until he couldn't even think of that dead kid. More Bluddites were still scrambling down the walls, dropping from the ceiling. He leapt into the bed of a pickup truck to get the high ground as they raced toward him in a flood of bodies. He was screaming as he pulled the trigger, but it was roller-coaster screaming—scared but kind of living for that fear. He knew it would be game over for him in that garage, but also knew his counter was going up. *Plink!plink!plink!*

Zav was out there, alone, and Wyatt was going to die. What a way to go. To hell if it hurt. That whole stadium was watching him scream and shoot with his teeth gnashed together in a grin. Make a GIF of *that*, he thought. Make a hero out of this moment.

He stepped toward the cab of the truck, keeping his finger down on the trigger to fire off a rapid spray. Most of his shots missed, and the rest only puffed out little bloody spurts when they hit the Bluddites' shells, but it kept them back. They were all screeching and shouting things he almost understood, but even if they'd walked up and used perfect English to ask him where the nearest public restroom was, he wouldn't have the time or thought to stop shooting. He was managing to keep them off the truck at least, but they were closing in on him from every side, fast.

"Every last one!" Wyatt shouted. He wouldn't think of that dead kid, or the blood still reeking in his clothes, or even the explosion all those months ago, or Zav alone without him after he'd hoped they could be friends again. Aim. Fire. *SH-SH-SH-SH-SH-SHWOOP!* Screeching that echoed. The scaly circle tightened around him. The counter rose.

The truck lurched as a Bluddite landed in the bed barely two strides ahead of him, splayed out on all fours. It only had time to screech a "*Blah-EEeeeeEE!*" before Wyatt shot it between the eyes. Everything smelled like blood and that old-sweat smell and the gasoline of the garage. The truck groaned sideways with the weight of Bluddites hauling themselves up. Wyatt saw three heads and six hands rear up on his left—he shot one, but the other two were pulling in. The truck's tail-gate slammed down to let a few more climb up.

The *plink!* song was gone now. Even in all the screeching and wailing, he heard the silence.

Wyatt turned, just as a massive, boss-sized Bluddite landed on top of the truck's cab. The metal dented in. The truck keeled forward. Wyatt's face lurched just centimeters from the Bluddite's. It screeched at him. He could see every single one of its teeth as a seemingly slow-motion wave of thick, bubbling blue spit came rushing up like puke. It splattered against his Goggles.

"Dick move," Wyatt heard himself say, but he didn't recognize his voice. The Goggles may have saved him from blindness, but now everything was blocked by fizzing blue too thick to evaporate quickly. He swept a hand off his blaster to wipe it away.

Something cold latched on to his upper arm. It took him a second to realize it wasn't actually cold, but *pain*. He dropped his blaster onto the sling (his spine ached from the weight—everything ached) to clear his visor with his other hand. It smudged into a greasy film, thin enough to see a blurry Bluddite clamping its mouth just below his shoulder.

Wyatt stared at the Bluddite. It stared at him, fluttering its gills happily while Wyatt's dry, peppery blood sprayed from the holes beneath its mouth. Streams of freezing, gasping emptiness coursed through his body in long pulls. He was being sucked dry.

The pain was fine, it was just pain, but the wrongness rocked him like a punch, especially as his water bar tanked.

Wyatt screamed and threw himself backward. The Bluddite's mouth unlatched—Wyatt slammed his boot into the center of its face as he fell through the open window of the cab. Its teeth crunched under his boot like tiny icicles.

"*Ow*," it said.

"Ow yourself, freak!" Wyatt screamed. He tumbled against the dashboard, scrambling farther from that little window back out to the swarming truck bed. His arm was soaked in thick, dark blood, seeping from the fabric of his fatigues. A wave of nausea sloshed up from his stomach, made his head ring and his fingers numb.

Wyatt was swaying, like Zav used to. His breath was coming out choked and short. He was *not* smiling or roller-coaster screaming anymore, especially now that the counter wasn't going up and his whole face felt slack and hollow. The world seemed to be squirming ahead of him, every edge coming apart. Was he about to pass out? Or was he dying? He was losing blood quickly. His water bar still inched lower. The huge Bluddite on the top of the cab swiped its arm in after him. He pulled his knife to stab wildly into the meat of its forearm. The Bluddite squealed and yanked its arm back, but more reached in, all of them slamming against each other. They were too busy shoving to actually get through.

He turned his head, hoping that (somehow?) he could escape out the doors, but more rammed the sides of the truck. Claws squealed across the windshield behind him. He flinched away from a Bluddite with its face smeared up against the breath-fogged glass. All he could hear was shrieking, and voices.

"*Wy-aaaatt*," they kept saying, in every sort of voice. "*Playyyy. Killlllllll. Everyyy lasssst—*"

"Shut it," Wyatt squeaked. He wanted it to be forceful, but it was a terrified moan. A Bluddite leapt into the driver-side window so violently that the truck tilted onto two wheels, throwing Wyatt into the passenger seat where he could only stare at more teeth and claws. He thought the whole thing was going over, but the truck slammed back onto all fours to send him sprawling into the middle of the cab. His head slammed off the dashboard hard enough to rock his concussion even through the helmet. Wyatt was sure he was going to puke, maybe going to cry, definitely going to faint. The windshield creaked behind him, surely ready to shatter and let them all through after him.

"No no no," Wyatt was saying, frantic now. *Please let this be over.* He signed a waiver, and he wanted to be a soldier, and he wanted to save the world or just help people and be kinder than he was or maybe just help Zav to apologize for avoiding him or even to selfishly feel like he could even do *anything* in such a horrible world, but *this*?!

A Bluddite shoved its face and front arms through the tiny cab window across from Wyatt. Before Wyatt could think to do anything, four butcher-hook claws sunk into the tense meat between his shoulder and throat, dragging him forward. The Bluddite screamed so loud Wyatt thought all the windows would shatter out. Its teeth lunged for Wyatt's neck.

The wave of fear was just that—a wave, like drowning in icy slush too thick to swim through, every muscle giving up at once. Wyatt's water level soared downward. But it didn't seem to be blood this time, or at least not all of it. It took him a moment to figure out what had just happened.

His pants were soaked in more than sweat and blood. The cold fear was quickly replaced by red-hot shame. He'd pissed himself, like a toddler. Like an absolute baby. On national TV, in front of everyone.

This was way worse than Pampers.

In the bleak moment when he knew it had happened and couldn't do anything to fix it, under the sound of the Bluddite still screaming and all the others ramming the truck, Wyatt swore he heard the audience laughing.

He'd only wanted to help, and now he was more terrified than he'd ever been. He was still being pulled toward the Bluddite readying to clamp down on his neck and drink him dry, like that other kid, like all the other kids, and Leo. Wyatt lost sight of its teeth as it drew him in so close he could only see its eyes. It was this monster's fault that he was here in the first place. Everything was their fault. That Leo was dead, that Zav was an orphan, that Wyatt's parents worked so much, that Wyatt was teased by other terrified kids jealous of the things he had and they didn't. *Everything* was their fault.

Something inside Wyatt snapped. A surge of rage swept through him like a Power-Up. Except it wasn't a Power-Up. More like a Power-*Down*, fear and anger being written over by a blank white void. He was cold, and calm, and felt nothing at all.

He liked the feeling a lot.

No guts, no glory. Pain was temporary. Victory was eternal.

Wyatt plunged his knife right through the Bluddite's eye. It collapsed like a deflated soccer ball. Over the monster's screams, he thought he might have heard cheering or maybe gasping or Davids shouting, "A great move from DoctorDoctor! Don't count him out yet, folks," but it didn't matter because he was tearing that wriggling Bluddite's claws from him, getting a grip on its kelpy shoulders to drag it into the cab. It was flailing to get away, not even trying to bite him, just gurgling and flopping and scratching at his arms and his legs and his torso. It was *pathetic*. Wyatt pulled his mini-blaster and fired four times through its belly until the last shot pierced thc shell. He kicked the corpse off and fired at the Bluddites blocking up the window.

"Take that, take that, take that," someone was saying, possibly Wyatt. He locked his fist into his palm and jammed his elbow into the flat nose of the next one, giving himself enough of an opening to tear back into the truck bed with his aqua blaster blazing once again. The Bluddites screeched and squealed as they scrambled away from him, diving for the open doors, back into the streets. Wyatt no-scoped three. The garage looked and smelled like a killing floor, like a good and real war zone.

"That's what you get," Wyatt said with no smile. Sweat ran hot down his face. His water was tanking lower and lower as his arm and shoulder pulsed blood across his clothes. There was maroon around the edges of everything. If this was how he ended the game, then maybe that was all right. It might even be all right if he didn't win, because he'd still go right up to Davids with this same cold feeling and tell him that he better give Wyatt a spot on the team, so help him, because Wyatt was gonna teach those monsters a lesson. Saving the world for glory was one thing, and doing it because "gee, it sure does sound like the right thing to do, sir" was another, but doing it because he was terrified seemed like he had plunged the right key into the right lock to keep everything in. He was angry and scared, yes, but now this was bigger. This was deeply personal. He understood why Ava Maraj was so serious. She'd known this already, maybe since her parents died, and so he didn't care if Davids thought she was some sort of loose cannon: Wyatt wanted her on the team with him and Zav. Not to be happy, but just to get even for how much had been taken from them all.

"Prove them wrong," he muttered. *Plink!plink!plink!* "Prove them wrong."

Wyatt kept shooting while his vision grew smaller and smaller. In that pinhole, there was nothing but his sights and bodies dropping, blurrier by the second until the Bluddites were just figures on two legs sprinting away from him, but it didn't matter because they were dying, and that was good. They were dying because they should die. Because it was right for them to die. Because they were better dead than stealing water that belonged to paying customers.

Wyatt's water bar dipped to nearly none, and then he collapsed into the screaming void of rage locked inside his skull.

LEVEL 26

WYATT SAW NOTHING BUT white and his utilities: 46 kills, 5 players still remaining, 10:02 on the clock; two red dots in the garage, one in the park, and another on the complete other side from where it had been last he checked, a speed that shouldn't be possible if you had to cut around buildings. And then his water bar, which was rising.

His whole body felt soft and heavy, like the foggy moment when he looked up to see paramedics gathering him off the floor. He must have passed out. There was a dull rushing, but based on his volume sensor, it was only in his head. Slowly, the sheet of frosty white across his vision began to melt away, bringing the silhouettes, then hazy outlines of two figures ahead of him. The air smelled like metal and gas. The garage?

"You should have just left him," one figure said. Wyatt tried to remember who he thought would be in the garage. He knew he had made a guess, but everything was juuuust out of reach. "He's cracked, we dunno if we can heal, and I'm pretty sure he pissed himself."

"Cool . . . and?" someone else asked. Wyatt knew *that* voice: Loop. He was honestly cheesed that Loop was trying to save him, both because he didn't take Loop very seriously, and because he'd already decided on his top three. Him, Ava, and Zav. "You want me to watch some other guy bleed out right in front of me?"

Wyatt had done that. He had no regrets.

"He's not *bleeding out*," the other voice said. It wasn't Ava, which was odd. The hazy figure was broader. "It's a *video game*, dipshit. It's a competition." It was more than that. As Wyatt's vision cleared, he did see Loop crouched ahead of him, and another guy looming behind. "And if it wouldn't tank my score, I'd friendly-fire him right now so I can get closer to winning."

"Try it," Wyatt heard himself say. His throat contracted around each word.

Both players turned to look at him, Loop at his level and B haunting behind. They were in the back room of the garage, where the windows were all boarded up and the TV was on the permanent fritz, shining grayish light over the worn-down couch and open mini fridge. The fridge was still humming, but empty now that two water bottles were lying at Loop's feet. Wyatt noted the red-and-white med pack Power-Up on Loop's belt, and a yellow shine in B's visor.

Loop smiled, close-lipped and tired. "You back with us, man?" he asked. The low, quiet concern felt like an accusation. There were bandages wrapped tight around Wyatt's arm, and a thick wad of gauze taped at his shoulder. "Gave you some water and patched you up."

True enough, Wyatt's throat felt cool and wet. Had he actually been given water onstage? It didn't matter: he was still in the game. The pain was only a far-down pulse. It was good. He was tired, and his body still felt a bit too numb, but he was *back*.

Despite watching that Army Cadet die, and making sure *Panda Parade* kid did too, Wyatt had been spared.

"Any other strays you wanna pick up?" B growled. He was speaking to Loop, but staring Wyatt down with his thick jaw shifted sideways as the TV light turned him cold and pixelly. "Wanna patch up a Bluddite too?"

So much for meeting your video game heroes. Wyatt wasn't surprised, or even disappointed, mostly because he just didn't care. In that blank white space, he felt nothing but determination to get this finished. He'd pulled through and had to make it count for something.

Loop rolled his eyes behind his visor and leaned closer. "He wasn't complaining when I was saving *his* ass five minutes in," he whispered to Wyatt, like they were in on the same friendly joke. They weren't friends, were barely friend*ly*. "Guess he's scared to be alone, but I'm not blaming him—the graphics on this are next level."

Wyatt said nothing, just stared at Loop's friendly smile despite the blue blood flecking his visor, and long limbs hanging casual even with a soaked bandage wrapped tight around his forearm. Even in all this, he still seemed so . . . so *unbothered*. "You could've left him," Wyatt said. Not an accusation, or a question, just a fact released from the cold static in his skull that muffled the memory of that dead kid in the alley, and the shame of his still-damp fatigue pants. He wondered how his IRL gym shorts looked onstage—he strangled that thought down. It didn't matter to him, not in here. "Maybe he doesn't have what it takes to win."

"And *you* pissed yourself," B added, before wandering off to kick at the TV and inspect a pinup calendar on the wall. Wyatt didn't care what he said—it didn't matter. The glitchy light hissed around the room.

"I'm not gonna watch someone die in HD," Loop said easily. He rocked backward, bringing himself up to standing with his forearm held out to Wyatt, palm ready. "It'd be like watching them die in *real life*," he said, looking very closely at Wyatt through their visors. Only Wyatt knew what he was getting at. But this wasn't real life, not yet. And once it was, would Loop have the guts to deal with it?

Davids was right: Loop was so soft. Part of Wyatt was almost jealous—how could Loop look so chill in a terrible, bloody, monster-infested world? How come he got to waltz through this without being piss-your-pants scared?

Loop was nice, had always been nice, but he wasn't serious.

Wyatt pushed himself up onto his own feet. His blaster tugged uncomfortably between his weary shoulder blades, and his legs were rubbery. It didn't really bother him. Once his boots were under him properly, his muscles and bones stacked up like a perfect block tower, he was all right.

"Thanks," he offered, in his new, flat voice. His map said he was close to Zav. And considering Ava wasn't with Loop, maybe she really was ready to make a better team. Wyatt turned for the door.

Loop's hand caught his arm, just close enough to the bandages to make the wound beneath seethe. Wyatt reeled back on him, face tight.

"Where the hell do you think you're going?" Loop asked.

"To fight some Bluddites," Wyatt answered. "I'm assuming that's what Ava's out there doing without you." For once, he meant for that to come off a bit mean. B laughed.

Loop's eyebrows twitched. "Come on, man," he said quietly. "You look rough. Let's wait it out a bit more; then we can get Lion together."

There wasn't time! "She ditched you. I'm right, aren't I?" Wyatt said. He tore his arm back. His voice never grew louder than an even speaking tone—he didn't need it. He didn't even have it in him. "She knew you weren't serious enough about this."

Loop shook his hand out, like he needed to get Wyatt off him. His smile had fallen away, eyebrows twitching toward anger that he refused to feed. He *should*. "I don't know what the hell he says to make you all act like this," he muttered. Who? Davids? Ava had been saying the same thing as Wyatt, that Loop was too casual. Now *he* was jealous of Wyatt, was that it? "I take this shit plenty serious, which is why I'm not happy seeing dead kids, you get me? That shit *sucks*."

"That's real life," Wyatt said.

"You're both crazy," B breathed from the peripheral.

Wyatt didn't even care if the whole Hydrexo Centre agreed with B, or everyone on national TV. They didn't understand, not yet, and there wasn't time to explain to people who weren't worthy of what Davids had confessed to Wyatt. "There's gonna be more death until we finish this properly," Wyatt said. "If you don't have the guts to do that, then maybe you don't deserve to be part of it."

Loop stared at him. Wyatt waited for him to yell, or curse him out, or just storm off. Whatever. Fine. Instead, he did the most expected and most infuriating thing in the world: the corner of Loop's mouth twitched back toward the usual smile, even if it didn't seem to brighten his face. It was a bitter, somehow condescending smile that made Wyatt feel even more angry.

"You think this is ever gonna be over?" Loop asked. He leaned his weight back onto one leg, shaking his head. Wyatt's whole body crackled. "What? You kill all the Bluddites out there, you beat yourself dead in the body and up in here." He tapped the side of his helmet. The *tock tock* shook down into Wyatt's bones. "Then what? Rainbows forever? Wake up one day to paradise and retire happily?"

That was simplifying it, but *yeah*, Wyatt did think that. "What the hell are you talking about?" Wyatt said. He shuffled his blaster into his hands, ready to storm out the door and back into the hostile zone.

Loop swung his blaster to ready position too. He leaned closer to Wyatt, both of them reeking like blood and sweat.

Loop's mouth was smiling, but his eyes most certainly weren't. They seemed years older.

"You know what I learned from working with Davids and Ava? There's no Final Boss," he said, low. Was he allowed to be talking this openly? Wyatt was certain that some Security Force operative was swearing under his breath and censoring the feed. "We can kill all them Bluddites out there, build another refinery, but shit was bad before it went down and it's still gonna *be* bad with it back. I'll take my paychecks for all this just like anyone else, but I still gotta live with myself."

Wyatt swallowed. He didn't have any words for that. Ava had been saying the same thing, that there was no happy ending here. Was there something else Wyatt was missing? But this victory, a chance to purge monsters from the world, it couldn't be a lie.

There had to be an off switch to all the bad things out there. *This* was it, even if Loop was too cowardly to do it properly. Hadn't Ava said Loop was missing a bit of info?

"It sounds like you don't want to do what has to be done, Loop," Wyatt said quietly. "Maybe you don't actually want to be on this team."

Loop took a slow breath. "Maybe I don't," he said, but didn't drop his blaster. "But I don't see much of a choice."

From the harshness of Loop's eyes behind his visor, Wyatt understood that Loop still wanted to win this just as much as anyone. Maybe for the money, maybe to stick with Ava. Wyatt didn't know, or care really. He was going to find Zav and end the Bluddite scourge. That would save humanity, no matter what Loop seemed to think. And if Wyatt was still a bit confused about what Loop allegedly didn't know, and perhaps worried that Wyatt didn't have the whole truth either, then it was better to ignore that until this was over.

"All right," Wyatt said. His voice was still sort of slow and low, very *proper*, like he was practicing for a speech contest. Was this how soldiers felt? Maybe he'd cracked something important in his head, and that should frighten him, but he was past fear. "I'm going out there, so you can come with me or stay here."

"Fine," B said, finally turning back to Wyatt with his arms crossed. His posture seemed a bit stiff. Clearly he wanted more protection, and Wyatt was set to provide it. Loop was eyeing Wyatt carefully, but Wyatt turned for the back door anyway, the one that would let them out to the west edge of the park. According to his map, Zav was waiting on the other side.

Also according to his map, the last dot that must have been Ava Maraj was on its way back toward them, weaving in a strange path Wyatt still didn't understand. She probably had her own high score, but he had his, and he'd make sure Zav did too.

Was that unfair?

Wyatt was going to decide what fair meant, on his terms, to make sure he was never as scared as he was in that garage. He'd do whatever he had to in order to finish this.

Let. It. End. And bring him the perfect paradise he was promised

LEVEL 27

WYATT WALKED OUT THE flimsy back door, his blaster already raised while he scanned. The warehouse stretched along his left, ending with a mostly empty parking lot. Ahead, the park sat quiet and crusty.

He hadn't been to the real-world location in a long time (not since Leo, he knew), but it looked as sad as he remembered: gray-brown trees without leaves, no places to sit asides from the crunchy grass that stabbed through your pants, a distant gazebo with planks over the windows, the public fountain ahead that had never worked, and garbage cans that were always overflowing. Wyatt wasn't sure whose job it was to empty them, only that they never did. When he'd gone to the park in real life, there were always tents strung up from trees or clustered together around makeshift firepits, with bikes and shopping carts waiting alongside.

Those tents were still there, but none of them were standing. Instead, the dingy fabric and litter scraps had been thrashed to the ground. Wyatt crept forward with his blaster ready. His boot crunched into something. When he looked down, he saw a poster board, the marker-scrawled words still legible under red, human blood.

SOMEONE LIVES HERE: DO NOT CLEAR

The *Fathom Fall* locations were so accurate. And yet, just off the path and into the dry grass, there was one of those big blue signs they put in historic locations, usually for important buildings, war memorials, things like that. There was never one here before, in real life or even in the *Fathom Fall* maps Wyatt had played before. He crept across the road to read it.

Hydrexo Community Park

To commemorate the brave commitments of Hydrexo's Security Force, for answering the call to arms and securing peace and fair water distribution for all.

A button appeared at the bottom of the sign, blinking. There weren't any further instructions.

"This is new," B added over Wyatt's shoulder. Loop kept his blaster ready, aiming down the open path. "Press it."

"Hold up," Loop said. "It could be a trap—"

Wyatt pressed the button.

"Bonus level unlocked," the woman's voice said from seemingly all around them. For a second, Wyatt could hear the cheering of the stadium. When he looked up from the sign, the park wasn't how he remembered it, not at all.

All the tents were gone, the grass was green, and a warm autumn breeze ruffled the orange leaves together. The garbage cans were emptied, and the fountain in the middle pumped shimmering water. Even the air seemed clearer, so Wyatt could see that the gazebo was white-painted and clean, with no more boards on the windows. Wyatt even heard birds—not just pigeons, but the chirpy sparrows you only found in the city's fancier parks, or maybe on private rooftop gardens with their own sprinklers. The air smelled sweet, like fresh-cut grass and buttery popcorn from an unseen snack cart.

"Damn," B breathed. He took a step forward, blaster beginning to lower. He reminded Wyatt of his own dad staring at *Fathom Fall* footage, getting all nostalgic about water guns. "I didn't know grass could look like that."

It was beautiful, one of those places that only existed in history and storybooks now. Or one of those places that would exist in the future, when the Hydrexo team fixed everything. Wyatt wanted to stare, to take in the sunshine. But for now, his map said that Zav was past the fountain in the small field, and it had a new countdown burned across it:

59 . . . 58 . . .

Whatever change had occurred in the park, it wasn't going to last.

"Nu-uh," Loop said. Why was he being such a pessimist? "We go in there to smell flowers or whatever, and then it's gonna snap right back to how it was and ambush us. It's a trap."

Not a trap, but incentive. All the blood, and shame, and anger, it would get them this. Maybe Loop didn't have the guts to get them there, but Wyatt did. He had one minute to find Zav in this paradise park, before Bluddite territory plunged in on him with a vengeance.

Good, Wyatt thought. Once he had Zav with him, they'd finally be able to work together, to bring in the stable future they both deserved, and to spare everyone else from the shame and fear Wyatt had felt today.

He'd get there. For now, there would be blood.

Wyatt sprinted forward, not caring if Loop or B followed. He held his blaster against his chest, running so fast he thought he might lift off from the ground. The park streamed by, trees rustling, fountain trickling. The destroyed tents had been replaced by picnic tables, somewhere you could actually sit, not even those uncomfortable arc-shaped benches at the bus and streetcar stops. And the people who had lived in those tents, surely they'd have houses. Zav too. Everyone would be all right once the Final Boss was defeated.

The counter spun lower and lower. Wyatt didn't know what the park would look like once it hit zero, but doubted it would be good:

42 . . . 41 . . .

Wyatt sprinted up toward the fountain. He was still cold, and yet he knew how much he wanted this. Something had made the park bad, and that something was Bluddites, and so they had to die. He knew it without emotion. It was just a fact. Eliminating them would make the sky bluer and the grass greener. Somehow, it would be true. Because there needed to be a way. They couldn't be powerless.

Wyatt jumped up onto the stone edge of the fountain and slashed through the water. It washed cold and thick over him, chasing off the reek of sweat and blood and being so scared he pissed himself like a child. The water rushed around him like a warm thunderstorm. He was sure he hadn't felt one of those since he was much smaller.

35 . . . 34 . . .

Wyatt tore out of the veil of water and leapt up onto the far edge of the fountain, staring out at a thick wall of trees and hedges that showed flashes of red dirt and chain-link beyond. They'd put in a baseball diamond on the other side. The only way past was through the gazebo. And, according to his map, Zav was at home plate.

Also according to his map, Ava was beelining her way to them too. Wyatt didn't like that. B and Loop were coming up quickly behind him. Wyatt suspected B was all right with sacrificing him, probably Zav too, and Ava might get on board with it all. He doubted Loop could convince them to be nice and work together, mostly because Wyatt couldn't be convinced either. He had to get Zav, take cover, and go from there.

But why? a voice deep in his head asked. It was the same thought he'd had before the competition, trying to creep forward again. He hadn't felt chilled by the water, but he was chilled by that voice. *You've been talking about letting the best people win . . . Is Zav the best, or do you just feel guilty? Ava might be more willing to work with you if you drop your deadweight too.*

Wyatt had no way to fight that thought. If he had his emotions left, he might have remembered that Zav was his friend, so was Leo. He should help, right? He thundered off toward the gazebo. He was running out of time!

28 . . . 27. . .

Wyatt was always told that other people were jealous, but he didn't *choose* to be a Water Baby. If anything, he was doing everything in his power *not* to be one. So should it be his job to help Zav? And who was more important? One boy he used to be friends with, or the entire world that might suffer if he played favorites to let Zav onto a team he wasn't ready for? He was finally thinking clearly, all those pesky emotions set aside for what really mattered: doing what needed to be done to get to the end of this, no matter the cost.

There are probably a thousand Zavs in Toronto. I can't drag them all with me.

The best thing he could do was make sure there was a good team. It was like sabotaging that kid—no, it was even more practical, like having water on tap versus buying by the liter. In the long run, it was better to make one sacrifice at the beginning than die by a thousand little cuts. If he let Zav win now, tried to push back his video game death, he could die in the battle to come. It'd be much more permanent. Maybe Loop did have a point: Wyatt wanted to spare deaths wherever he could. If that meant being ruthless now, shouldn't he?

People were so small, and fragile, and complicated. He needed to put that aside and think logically.

Wyatt watched the dots in his map getting closer and closer. They were converging on the baseball diamond. He tore up the stairs into the gazebo with only twenty seconds to spare. He was still damp from the fountain, invigorated as his lungs tightened and heaved. There was a large metal box on the floor of the gazebo, right in the middle. He dropped to open it, hoping it would give him more time before this "bonus level" paradise ended and threw him into the next terrible trial.

Special Item unlocked!

Friendly Fire

You are now able to eliminate ONE competitor of your choosing, without invoking a half-score penalty.

The blaster hanging from Wyatt's chest glowed. When he looked down, the colors had been inverted—the usual gold-orange body had changed to blue, and the wave patterns to flames.

One shot. One competitor thrown from the game. It felt like a reward. As if Davids had noticed the hard calls he'd been making, somehow heard the decisions he'd been cooking up, and understood. Someone was hearing him, after so long screaming.

Wyatt, his mouth a straight line and his breath coming slow and even, looked to the baseball diamond, and to the figure on home plate. Zav craned his neck up to the shimmering blue sky, then to the green, green grass with awe. Instead of the usual fatigues, he was wearing something navy blue. Was it a Power-Up? Better body armor? Camouflage? That would explain why a rookie had lasted so long.

There were no Power-Ups in the real world. They needed to be serious.

Loop and B came thundering up the gazebo steps behind him. Wyatt leapt into the grass and sprinted for Zav, the Friendly Fire blaster heavy in his hands. His boots kicked up clots of red baseball dust. Wyatt wouldn't be swayed from answering the call to arms. That moment in the truck had made him sure: it was humanity or Bluddites, and he wasn't going to let everything and everyone he knew and loved be taken away. Maybe that meant letting Zav go now, to save him. He'd turn off his emotions and bring them back when this was all over. Because it *would* end, regardless of what Loop or Ava thought.

And then, Zav turned to see Wyatt running for him. He smiled under his Goggle-visor—relieved, exhausted, excited, all things Wyatt knew in a faraway way. Did Wyatt still care to save him? To help him?

Zav ran through the shimmering dust to meet Wyatt, who noticed two things:

First, Zav didn't have new clothes. What Wyatt had mistaken for blue armor was actually one big blue stain. As Zav ran closer, the sweet smell of the park and grass and dirt was replaced by the metallic reek of Bluddite blood. Zav was covered in it, head to toe, even his face below his visor. His big eyes peered out, alert like an animal caught in a snare. He seemed terrified, and yet ready to keep fighting, probably ready *because* he was terrified. Wyatt realized he felt the same way, deep down.

Second, Wyatt noticed someone else was sprinting toward them from Commissioner Street. Ava, as he suspected, and she was running *fast*. She was holding her blaster to her chest.

No, Wyatt realized, just as Zav reached him on the pitcher's mound, his timer dwindling down (5 . . .), the heavy footfalls of B and Loop racing over the packed red dirt. Ava wasn't holding a regular blaster.

It was blue, with orange flames: a Friendly Fire Power-Up.

There were five players left, and it was up to them to pick who'd join forces for the last leg, who'd raise their scores together until the heroic end. They would be brothers-in-arms, not a big, happy soldier family but one ready for war. They had to put aside emotions, and *Zip-Monsters* memories, and pick who they trusted to kill every last Bluddite. To make a difference.

Wyatt held the Friendly Fire blaster tight and rounded on Zav Silva.

LEVEL 28

THE MUZZLE OF THE Friendly Fire blaster turned on Zav. In those microseconds, Wyatt saw his only friend's smile fall, eyes fade. Would it burn, a shot of blaster laser? Or would it be quicker than Bluddite teeth? Zav's mouth started to wrinkle, not with sadness, but anger. It speared into Wyatt, enough to hurt him through the staticky noise. He figured it was wrong to be sympathetic, it was selfish, and so what if he cared about Zav? So *what* if he wanted to be friends again? What place did *feelings* have in a *war*?

Zav's lips wrinkled nearly to a snarl, looking angry like he had last night when Wyatt had shown up out of nowhere asking for help. Zav had helped him for no good reason, or maybe for the most obvious reason: because it was the right thing to do even if there was no logical sense behind it. Because the world was so bleak.

Compassion burned up through Wyatt. He despised it, sure this was opposite to how a good soldier was supposed to feel. But he wasn't going to be cold like Ava, and yet swore he wasn't soft like Loop. He didn't know what the hell he was when he collided with Zav, grabbing his shoulder and turning them both to run for the dugout together. Would this save the world? Was it selfish, or heroic?

Did any of that even matter? Did it have to matter? What if nothing did?

"Dude," Zav said.

"Run," Wyatt snapped, shoving him backward. But it was still too late.

The countdown in Wyatt's map hit zero. The bonus level was over.

Wyatt thought the nice park would fade slowly, or there would be a big wipe that would go all the way around them and dissolve everything to gross old ruin. But it was like when he woke up in that room.

One moment he was turning toward the dugout, to get cover so they could open fire on whoever he decided needed firing on, and the next there was no dugout at all. He hadn't even blinked. There just *was* a baseball diamond and nice grass and birdsong and the distant sound of that fountain, and then there wasn't. Even the lingering water disappeared from Wyatt, along with the clean smell, and he was back to bloody and reeking. They were standing in the dry field, circled distantly by stomped-in tents, overflowing garbage cans, and all the things that made a good park look like a bad one (or so Wyatt had always heard people say). That might have been fine, more terrain to hide in, except Loop was right about one thing:

The park had been a trap. Where the edges of the diamond

had been, there were now dozens of pacing Bluddites, even more than in the garage, corralling the five of them in. None of them charged. They seemed to just stare, waiting, but it meant they'd all lost their chance to leave.

Now, with the timer at zero, there were no exits from the final showdown. Past the skeletons of dying trees, the air was green black with pollution, and the buildings in the far distance had begun to crumble. This wasn't just their world now, but a promise as well.

They either fought for paradise, or lost to this hellscape.

B and Loop ran to join Wyatt and Zav. They didn't even slow their sprint—they hadn't noticed the Friendly Fire blaster yet. But Ava kept her distance, holding back as far as the silent, pacing Bluddites would let her. Wyatt wondered if there was a time limit, if they had to sort this before those things would leap and kill them all for hesitating, just like with the brood mother. They were being trained to act quickly—don't think, just move.

Ava's blaster came up at the same time as Wyatt's. They both aimed for each other's heads with no hesitation. Wyatt stepped ahead of Zav. Ava eased closer to them, trying to step for Loop.

"No," Wyatt said, calm. The park was silent: the click of his safety button turning off was as loud as a snapping bone. She stopped moving, clicked hers too. Wyatt had to go about this carefully. "You left, Ava, so you don't get to cover him."

She sucked her teeth. All around them, the Bluddites clicked, made curious "*Kehh?*" sounds. There was no way out. If B and Loop and Zav were confused before, Wyatt was sure they'd just clued in. Neither Wyatt nor Ava was going to give up their spot on the team. Now it was just a matter of figuring out who they'd take with them: Ava's friend, or Wyatt's?

B was no one's favorite—he took one look at the two guns, then backed away from Loop, maybe thinking to run. But it was suicide to try, for Wyatt too. But wasn't it suicide to stay? Wouldn't Ava just take Wyatt out, then wait for the Bluddites to catch up with Zav? But in the edge of Wyatt's vision, he saw Zav covered in the blood of his own kills, with his blaster aimed for Loop as he tried to ease into Ava, as if Zav might really shoot Loop out and tank his own score. Maybe he wasn't deadweight after all? Was Wyatt the deadweight with his 46? It was a good score, but he couldn't see anyone else's.

"Let's just keep'r easy," Loop said. His voice was low, so quiet his volume sensor probably didn't go above yellow. "Obviously we're not all getting out of this, so let's just pick three. B, what's everyone's scores?"

B stared at them all from behind his yellow visor: he must have been able to see their stats, including their scores. This seemed like a fair way to judge who should win a video game competition, but it didn't take anything else into account. Like who actually knew what this competition was about. Maybe Zav and B were the odd ones out. Or it was B and Wyatt, because they were the spoiled kids? It could be Loop and Ava, because Davids had said they needed new tricks.

"I've got a fifty-one," B said.

"He could be lying," Zav added. Wyatt swallowed slowly. There was a reason Zav was still in the game. He had a good brain for strategy, asking the right questions and moving carefully. "We can't tell if that's the truth."

"You'll just have to take my word for it, *twenty-five*," B said.

"I've got a forty!" Zav snapped, voice shrill like claws on glass. "I cleared this whole park before you guys showed up." A 40 wasn't bad at all, but it only mattered what everyone else had in comparison.

"DoctorDoctor has a forty-six," B said. That was true. "So does Loop."

Wyatt moved his lips against his braces. His teeth grated against each other, so tight his muscles wanted to cramp and send tremors through his aim. He knew the second his sights were off Ava she'd shoot him down, so he fought to keep his cool. He could do this.

"And Ava?" Wyatt asked, in his slow, low voice. *Keep it together, Doc. Keep it locked down, soldier.* "What does she have?"

There was a pause.

"N-nothing," B said.

That couldn't be right. Ava's expression stayed the same, that usual flat line. Her clothes were rumpled and damp, her boots caked not with dirt or grass or gravel, but mud. She'd clearly been doing *something*; Wyatt had seen her dot sprinting around the map. And yet there was no Bluddite blood on her, just one strike up her visor. It was red. Human. Probably her own, but where was the injury?

"It's a trick," Zav said. Ava's lip twitched. If they shot her out now, and she had some ridiculously high score, could Wyatt and Zav even get that many before their own runs ended? "She must have gotten a Power-Up, some sort of cloaking—"

"We all know she has the best high score," Loop was saying.

"I thought you wanted everyone's *current* scores," Wyatt said, almost sweetly. "Are you going back on that now that she's losing?"

"So we go off our old Leaderboard high scores," B said. That would mean him, and Wyatt, and Ava. No Loop, no Zav, just the three with the top scores they had all worked so hard to get. Didn't that just make sense? Reward for months of work? Wyatt could just give the prizes to Zav.

The silence held. It was agonizing. Wyatt resisted the urge to shake his hands out, and yet in the quiet, every worry became louder. He couldn't stand doing nothing, knowing that every second he spent hesitating was another second they were losing water.

B took a few steps closer to Ava—her eyes darted to him for half a second to mark his position before they were back on Wyatt. "She's not tricking us," B said, a bit louder. Wyatt's sensor spiked to orange. One of the pacing Bluddites gave a warning click that rippled through their ranks. But B didn't shut up. Maybe he hated the stillness too. "She really does have a zero."

"Easy," Loop said.

Ava said nothing.

"She's not even arguing!" B said, gaining resolve. His blaster was still hanging heavy off its sling. Zav shifted his aim to B. Maybe this was a trick, just a distraction. "She's probably been hiding this whole time. Why's it so hard to believe?"

Because Wyatt had seen Ava moving all over the map, like she was flying over the buildings. But her boots were too muddy for the rooftops, and there was grime streaked on her shoulders and knees too.

Wyatt's breath caught. She hadn't been on top of the buildings, no way.

Wyatt was sure that Ava "Alpha_Test" Maraj had been in the sewers, where the highest Bluddite population was. Her score could be well into the hundreds, not that she'd let them know. That matched the intense, driven, perhaps unnervingly ruthless person Wyatt knew. Zav started to speak, but Wyatt kicked his shin to get him to stop. Ava kept darting her eyes to B. The distant Bluddites grew restless, chittering and clicking. There came a rumble from the distance, as if a building had caved in.

"*Wyattttt*," a distant Bluddite muttered. "*Xavierrrrr . . .*"

"Wyatt," Zav whispered.

"*Stop*," he said, because Zav was hanging on to the thinnest thread of Wyatt's compassion, fraying the longer they stood motionless. Loop's coward talk kept cycling through his head. Would killing Bluddites actually make the sky bluer? It would leave more water for Hydrexo consumers, but it wouldn't *create* more water, or filter the pollution, or stop the climate from dive-bombing into chaos. So what then? Who had to die to fix that too? And how could Wyatt, in this moment right here, ensure they did?

"Did you get scared?" B was still saying. His voice was getting higher, sort of squealy. A Bluddite gave a warning shriek. Loop was telling him to calm down again, but B wasn't listening. "Crying in the corner waiting for Loop to come save you, huh? Do you even *play*? Or did you get him to do it for you and that's why his Leaderboard score's crap, 'cause he's been carrying you? Maybe he's Alpha_Test and you're Loop_D. Just playing to impress him, huh?"

Ava's eyes lit up so bright behind her visor that Wyatt swore she'd combust. Her blaster barrel started to shake. Wyatt kept his mouth in a flat line, but he wanted to grin. She was going to lose her cool before he did. He was going to win this thing. He just had to focus.

"*Zav! XAVIER! WYATT!*" The Bluddites shouted louder, voices garbled like radio static. The circle was tightening. Wyatt's bone marrow shivered under the case of cold focus.

"Why the hell would a girl want to play anyway?" B nearly shouted. Ava's mouth curled for one single millisecond. She looked like a fourteen-year-old kid, not like the blank, intense person Wyatt had known. But then it was gone. "Why do you even care about *Fathom Fall*?"

Wyatt knew. It wasn't about a bright future, or even helping people like Loop said.

It was about vengeance. Every. Last. One.

"Ava," Loop started to say, a careful warning.

There was so much to prove, so much control to regain after waiting so long for any sense of hope. Wyatt understood.

Ava rounded on B and pulled the trigger. The wide spray of buckshot-like laser blasted forward across B's chest and head. It burned and scraped, tearing his skin up to battered pink and red singeing across white teeth. Zav gasped. Loop looked empty. Wyatt just stared as B "died." His digital corpse fell backward and was gone before it even hit the ground. Onstage, B was probably removing his Goggles while the stadium roared in applause or hissed and jeered.

But here, where it mattered, Ava's face hadn't changed at all, still the flat mouth and distant eyes, like a robot who got the emotion programmed out of it.

Wyatt recognized himself. It scared him, and the fear fought with the nothingness, and he felt like he might go insane.

Ava's blaster flashed back to the usual blue on orange. Now it was only Wyatt left with a Friendly Fire gun. And while she had been shooting B, he had swung his aim to Loop.

"Drop yours, Ava," he snapped. "Or I shoot Loop."

"Come on," Loop was trying to say.

But a strange thing happened then. Ava Maraj *did* drop her blaster. She let it hang from the front of her chest, and held up her hands. Wyatt hadn't expected her to give in so easily—should he aim at her now? What was she planning?

"All right," she said, feet braced apart, torso exposed. Wyatt paused. "What now, Water Baby? You're in charge." Her eyes seemed strange, frightened and jittery for a moment. She was going to lose. *Wyatt* would win, finally. But he knew she couldn't let that stand.

Ava's mouth turned into a smile, for the first time ever. She knew something. She said he was in charge, but he wasn't.

"What?" Wyatt asked. She didn't move. A small flare of panic tried to make itself heard. *Shut up!* "What?!"

Her smile warped to a terrifying grin. Was she bluffing? "Shoot him, you and your friend win, but they'll never tell you what I know," she said. He started to think that wasn't her own blood on her cheek, but he couldn't understand why. "They haven't even told Loop."

The Bluddites were still shouting. "*WYATT!*" His name was almost impossible to hear, hidden under all the impatient screeching and chittering and *bugga-bugga*, *wuh-oh* cartoony sounds. "*ZAV!*"

Loop's eyebrows had drawn in tight, more confused than frightened. "Ava, what—"

"You don't wanna know, Loop. You won't like it," she said. Wyatt thought he caught another twitch of her face, something kind, but she locked it away. "Win or lose, I know everything. Why do you think they keep an eye on me? They're scared I'll tell. But I don't need to—I don't *care*."

Loop looked up above him, as if some military chopper would gun her down for talking about the mission on national television. His hands were shaking. Screw it: Wyatt swung his aim to her.

"What the hell, Ava?" Loop said. Even he sounded scared. The Bluddites slowly tightened the circle. "Nize it with the creepy shit. Can we just team up and get out of this?"

"There needs to be winners," Zav said, hard.

"Winners," Ava scoffed. "So they can tell you what to do? I'm tired of it. Let me be real with you, 'cause you can bet *Davids* won't be: they put the Goggles on 'cause they know you can't handle what it *really* takes to win. When those come off, you'll run home screaming."

Wyatt's Goggles were locked in; he didn't want them off. The Goggles were protecting him. The Goggles *were* him. In here he could hurt, but not die. In here he was powerful.

"I can win," Wyatt said, meaning so many things. "I can *help*."

Ava still smiled. "You still think this is about helping people," she said. She sniffed, as if she might cry, but there were no tears. "I'm here to get even, no matter what Davids thinks I can or can't handle." Her eyes were still jittery and panicked, but her smile was set. Her hand twitched. Wyatt's fingers readied at the trigger. "And if you think you're tough enough to know the truth, then how 'bout you prove it?"

There was so much to prove.

"I am," Wyatt said, and swung his aim to Loop.

As he did, Ava reached for something. Her blaster would have taken too long to pull, but her knife came out in a flash of light. Her empty eyes fixed behind Wyatt. Her smile disappeared. She was cold again before he could get the Friendly Fire gun to Loop and pull the trigger.

"Wait—" Zav was shouting, just as Wyatt heard a Bluddite screech, like a human scream, getting closer.

Ava threw the knife—not at a monster, but at a kid just like her—to prove she was tougher than Wyatt ever could be.

LEVEL 29

IN THE SECOND WHERE Ava's knife whistled past Wyatt's eyes and blocked out Loop's head, he saw how sharp it was, down to the teeniest, tiniest pixels. The graphics were scary accurate.

There was a squishy *thunk* as the knife struck Zav. *Damn.* All right, screw it, maybe it *was* better to have Loop on his team than Ava, someone a bit less serious but not totally off the rails. If Ava's score *was* more than zero, then this was the perfect time to get her out. He turned his aim on her, waiting for her to flash red to announce the penalty.

But she wasn't glowing, or anything. She just stood there in the dry grass, still as a frozen glitch, blank-faced while all the Bluddites paced a dozen steps behind her.

Her eyes shone, like lightning in black skies. No answers, no saviors, no heroes, no monsters, no rhyme or reason to the suffering. Just this moment here.

Finally, Wyatt turned his head.

In the seemingly slow-motion arc, as his eyes swept across their little circle, from Ava toward Zav, the Bluddites began blipping away behind them, one by one, like the game was powering down. The buildings in the distance blurred, fading back to how they looked in real life without any collapse damage. Loop tried to pull his med pack from his belt; it disappeared from his hands in a spattering of pixels. His jacket faded, his boots, his fatigues, his blaster, the gauze on his arm, and the blood there too. He was left wearing only the motion-capture suit and Hydrexo clothes, the helmet and his Goggles, holding nothing. Wyatt's own digital clothes unloaded, the weight stripping away layer by layer. He expected the ground to dissolve any second, or for his vision to snap to black, but it didn't. The utilities all stayed, like the Standby Mode screen, with red words blinking across the bottom:

Emergency Error: CONNECTION PAUSED. Standby . . .

They were no longer transmitting to the stage screens. Why? Was the game over? Didn't they all have to die to set their scores?

Loop looked at Wyatt through his Zip-Go Gaming Goggles. His lips were fading to terrified gray, his jaw beginning to shake. Wyatt waited for Loop to blip away too into calm nothingness, to give Wyatt a moment to breathe before he pulled the Goggles off and found out if he'd won, if Zav had too. But he didn't.

A faint breeze drifted through the fabric of Wyatt's motion-capture suit. The loose threads on Loop's bracelet twisted in the wind. The ground still pulsed beneath Wyatt's feet, a sluggish heartbeat. Loop locked eyes with Wyatt, looking just as shocked.

Loop was supposed to be one of Davids's testers, but even he hadn't been given the whole truth.

"What the hell . . . ?" Loop breathed. His eyes turned behind Wyatt, to Zav, and widened. Wyatt knew he needed to turn around, but he couldn't look away from the dry tree branches, the dust in the air, the faint movement in the clouds as the Bluddites all disappeared. He was looking for some sort of digital shimmer, something to say it wasn't real. But it was.

They were in the park. *Actually* in the park. The air smelled smoky, and the wind creaked through tree branches, and the ground chug-chug-chugged as the augmented reality powered down to strip away all the digital tricks. Sometime between turning the system on in the glass cubes and waking up in the apartment building rooms where he'd started playing, they'd all been transported. It was just an illusion, visual tricks and simulations of pain and movement through the strange tech of their suits, using fake weapons on fake monsters. A game, sure, but not all of it. Not all of it *at all*.

Wyatt felt his knife sitting reverse against his hip, hidden under his shirt and still-damp shorts. He'd brought it just to be sure, to be safe, and he and Ava were so much alike. And yet she did know something he didn't.

"Stay exactly where you are," a voice said from inside Wyatt's Goggles. It was the woman's voice. She was speaking much faster than usual, more urgent than the steady instructions. "Emergency evacuation teams are on the w—" Her voice fizzled, like a bad connection. "Stay wh—"

B appeared near the end of the field, trudging up to the road, probably toward some meeting spot he'd been signaled to. He didn't turn around to see them, didn't even know the game had ended. Had that little kid stood in the dusty alley, watching Wyatt watch his corpse? Had the kid in the cement silo actually gotten all the way up there?

The ground pulsed. The Bluddites were still disappearing one by one, leaving only the dry grass under the too-hot breeze, in the park cleared of all people with only the distant shapes of kicked-in tents. This was supposed to be a cool surprise, one that would make them all laugh and cheer about how *cool* AR was. Or, at least the people in on it, at the Hydrexo Centre, they were cheering. Down in the heart of it, Wyatt couldn't make a sound. Was this to make them better soldiers?

Or were they trying to see how far you could trick someone, how much you could make someone believe?

When Wyatt turned, he saw two things that took all the air out of his body. Two things that cracked through the cold shell of the game and tore into the fleshy stuff inside him, ripping it up like shrapnel. Zav was still there, standing in the dry, empty field and holding his Goggles. That must have been the first thing he tried to do—take off his Goggles, end the game, accept his defeat, grab his merch, and move on until he couldn't remember what a knife blade felt like. But as he squinted up at the dark sky above them like he didn't understand it, the knife handle wobbled from his stomach, bobbing as he breathed. Slick maroon crept over his bright-blue shirt; the smell of blood hung thick and metallic. A dark red drop crawled down the side of his mouth. He wiped it away with the back of his hand.

The park was real. Zav was real. And that meant the knife in his stomach was real too.

And yet, Wyatt knew people survived gut wounds. Surely Davids had shut the game down to send paramedics right away. It was just an accident, the kind of thing you didn't plan for but knew *could* happen. The kind of thing they had signed a waiver for in the first place. They hadn't checked the players for real weapons because, what? Davids wanted to show how much he trusted them? How grown up they were?

Grown up enough to be moved without their knowledge? To think his leg would break, to be so scared something in him shattered? All to make them believe that enough blood would stop that pain forever? Ava knew everything, and was no better for it. For a brief moment, Wyatt understood why his mom thought he shouldn't play these kinds of games, because maybe it was sick to be so used to blood and death that it didn't feel that gross anymore. For the *plink!* to be its own addicting reward, to feel nothing when the player counter went down, to think any of this was good.

"Teams on—don't move—" the woman's voice struggled to say. It came back quieter, as if she was speaking to someone on her end. "I don't know—interference—radio scrambler. I thought they cleared the area—"

“Get them out of there now!” a voice screamed. Davids.

“It felt pretty real. It doesn’t hurt now,” Zav said distantly, looking at the blood on his hands. His skin was fading to gray now too. Shock, Wyatt realized. “I . . . I don’t know why the blood’s still here.”

Wyatt tried to get words out of his mouth. They’d signed waivers for accidents, but not for being a few kids alone in the industrial zone, with one smelling like blood, and open sewers all around them.

The digital Bluddites were all blipping away, their details fading until they disappeared entirely from the real world in front of Wyatt. But not all of them. Even when the second-last Bluddite flickered away in a shattering of pixels and glitchy lines, there was still one left. And it was running right for them, from the open grate on the road. Wyatt waited for it to disappear too.

It didn’t. It just kept coming, scaly arms pumping, clawed feet slamming into the grass as it ran closer and closer, zeroed in on Zav.

Shooting fake, digital Bluddites? That’d been scary, but maybe fun.

Wyatt wasn’t having any fun now. All the fake monsters had disappeared. But he knew this one running for them had somehow slipped past whatever “clearing” Hydrexo had sent.

This part was real, or at least Wyatt believed it was. It was impossible to be sure of anything now, besides gut-wrenching fear, and the knowledge that he’d never had a real blaster to protect himself with. He kept waiting for Davids's voice, but there was only digital static. He'd heard something about radio scramblers. Why would water monsters have radio scramblers?

Zav quirked up the corner of his mouth, like the situation was sort of funny. He was starting to sway again. "Y-you can take the Goggles off now," Zav said, but it wasn't true. The Bluddite was barely a meter from them now, close enough for its huge shadow to cut over Zav.

Wyatt tried to rush into attack mode again, but he felt exhausted, betrayed, hopeless. He thought to raise his blaster, realized he didn't have one anymore, and reached for his hidden knife. He was moving in slow motion—the real-life Bluddite's scaly arms swept in on either side of Zav. In its great, bulbous eyes, Wyatt's reflection stared back with a flat expression. Over his shoulder, he expected Ava and Loop to be leaping into action to defend him.

They were supposed to be a brotherhood. To kill these things. And save everyone.

Instead, Wyatt saw that Loop had thrown his Goggles off and locked his arms around Ava's middle, trying to drag her toward the safety of the trees. She was looking past him, her hands balling up the back of his shirt, eyes staring Wyatt down. Her mouth was hidden behind Loop, but he thought she might have been grinning at him still, that smile that knew something. The blood swished up her cheek seemed startlingly scarlet, now that her Goggles and helmet were gone.

When those come off, you'll run home screaming. Ava Maraj

knew something Loop and Wyatt hadn't, and it had shattered her.

And yet, all of this became background noise in the shadow of something worse.

The Bluddite ripped Zav off the ground, turning him away from Wyatt so fast that the knife flew from Zav's stomach and went thudding into the grass. In the split second before he was torn away, Wyatt could have sworn Zav was smiling. The Bluddite's gills splayed out; blue spit sprayed from its mouth.

"*WYATT!*" it screeched. How did it know his name, if it wasn't coded to know? If it was *real* and not pixels like the others? How did the one in the bathroom know too? Zav's sweat-slick hair fell away from his forehead, revealing that strange bruise. If they'd played together, that first day, then Zav would have known Wyatt was occupied with his game. And hadn't Zav spent so many days on that fire escape? "*WYYYYYAAAAAATT!*"

Wyatt didn't have time, only panic. He pulled his knife and slashed. The blade swiped uselessly along the Bluddite's tough side. Wyatt screamed and stepped after it, watching Zav dangle from its arms, unconscious now. Wyatt was suddenly crying, tears pouring down his cheeks all at once. He kept trying to stab, but every strike hit the Bluddite's shell and didn't pierce. It kept saying his name ("*Wyatt—Wyaaatt—st-t-op-RAHHH—*"), stepping away from him with Zav hanging like a rag doll. He tried to reach the thing's gills, but he was too short. That filled him up with a surge of emotion, a feeling of deep *uselessness* like he'd always felt seeing Zav or the Outpost prices. *This was supposed to fix everything!* He grabbed a handful of the Bluddite's kelpy fins and pulled, but even when they came off in his hand, the Bluddite did nothing but hold Zav and step away, screeching back at him.

"*Wyatt!*" it screeched, so clear. "*Raah-Goggl—RAHH!*"

A heavy *whomp-whomp-whomp* sound joined the chugging heartbeat. The dry grass and dusty dirt began to spiral up around them. A beam of helicopter searchlight burned down upon them all—the Bluddite looked strange, scales still dim for just a moment before they lit up too. It spit out some word, like how a human spits out a curse, then lifted its foot. It slammed hard into the center of Wyatt's chest, knocking all the air out. He didn't feel the impact of the claws, but something wide and hard. Like a boot.

Wyatt tipped backward, hit the spiky-grassed ground, and couldn't move anymore. His vision jarred once, then pixelated, turning the Bluddite to a pink-and-green blur before it was again a scaly monster holding his nearly dead friend. Through a spattering of concussion-induced splotches of light, Wyatt watched the two of them run off to disappear down the grate.

Why would a Bluddite retreat with Zav? Why not eat him right there, like the simulation had shown him?

Every bit of exhaustion had finally caught up with Wyatt; all he could do was roll onto his back and look up at the dust and grass whirling below the hovering chopper high above. The clank of the sewer grate falling back into place echoed out through the very real industrial zone. Zav was going to die.

A Bluddite had just killed his only friend. Even if Wyatt was a hero after this, what did that matter now? If he had a blaster, he would have shot it. That was supposed to be a good thing, a proud thing, but he was just tired.

There were ambulance sirens out there, in the distance. Wyatt lay alone, breathing in and out, in and out, slowly in through his nose and out through his mouth. He reached up to pry his Goggles from the helmet, which took some effort; only once he'd tossed them into the grass with Loop's did he realize he was still holding a fistful of Bluddite fins. That wouldn't be good, he thought. They had to keep people from knowing this was real. Only the trusted three could know.

Trusted? Or tricked.

Wyatt opened his hand in front of his face to inspect the fins. Except they weren't fins. There was nothing lifelike about the thing in his hand. Through the shock, his throat tightened with overwhelmed tears. He wanted this to pixel away too, for that Bluddite to be as fake as all the others he'd killed, but his Goggles were off.

This was real.

Wyatt was holding a faded scrap of fabric. A patch, to be exact. There was mud in the loose threads, a splatter of blood across it, but it was still clear: a black cat, with one word beneath it.

"*Solidarity*," Wyatt read. He stared at the screeching cat face. It looked so much like a Bluddite.

The black dreamscape closed over him anyway, shutting him into the sick panic in his stomach, and the knowledge that no one would believe him when he told the horrible truth.

The world would want an easy answer, someone to kill, but it was all so much more complicated than heroes and monsters. Ava Maraj had been ruined by that truth.

Maybe Wyatt would be too.

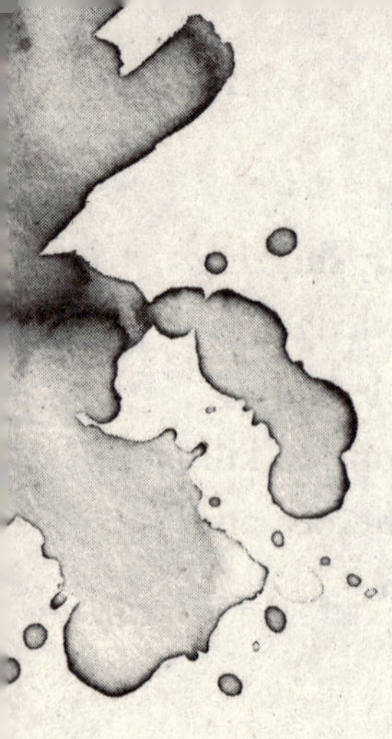

CREDITS

WYATT WON, AND IT had been a hell of a victory too, at least the parts they'd bothered to air. When Ava crashed the game into emergency mode, the feeds had all cut out, replaced by dramatic music and a national TV message to "TUNE IN TOMORROW TO SEE THE END BEFORE OUR AWARD CEREMONY!" The audience just thought it was a cheap ploy to get more views, but Wyatt knew: they were trying to buy time, to decide what to do about Zav. But Zav didn't have parents to ask where he was, didn't even have a big sister. If he just fell off the face of the planet, who would know?

Hydrexo only had to find a way to smooth it over into the answers people wanted to see. Wyatt understood that even when he alone was picked up by the chopper, flown back to the stadium in what should have been the coolest journey of his lifetime, and put back in some dressing room. He kept watching the door, thinking Davids might walk in to explain what they were going to do next, or even where Loop and Ava were. Had they been flown back too?

But he didn't. Instead, Wyatt's parents had been given the day off to come pick him up. Wyatt didn't even know what to say to them. He was uncertain whether his voice even worked anymore, if it made any difference.

They drove him home and tried to have the "we're upset that you disobeyed us, but we're also proud of you for winning at something you like" talk, which was as bumpy and confusing as Wyatt expected it to be, especially because they didn't know the half of anything, including what happened to Zav. Wyatt's dad kept asking if he actually won after the feed cut out, promising that they'd take him to get professional photos with the trophy. His mom was mostly silent, nodding and *hmm*-ing.

The only time she said anything was when she looked at him in the rearview mirror. "So are you and Zav going to hang out more? We can invite him over for dinner, and Leo. Do a little party?"

Wyatt had smiled then, easily. "Oh, maybe," he said. And then they'd taken him for lunch, offered to take him go-karting to celebrate, but Wyatt just wanted answers. He'd said he was tired from all that running and jumping, so he went home, curled up in bed, and found the playbacks on his phone. He'd hoped for some answers. What he learned was this:

The audience knew this was AR. Davids told them right away. "Our heroes are test running a state-of-the-art battle simulator," he said at the podium, eyes all shining under his glasses, in his cool-casual T-shirt. "But what they don't know is that this isn't virtual reality, but *augmented* reality. That's right—we're bringing them *live* to the Hydrexo property, to run, and climb, and shoot. They'll also be able to feel the Bluddites, but don't worry . . ."

The audience was trusted with some of the truth, but not all of it.

"The pain simulation is no more than some rumbles," Davids lied. "And for parents watching at home, please be assured that we have personnel standing by to steer them out of any sticky situations. Their safety is our number one priority."

He'd wondered how they were going to handle Ava going into the sewers. Surely that would prove that they weren't exactly being safe with the competitors, even if he felt certain that Ava wasn't supposed to be down there at all. She'd gone rogue, to find *real* Bluddites, but that couldn't be aired. And so that was the first time Wyatt saw how the feed was changed: Ava arrived in the game, sat herself down in the corner of a restaurant, and stayed put. No hunting, no shooting, just a big fat score of 0. Wyatt knew she'd been on the move, and yet the feed showed something different, so why question?

Of course, the online forums were full of people saying dumb shit about Ava being a coward, a silly, cowardly little girl. They were all the same people saying how *cool* the AR thing was, how they wished they could play it too, that the competitors were *so lucky* to test run it. Wyatt watched his feed, every heroic moment split between his game feed POV, and some sort of game camera that caught other dramatic angles: sidelong when the Bluddite was stomping him, overhead as the

Panda Parade kid died, a dramatic upshot of him on the truck bed. The footage seemed slightly strange, slimier than reality. *AI smoothing*, some online nerd said. *Cool*, Wyatt might have thought before. But watching yourself get thrown around a truck cab, screaming and flailing? It was hard to enjoy that. Or the clipped-up conversation with Loop—in the playback, he noticed how exhausted Loop seemed despite his smile.

Loop had clearly known something was wrong. Maybe not the whole truth, not like Ava, but he was catching on to them all being pawns in a game bigger than they'd been told. Wyatt *had* hurt himself for this, thinking it would fix everything. It wouldn't.

And then he watched himself run through the park with Loop and B, make his way to Zav, confront Loop and B and Ava (who finally got up just in time for the showdown), until the feed cut out dramatically.

No answers.

He'd slept the rest of the day, eaten dinner, and then the next day, he rode with his parents to Hydrexo, to their auditorium where the award ceremony was being held. He saw all the competitors, without Zav (of course), but strangely, without Ava or Loop either. His stomach churned, but he didn't know what to say.

In the audience, he watched Hydrexo's truth.

B was shot by Ava, Zav was eliminated by Ava's knife, Wyatt shot Ava out (as he'd planned), then the Bluddites closed in on him and Loop. The graphics were slimy smooth. A Bluddite tackled Loop to the ground, but rather than even *try* to shoot it, he ripped his Goggles off. His score tanked to 0. Disqualified. Almost immediately, the sidebar chat lit up with accusations of Loop rage quitting, and how every random anonymous player wouldn't have been so scared. Wyatt wondered if he should get out his phone and type something, say, "I'm Wyatt Docherty, and this is NOT what happened! We really could feel it!"

He knew no one would believe him. Wyatt just watched the screen, where his own footage showed Bluddites ripping him to pieces too. But still, as he died, his score glowed bright.

In front of quite a few camera crews, B took third (he'd lied about his score at the baseball diamond, obviously), flashing peace signs and smiles to the audience of mostly Hydrexo Cares employees and sponsored fans. Loop would have taken second if he wasn't "disqualified," which made Wyatt feel a bit sick. Where was he now? Or Ava? Was there any sort of justice for her killing Zav?

How could you punish or control someone like Ava Maraj, who had been pushed so far that rules didn't mean anything anymore?

None of it made sense, which was even worse than a bad answer. Wyatt didn't know where Ava and Loop were, and knew no one would ask beyond saying shitty things in the forums, which made him nervous.

Instead, the *Panda Parade* kid took second, which might have been a win for the little guy if he stopped crying on the podium. Wyatt took first, grim up there while he received his trophy and a package labelled "TOP SECRET" from some generic Hydrexo employee. Davids hadn't appeared, surely because he knew Wyatt would demand answers.

Wyatt had gone home and opened his package to find a check (right into the bank to earn interest, to sit uselessly), a Hydrexo Outpost card with a monthly balance, and nothing else. Not yet. And then, the world turned ever onward. Ava and Loop and Zav would fade out. No one was looking for them.

As for Wyatt, he was still in on this, even if he wasn't sure what he'd do once Davids finally reached out for the next phase. *Was* there a next phase, or was that a lie too? What if that was it, just some trickery out there in the industrial zone, some lies about Wyatt being a hero, and then nothing more?

This was so much bigger, but who would believe him?

■ ■ ■

It had been two days since the awards ceremony, and Wyatt was in his room, curled on his side in bed. His *Fathom Fall* trophy stood aqua blue and gold orange next to his TV, with a first-place medal hanging off its laurel-shaped arm, but Wyatt didn't want to look at it. He just lay in the dim room, staring at the full water bottle on his nightstand. His brain pounded deep in his skull. He felt exhausted, with the tiniest shiver of defeat trying to ripple out through his cold skin.

No. It wasn't over. It couldn't be.

Wyatt dragged his legs over the side of the bed, sat up in a soupy rush that made the room swirl ahead, then reached a stiff hand into the pocket of his pajama pants.

Since he found it in his fist, the patch hadn't left Wyatt's pockets. Even now, he cradled it between his fingers, like it might be seen through the windows. The stitches bumped under his fingernail; there was a brown-red stain on one edge that was maybe mud, or maybe blood, but was certainly real. He'd pulled it himself from a Bluddite, one who wasn't wearing any patches. But, as Ava had said, the Goggles had come off. Wyatt had tried looking at the patch through the Goggles in Standby Mode, but it was still just a patch. He had a horrible suspicion.

Wyatt swallowed stiffly and closed his eyes to breathe back a wave of nausea. He wanted to be wrong, but he knew this was deeper. Even if no one would believe him, and even if he was certain he couldn't solve this problem so easily, admitting the lie would be the first step in fixing something. Not everything, but he could start.

Wyatt opened his eyes, put the patch back in his pocket, and forced himself to his feet. His movements were sluggish and prickly. He'd been faking sick to his parents for the last two days, but really had started to feel ill now. He looked out his window and caught sight of the dying plant on the fire escape. The poor thing was looking swampy.

Not underwatered, but overwatered.

Wyatt stepped up to his mirror. By the light of the desk lamp bright enough to make him wince, he inspected the thick bruises under both eyes, how the whites were turning red. He looked like hell warmed over, as his dad always said. When his reflection loomed so close that his breath bounced off the glass, he could smell the sourness. *Two days*, he thought, wincing when his head panged angrily. Two days for this Water Baby to eat nothing but saltines and dry bread, to dump his water out the window until he was dehydrated. The fall was much faster than he thought.

He was doing this. "O-okay," he said to himself, face tired but stern. He lifted a weak arm to grab his Zip-Go Gaming Goggles off his desk. He held them in front of his chest, taking a good long look at himself again. His face was sunken, his eyes red behind his glasses, his hair limp, but he was still Wyatt.

Wyatt Docherty, son of Hydrexo's head engineers, champion of the *Fathom Fall* Operation Hostile championship and a Water Baby, closed his eyes and carefully pulled his Goggles up in front of his face like a camera. He turned them on to Standby Mode.

He wanted to be wrong, because if he wasn't, life was going to be so much more complicated than a monster infestation and a tri-kid league of champions sent to destroy them. Somehow, that was the easy option.

Wyatt took a deep breath and opened his eyes to watch the world through the digital screen.

In the mirror, Wyatt saw a figure holding its hands in front of its face, just like him, except there were no Goggles raised in front of its eyes—they'd been edited out. And instead of having hands, the thing in the mirror had claws, scaly and bright blue, and milky white eyes like Ping-Pong balls, and a round opening of pointy eel teeth.

Wyatt's dehydrated mind rang and lurched. His body ached. *No no no no.* He stumbled back from the mirror; the Bluddite did the same. It matched his movements precisely. Wyatt knew his face was all panic now, could feel himself shaking, but the Bluddite staring back at him was expressionless. A monster, something to shoot without remorse. And he *had*. With just a gun made of pixels, yes, but he was meant to have a real one soon. And to rack up a kill score with the familiar *plink!plink!plink!*

The Bluddite in the mirror looked as real as the one drinking from his bathroom faucet, and the one in the skate park. It looked as real as Zav Silva with that weird bruise on his forehead, awkwardly apologizing.

Wyatt had never kicked a Bluddite. There had never *been* Bluddites.

Wyatt fell backward into his bed and dropped his Goggles. The Bluddite fell away with them. Then it was only Wyatt in the mirror, looking back at his body collapsed against his bed. He looked like Wyatt, but not really.

He looked not much different than the desperate people who gathered around Hydrexo, in public parks, and who he was now sure were opening hydrants all over the city. Who were joined by Hydrexo employees, scrawled warnings in graffiti, looking for a way to give everyone what they needed. *To drink*, exactly as it had been said. But they weren't monsters. He wasn't even certain they'd blown up the refineries, or that they were killing soldiers sent to Lake Superior. He wasn't certain of anything now.

"It's all AR," Wyatt breathed.

Sure, kids were more resilient, had more to prove. But they were also easier to ignore, which meant no one would believe Wyatt if he said Hydrexo CEO Peter Davids wanted to train him and other kids to kill the real, water-desperate people threatening his water empire.

They hadn't had real weapons in the competition, but that was only the beginning.

Fathom Fall was a trial run for annihilation, and the whole country had cheered as they watched.

Wyatt felt so sick he swore his insides were gone. DoctorDoctor had nothing but *Fathom Fall*, nothing but his new title of champion—not even friends. He'd just wanted a chance to feel like he was in control. Wyatt's chest was tightening, eyes burning worse even if he had no tears to cry. The world was swaying ahead of him. He kept blinking, hoping it would be different when his eyes opened, but it wouldn't be.

Maybe Ava had cracked under the pressure, maybe what she wanted seemed even sicker now, but she had one thing right: this plan saved *no one*. It would only keep hurting more and more people. Wyatt couldn't just sit here. And that bit about no friends wasn't quite true now, was it? Wyatt looked at himself in the mirror, where the dark circles were still there, and the headachy sway. He had no idea what the hell he was supposed to do, but it did give him hope for one thing.

If the Goggles were a lie, then there hadn't actually been a Bluddite there that day when Ava threw the knife. And that meant Zav could still be alive with whoever had scrambled Hydrexo's radio reception.

"I gotta find him," Wyatt said to himself, while his trophy stared and the Goggles seemed to grin on the floor in front of him. In the park, there'd been a glitch in his Goggles. He'd seen Bluddite-green, but he'd also seen pink. And he knew that patch that he'd ripped from the only "real" Bluddite that day in the competition.

He hoped someone had been there to save Zav, and he hoped he knew who.

Wyatt swiped his water bottle off the nightstand to take a gasping drink, hoping he could rehydrate his brain fast enough to make a plan. He pulled the patch out again, tracing his eyes and his thumbnail across the edges to ensure it was still real. It helped him keep calm, or at least as calm as he could be.

If there was anyone who'd believe Wyatt, someone he could trust to help him prove the lengths Hydrexo would go to keep its hold on all the water, it was Leo Silva, and she was alive, and he was going to find her.

THANKS FOR PLAYING

ACKNOWLEDGMENTS

Thank you firstly to the people who made me who I am today, in all sorts of ways. I owe this book to the Canadian Cadet program, who taught me how easy it is to get swept away into a hierarchy that thrives on heroes and monsters. So thank you also to the people of York University's TBLGAY queer service group, for showing me that community isn't about domination, but about togetherness, and being loved for exactly who you are. Thank you also to the various activist circles and movements and marches and random meals in random parks with wonderful people who remind me again and again why I do still love Toronto even when it kicks us. This home is worth fixing so I can keep sharing meals and moments with you. I'll remember my OPSEC and leave your names out of this, but hopefully you know who you are.

Thank you to my fiancé for keeping me up to date with what the #youths are saying these days, and also keeping me grounded during the hardest parts of writing. I've gushed about you in enough of these. Surely you're tired of it by now so we'll move on.

Thank you to my parents, Wendy and Giuseppe Cerilli, two engineers who worked in factories all my life. I don't say it often enough, but you have pretty cool jobs that everyone is right to be jealous about. Thanks for keeping me safe and for accepting all my annoying childhood phone calls while you were in the middle of fixing a giant machine. Thanks also to my little sister, Megan, for being the reason I was calling you. And thank you to my early childhood best friend, Josh, who will probably never know this book exists, but who was integral to the baby gamer nostalgia baked into Zav and Wyatt. Sorry for stealing Pokémon off your Game Boy when you lent it to me. I should also thank my cousin, Jake Shultz, for all the times we not-so-secretly played gory first-person shooters in your basement. I was totally pathetic at them (I still am) so I appreciate the help.

Thank you to my agent, Ali McDonald, who accepts every weird project I throw at her. Also to Olga Filina and Cassie Rodgers of 5 Otter Literary, and to Jess de Bruyn who can fix my writing with one word (often "Why?" or ". . . Stop" or "No"). Similarly, thank you to my professors at York University for forcing me to take myself seriously, and for encouraging me while I try to find my way in the literary scene. Thank you to all the writer friends I've made, and the librarian and teacher friends, too. You all remind me why this matters.

Thank you to the fabulous team at Bloomsbury! I had a

truly amazing time sharing Toronto with you. Thank you to Camille Kellogg who picked this story up, Sarah Shumway who carried it forward, Regina Castillo and Rebecca McGlynn for their sharp eyes, John Candell for the design, and Chase Stone for turning my scratchy Bluddite sketches into that *brilliant* cover. There are surely publishing people I'm leaving off this list, so thank you to all the names I don't know who get this book from idea to print.

Thank you to the bookish community at large. Booksellers, librarians, teachers, reviewers, and readers. You're why we do this. Thank you also to the *community* at large. Every TTC driver, mail delivery person, park gardener, and barista made this book possible. I really mean that. To anyone reading this, I promise that you've somehow carried me closer to this story, or carried the right people closer to me to make this story possible, and for that I'm eternally grateful. Each of you matters. Each of you is making a change in the world just by existing. We can't always see the products of our work, but they're out there. I know that's as terrifying as it is empowering. We can let that fuel us.